LONG IRON ROAD

by

Thomas Willis

Tifton Press

First edition published in 2025 by Tifton Press, West Palm Beach, Florida.

This is a work of fiction.Names, characters, businesses, places, events, and incidents are either the product of the authors imagination or used in a fictitious manner. No identification with actual persons (living or deceased), places, buildings, and products is intended or should be inferred.

Library of Congress Control Number: 2025914206

ISBN: 979-8-9893052-4-7 (Paperback)

ISBN: 979-8-9893052-5-4 (E pub)

Book Cover by Stewart A Williams

Logo by Bill Baffa

Printed in the United States of America

The more I know men, the more I like my dog.
Madame De Sevigne, attributed

Chapter 1

Keri had only stopped at the rest stop on I-95 to use the restroom and wait for the storm to pass. Now she was lying in a coma in an intensive care room with her head wrapped in bandages like an Egyptian mummy. Tubes snaked out from all parts of her body, leading to blinking, flashing, and beeping machines. The good part, if it could be called good, was that the doctors had placed her in a deep coma, so she was mercifully unaware that her very life existed only because of the hardware that surrounded her.

Sharon Gillis, a critical care nurse, stood a few feet away watching an orderly empty out a bin with an image identifying it as hazardous waste. As he left the room, he had an unspoken question in his eyes as he exchanged glances with Sharon. Her answer was only a sad side to side movement of her head.

The rain had started less than half an hour after Keri left Jacksonville. First a few drops helped to clean her windshield before she met a sudden wall of rain that nearly obliterated her view of the road. An eighteen-wheeler blew by on her left, throwing up more water and making it harder to see past the hood of her car. Easing the pressure on the accelerator and holding the steering wheel in a death grip, she slowed down to a crawl.

A road sign on her right flashed by, and she recognized the REST AREA sign. She breathed a sigh of relief while silently thanking the State of Florida for its frequent rest stops and that I-95 had a rest area located every forty to sixty miles apart.

She carefully moved over to the exit lane and drove into the parking area designated for cars. In retrospect, she should have taken one of the St. Augustine exits, because she was now facing a long stretch of highway that ran through a deserted area of Northeast Florida. There were few signs of civilization. Both sides of the road were lined with thick slash pine forest filled with palmettos and wild myrtle.

As she approached the building that contained the restrooms, her sense of relief was replaced by a twinge of concern as she realized that the rest area was deserted except for three older vehicles. One was an older model GT Mustang that had been extensively modified. It had a large bulge in the front hood and flames painted along the sides. The second car was an older model Mercury sedan that was parked in a handicapped space next to a sidewalk that led to a narrow entrance into the building. An older model Ford F-150 pickup truck was parked on the opposite side of the parking area.

After parking directly in front of the entrance that led into the covered area, she began having second thoughts about using the restrooms until she realized there was a security guard standing just inside the covered area that connected the men's and women's restrooms. He was barely visible through the driving rain, but she was reassured enough to reach for her umbrella on the seat behind her. Clutching her car keys in one hand and her umbrella in the other, she took a deep breath and opened her car door. Her purse strap was wrapped tightly over her shoulder. The umbrella provided scant protection from the driving rain that was blowing sideways. One half of her body was soaked before she could reach the sidewalk.

Leaning into the wind but afraid to run because of the slippery concrete surface, she moved toward the cover of the entrance. The moment she entered the covered area connecting the two restrooms, a blinding streak of lightning was accompanied by a deafening clap of thunder. Following the lightning strike, a transformer directly in front of the parking area exploded in a burst of fire and sparks, resulting in loss of electricity for the entire rest stop. Standing still, she tried to acclimate her eyes to the sudden darkness.

After a moment, her eyes adjusted enough for her to see the shapes of walls. Holding her umbrella in front of her, she took another step toward where she remembered the security officer had been standing while asking out loud, "Hello, does anyone have a light?"

As she uttered the words, she stumbled over something on the ground in front of her, causing her to pitch forward onto the wet concrete floor. When she hit the floor, her umbrella and car keys flew out of her hands, but she held on tightly to her purse. Fortunately, her head avoided contact with the hard floor, but she knew she was going to lose some skin off her elbows. Quickly reaching into her purse, she tried to find her cell phone but remembered she'd left it in her car. When she realized what had caused her to fall, she recoiled in horror.

The security guard was sprawled out on his back and the pool of blood around his head accounted for the wet concrete under the cover of the roof. All of her instincts were telling her to run like hell when she realized she'd dropped her car keys. As she desperately felt for her keys on the floor around her, all of her fears were confirmed by the two pairs of feet standing within arm's reach next to her.

Looking up in the dim light, she realized there were two figures staring down at her. As her eyes followed the pair from their feet upward, it was not the laced-up granny boots, the long loose dress, or the rainbow-colored hair the woman was wearing that sent chills down her spine. Outlined by another flash of lightning, it was the young woman's face, contoured into a maniacal grin that was imprinted on Keri's brain just before one of the laced-up boots crashed into her face.

Her last conscious memory as the blows continued to rain down was the voice of the man saying, "That's enough, Shela."

Chapter 2

Three days earlier, Keri Smith had accepted an invitation to spend the weekend with her friend Mark Price at his home in Jacksonville, Florida. She had only known Mark for the last three years, but it seemed as if they had been friends for much longer. She had been instrumental in helping Mark find the person who had been responsible for the brutal murder of her sister, Tanya. In doing so, it had freed a man who had been wrongfully convicted for murdering her sister. He was only a few days away from being executed in Florida's electric chair.

This was not the first visit to Mark's home in Jacksonville. He had visited her at her home in Orlando as well. They both had no illusions about their relationship. Each of them was accustomed to living alone, and they both enjoyed the independence and freedom it brought. Neither of them wanted to give it up, and they had no intention of doing so. It was a unique relationship, but they enjoyed each other's company. It worked well for them both.

Earlier, when Mark had called her and asked if she could come up to his home for the weekend, he had cautioned her by telling her it would be a full house. She had met Roe Estes on a previous visit. Roe would be there, as would Roe's friend, Angel Ruiz. Roe was for all practical purposes Mark's adopted daughter. But Keri was really intrigued when Mark told her his son, Mark Gomez, would be there as well. It was only recently she'd learned that Mark had a son.

As she drove through the open iron gates and into the parking area of Mark's home overlooking the St. Johns River, she was always impressed with its size and beauty. Built out of native Florida lime rock accented by massive beams of timber that had come from some dismantled railway, it blended into the lush surrounding vegetation of native Florida plants. Even with its massive size, it seemed to be a part of the hillside that sloped down to the river.

She parked in the courtyard adjacent to the two-story garage. Before she got out of her car, she saw Mark coming toward her.

If it were not for the wide smile on his face, most people would instinctively want to run from him as fast as possible. He was big. Not only large, but tall with broad shoulders, slim waist, and long arms that made the sweatshirt he was wearing look as if it were a size too small. Although he was in his fifties, he could have easily passed for forty. His full head of hair was a few weeks past needing a trim, but it was his face you couldn't ignore. His nose was off-center, as if it had been broken and never set straight, and a large scar ran across his forehead, down, and around his right eye. All of this was offset by his blue-gray eyes combined with a wide smile that made you feel like he was a lifelong friend. If it were possible to read behind the smile, you would know the violence he had been capable of, and you would pray to God that he was your friend and not your enemy.

As soon as she was out of the car, Mark enveloped her tall slim body in an affectionate hug as he spoke. "Keri, I never realize how much I've missed you until I see you. I see you didn't bring Brutus?"

Keri, herself a beautiful woman just as her deceased sister had been, replied, "No, when you told me there would be other guests, I thought it might be best to leave him with my mother. You know from experience that Brutus doesn't make friends very easily." Keri was referring to her Dobermann Pinscher who was overly protective of her.

Taking Keri by the arm, Mark led her toward the entrance into the main house. "I'm looking forward to you meeting my son."

It had only been a few months earlier when Mark had told Keri he had a son. Keri was somewhat surprised, because Mark had never mentioned any children other than his daughter Kim, who had been killed years earlier. She hadn't asked any questions, feeling that Mark would tell her more if and when he felt like it.

They entered through a foyer that opened up into an expansive great room. The entire wall facing the river was floor-to-ceiling glass providing a panoramic view of the St. Johns River. On the other side of the glass, a flagstone patio ran the entire length of the home. As they approached the doors leading onto the patio, Keri could see three people sitting in deck chairs.

As they stepped onto the patio, all three stood up in unison to greet her. Keri immediately recognized Roe Estes. Roe had long dark hair that was pulled up into a ponytail that accented her dark eyes and narrow Roman nose. Knowing bits and pieces of Roe's traumatic past, Keri was always amazed at the strength and confidence that emanated from her. Standing next to her was a large handsome man with brown, tanned skin that indicated a lot of time spent outdoors.

It was neither Roe or the man next to her that caused Keri to take a step backward and stare at the third man. There would never be any doubt about the lineage. This was Mark recreated at an earlier age. The only difference was the lack of scars or the offset broken nose. In every other way, he was Mark's clone. Just like Mark, even his hair was overdue for a haircut. He was dressed casually in khaki slacks and a polo shirt.

Stepping toward Keri, he took her hands and kissed her on the cheek. It was an effortless movement that people of Spanish heritage did so well. "Keri, I'm so pleased to finally meet you. My dad has told me so many nice things about you. Now I can see why."

Keri could almost feel herself blush. She felt the compliment to be sincere and not just a polite gesture. Almost immediately, Roe took her arm and directed her attention to the large man standing with her.

"Keri, I'd like you to meet my friend, Angel. Don't be fooled by his name. He's not an angel, but he is a good guy."

Angel put out his hand in a formal way and shook Keri's hand with a smile. "Good to finally meet you, Keri."

With all of the introductions completed, the group spread out in deck chairs drank good wines and watched the traffic move up and down the river. It turned out to be a congenial group, and everyone seemed to relax and enjoy the moment. Keri remained alert for any conversations that might shed light on the sudden appearance of Mark's son in his life. Everyone present acted as if Mark Jr. had been there all along, but Keri was certain that he had not. What she did learn from the ongoing conversations was that Mark Jr. was a lawyer living in Atlanta. He worked for a group that specialized in criminal defense cases. He'd attended college and law school in the US, but before that, he'd lived in either Mexico or Colombia. She couldn't quite tell, and she was wary of asking any pointed questions.

Later in the evening, after steaks on the grill and a lot of drinks had been consumed, Mark and Keri went down to the dock that reached out into the river.

"Keri, I owe you an explanation. I know you're wondering how a son appeared out of nowhere. I'm going to give you an abbreviated explanation. The details are of little concern."

Mark continued to tell Keri that Mark was the product of an affair that had occurred during the time he was serving in the Army. Mark Jr's mother, who was originally from Mexico, was thought to have been killed in a special ops mission, but she had somehow survived. Because of her memory loss and family ties, she had remained in Mexico. She was also pregnant with Mark's son. By the time she had made a successful recovery and well after Mark Jr had been born, she discovered that Mark was now married. Not wanting to interfere with Mark's life, she chose to remain in Mexico and raise Mark Jr. with her extended—and very wealthy—cartel family. She had made arrangements with her attorneys that upon her death, both Mark and Mark Jr. were to be told of the existence of the other, and what they might choose to do at that point would be up to them.

"As you can see, we chose to meet. It has been a wonderful thing for us both. I think it might have also helped Mark deal with the loss of his mother Rosa, whom he loved dearly. It's a strange story, but as you know from your sister's life, truth can be stranger than any fiction."

"Thanks for explaining, Mark. It's obvious that you two have bonded well. I'm really happy for you."

The group spent all day Saturday at Crescent Beach just south of St. Augustine. They put up a large tent and enjoyed the white sand and crashing surf. Under the tent, there was ample deli food along with lots of ice-cold beer, which they were careful to keep out of the sight of the ever-present beach patrols. Later in the day, Roe proposed that Mark Jr. should be renamed.

"Mark Jr. is just too stilted. We need a different way to recognize you."

Everyone unanimously agreed that Mark Jr. should be renamed. Mark Jr. just seemed awkward, especially since he'd never been a Jr. until recently. At the time of his birth, his mother compromised with her brother that she would call him Mark and he could use his name of Mendez and Rosa's name of Gomez. His name was Mark Alfonso Mendez Gomez until he came to the US for school. For simplicity, he started using Mark Alfonso Gomez as his name.

Mark Jr. added, "I do have to agree. Having two Marks is confusing. Some of my friends in college called me Alfonso because they thought it sounded cooler than plain Mark. Why don't you just call me Al? Just like the song."

And so, it was decided. Al it would be.

Keri had originally intended to leave early Sunday afternoon and drive back to her home in Orlando, but Mark had somehow acquired tickets for them all to attend a Jaguar game on Sunday afternoon. There was no way she was going to turn that down. The only downside was she had to drive back late on Sunday. She needed to be home for an early business meeting she'd scheduled for Monday. So it was that Keri left Mark's home late Sunday afternoon and drove south on I-95 into an approaching thunderstorm.

Chapter 3

Mark had just dropped into a deep sleep when he was awakened by his cell phone. Initially, he had a hard time understanding the caller. He quickly recognized the voice of the caller as Keri's mom, Vera Meyers. Urging her to slow down and take a deep breath, he tried to understand what she was trying to tell him.

"Mark, I just got a call from the hospital in St. Augustine. They said Keri had been admitted and was hurt really bad. The man said I needed to come as quickly as I could. Do you know what happened?"

"Vera, do you know who the person was that called?"

"It was the sheriff's office that called. They said they got my phone number from Keri's wallet. They only would tell me she had been involved in an incident at a rest stop and had been taken to the hospital in St. Augustine. I'm going to leave now and drive up."

"No, Vera. It's late, and the weather is bad between here and Orlando. I'm much closer than you. I'll leave now. I'm only an hour away from the hospital. Let me call you back as soon as I get there and find out what's happened."

"Okay, Mark. I'll wait to hear from you. In the meantime, I'll be getting ready to drive up."

Before he closed the call, Mark was moving. Quickly dressing, he wrote a note and left it next to the coffee maker in the kitchen. Trying to remain as quiet as possible and not wake up any of his guests, he left his compound and drove south toward St. Augustine. Vera had given him the name of the hospital. There was only one main hospital, and he had no problem finding it and its main entrance. At 4:00 AM, the place seemed deserted. A sleepy receptionist inside the lobby directed him to the emergency room area.

This part of the hospital, as in most emergency rooms, was alive with activity at this hour. Victims of bar fights, drug deals gone bad, and accidents resulting from drunk drivers created a chaotic atmosphere. Mark was somewhat surprised at the large police presence as well as several Florida state troopers. Having some familiarity with the system, Mark approached a harried lady at one of the reception desks and waited for her to finish her phone call.

"I just learned that a friend of mine was just admitted. Can I talk to someone who knows what's happening? Her name is Keri Smith. My name is Mark Price."

"Just a minute, let me get someone," she said as she picked up her phone again. In less than a minute, two state troopers were walking rapidly toward the desk where Mark was standing. One of them was a tall, thin man and the other was a woman who obviously was a weight lifter. The bulges in the arms of her uniform were hard to miss. She was a formidable figure even without her sidearm. There was no small talk. The lady trooper only said, "Come with us."

Mark followed them down a side hallway and into a small conference room. There was an oval table ringed by six plain chairs. Two men dressed in suits were standing on one side of the room engaged in a quiet conversation. Mark had a foreboding feeling as he realized that this was probably where they took family members to deliver the worst of news. A single box of Kleenex in the center of the table added to his growing concern.

The moment Mark entered the room, the two men in suits both directed their attention toward him. The two uniformed patrol quietly closed the door as they left the room. Both men were dressed in nearly identical dark suits that were certainly not tailored but had come from a rack in a big box store. The ties of both men were loosened, blending well with bloodshot eyes. It was obvious that both men had been working without sleep for some time.

The older-appearing one of the two spoke first and simply said, "Please sit down. You identified yourself as Mark Price, I believe?"

"That's correct," Mark replied as he took a seat at the table.

Both men sat down on the opposite side of the table, their haggard expressions further emphasizing their lack of sleep. The older man who looked to be in his fifties was futilely trying to hide the extent of his baldness by combing hair across the bare area, making it even more obvious. He seemed to be the one in charge, and continued, "Mr. Price, I'm Detective Luhrs, and this is Detective Adams. How are you related to Ms. Smith?"

Beginning to feel a little anger at the abruptness of the way the detective was starting the conversation, he instead replied, "Is she okay?"

The younger detective who had a full head of jet-black hair in marked contrast to the older man angrily replied to Mark, "We're asking the questions here."

Mark started to stand up, but Detective Luhrs held his hand up. "Easy, Adams. The man has a right to know what's going on. Mr. Price, let's start over. Ms. Smith has been admitted to the hospital in critical condition. You can understand why I need to know your relationship with Ms. Smith before we go any further."

Mark eased back down into his seat. "Keri is a very close friend. She has been visiting me at my home in Jacksonville for the last few days. She left earlier this evening to go back to her home in Orlando. Her mother just called me and told me Keri had been in some sort of accident and had been admitted to this hospital. I told her mother not to drive up tonight until I'd found out what had happened. She's a total basket case right now, waiting for me to call her back. I'll get her on the phone and let her give you permission to tell me anything if that's what you need."

Both detectives looked at each other and nodded.

Luhrs spoke first. "A 911 call came in around 10:30. A trucker had just parked and gone into the building to use the restroom. He realized that the lights were out before he even got out of his truck, so he took a flashlight. As he started walking toward the building, he saw two vehicles leave the rest stop at a high rate of speed. The minute he entered the covered arcade, he saw two bodies on the floor. That's when he dialed 911. He backed out and waited. Fortunately, he also kept several other new arrivals from going near the arcade. A state patrol car arrived within two or three minutes. It only took him a moment to realize he needed a lot of help, including EMTs.

"They found Ms. Smith lying near the security guard. The guard was deceased, but Ms. Smith had a faint pulse. An elderly man was sitting near the exit from the men's room with his wife holding his head in her lap. He was conscious but incoherent. He's being treated here as well as Ms. Smith."

Almost afraid to ask, Mark spoke, "How was she hurt and how badly?"

"Mr. Price, the only thing I can tell you is that she has severe head injuries that suggest that she was badly beaten. She's alive, but the head trauma she suffered is very serious. I'm not the doctor, but from what I've been told, you should get Ms. Smith's mom up here as soon as possible. One more question: What kind of car was Ms. Smith driving?"

"She was driving a newer model gray Toyota Camry. I don't know the tag number. Is her car missing?"

Detective Adams had mellowed, and he answered, "We weren't sure until now, but yes, it is missing."

"So, you think robbery was a motive?"

"We don't know. They didn't take the old man's wallet or the security guard's wallet, and the keys to his truck were in his pocket. We're hoping the surviving man, or his wife, will be able to tell us something."

Knowing what the answer would probably be, Mark asked, "Can I see Keri?"

Detective Luhrs shook his head and replied, "Not now. We've been told that she's in a coma on a ventilator and they plan to keep her that way for now."

Mark felt a chill as he realized that the detectives were not considering Keri to be a source of information anytime soon, or maybe not at all. It was not a good omen.

After his meeting with the detectives, Mark tried to find out more about Keri's condition, but he was met with an impenetrable wall of HIPPA regulations since he was not next of kin and there was no directive allowing him access. Mark called Keri's mom back, telling her what he'd learned without letting her know the full extent of Keri's condition. "Vera, wait until morning and then drive up.

Go straight to the main desk here at the hospital. If I'm not sitting in the waiting area, ask for me at the desk."

Mark called Roe and told her what had happened.

She came awake fast. "Mark, I'm so sorry. What can I do?"

"Nothing at the moment. I'm going to wait here at the hospital until Keri's mom drives up. I know she's going to need support. Also, maybe I'll learn more details about Keri's injuries then. They've only told me that her condition is critical."

"Mark, I'll wait for you to call back. You know we're all ready to do whatever is needed."

"Yes, I do, Roe."

He returned to the waiting area outside the emergency room and tried to ignore the commotion. The thought crossed his mind that if he were ever really bored, he could sit in a hospital emergency room and just watch. He sat in one corner until the family of a gunshot victim who had apparently succumbed to his injuries were confronted by the family of the shooter who had suffered a less grievous gunshot wound. At that point, Mark made a strategic decision to leave before there were more gunshot wounds to be treated.

He returned to his car and dozed off in the driver's seat. At 5:00 AM, he went back inside. By now, the main part of the hospital was waking up. Surgeons and nurses were coming in to prep for early surgeries as the night shift people were leaving. He found a kiosk serving coffee and sat in a comfortable chair in the main waiting room.

He was glad he'd come in early, because at 6:00 AM sharp, Keri's mom walked through the door.

She went straight to Mark and tearfully gave him a hug. "Do you know how she's doing?"

"No more than what I told you last night. I'm sure someone will tell you more than they've told me."

"Mark, I can't lose another daughter."

"Vera, let's not even think that way."

Vera had brought paperwork proving who she was as well as documents showing that she had been designated by Keri to have access to her personal medical information. She insisted on having Mark stay with her when she was finally able to meet the physician who was directly responsible for Keri. Mark immediately liked the doctor, who inspired confidence by her demeanor. Mark was glad for Vera's sake. Although a young physician might be as good, better, or worse than an older one, Mark knew that Vera was more comfortable with the older image.

The doctor looked to be between fifty to sixty, wearing a white coat over a green scrub suit with the traditional stethoscope hanging from her neck. Her hair, pulled up into a tight bun, was hidden by a surgical cap. Although she had a somewhat haggard look about her as if she'd been up all night, which she had been, she projected not only strength and confidence but compassion as well.

"Mrs. Meyers, I'm Dr. Goldblatt. I'm sorry this is happening. I understand your concern and your fear. The first thing I want to assure you is that Keri is getting the best care possible. Although this hospital is not the largest, we're part of the medical center of the university, and her care is being overseen by several different specialist. At the moment, we're keeping Keri's movement to an absolute minimum. She has had some internal bleeding in the abdominal area, but it's her head that we're focusing on. We've had to relieve the pressure, and we're keeping her in an induced coma for the time being. I must tell you that presently, she is barely hanging on. Her injuries are severe.

I can't make any promises. If you're so inclined, I would pray as well."

Mark was surprised how well Vera held up after listening to the doctor give her summary of Keri's condition. Dr. Goldblatt gave permission for one person at a time to sit with her. Mark watched as Vera sat next to Keri's bedside. Keri was not recognizable with the wires, tubes, and bandages covering her head. As he watched, Mark couldn't shake the memory that he'd carried in his head for so many years. When he'd had to identify his daughter's battered body as she lay on a cold metal gurney in a morgue, the image had been etched in his brain forever. Although several years had passed, the emotions he'd felt then resurfaced again. Sadness, a feeling of hopelessness, but most of all, a burning anger overwhelmed his senses.

He left Vera sitting alone next to Keri. He'd reserved a room for Vera at a hotel within walking distance of the hospital because he knew she would be staying close to Keri's side. There was really nothing he could do by staying at the hospital.

As he drove back toward his home in Jacksonville, he knew he had to do something. When his daughter had been killed, he waited longer than he should have for the authorities to do their job before he acted on his own. As the rage inside began to grow, he didn't know what he was going to do, only that he would not wait as long as he'd done before.

Chapter 4

Gary Anders had never been as scared as he was now. Even the time he was sitting in a small boat fishing in a creek off the St. Johns River and a hornet's nest dropped from an overhanging branch, almost into his lap, didn't compare to this. In the incident with the hornets, he simply dove into the river and swam to the bank to escape it. Now he realized he was in over his head and trapped. There was nowhere he could go to escape what he'd just witnessed. Curt had promised him they were only going to steal a car and take it someplace where someone would pay good money for it. It would be, as he'd said, "easy-peasy."

Now he was not only a car thief, but an accessary to one or possibly two brutal murders. Gary had been nervous from the moment Curt had picked him up at his mom's trailer park in Palatka as he realized that Shela was going with them. Shela was a timebomb. He was more afraid of her than he was of Curt. Her tattoos alone were enough to give anyone pause. A dagger dripping blood on one side of her neck was balanced by an axe dripping blood on the opposite side. He suspected there were many others he'd never seen because it was winter, and she'd been wearing long sleeves and long dresses.

Gary had heard the screeching tires before he saw Curt come around the corner in his older model, souped up GT Mustang, sliding to a stop in front of his mom's trailer.

Shela opened the door for Gary so he could contort himself into the back seat, laughing as she did. "Climb in, Gary. You ready to have some fun tonight?"

Curt laughed. "Don't pay her any mind, Gary. She's been hitting the pills a little too heavy tonight. She'll sober up soon enough," he said as he spun out of the trailer park and headed east.

Gary really never had a chance in life. His dad had died when he was only three years old leaving his mom, Dot, to raise him and his older brother. In her desperation, she'd latched onto a no-good asshole of a man. Howard Epps was a drunk and a womanizer. But worst of all, he had a cruel streak that he directed toward Gary's mom and both boys.

Gary's older brother, Lucas, tried to protect both Gary and their mother and paid a heavy price for it. But Lucas grew up. As a middle schooler, he started playing football and lifting weights. He had a large frame that was amplified by the weights, and by his freshman year, he was starting as a tight end on the high school's football team.

Howard Epps subconsciously realized at some point that Lucas was no longer a vulnerable target, and he refocused his attention on Gary and Dot. Gary was just starting middle school, and he'd been dealt a poor hand out of the athletic gene pool. He was a small kid, and he simply wasn't destined to be an athlete like Lucas. By the time he was sixteen, Gary only weighed a hundred thirty pounds wet. Surprisingly, the one good thing the gene pool had dealt him was a surprisingly high IQ, although no one realized its presence.

All hell broke loose on a hot summer afternoon. Gary had just gotten home from school and found his mom sitting on the floor crying. He'd knelt down next to her and put his arm around her shoulder when he felt a stinging jolt of pain as a leather belt laid a welt across his face.

He tried to stand up to defend himself, but Howard shoved him back down and swung the belt again. "You little shit. She deserves what I give her. You need a reminder of who's in charge in this house."

Gary could smell the alcohol reeking from Howard, and all he could do was try to cover his mother with his body as another blow hit him across his back.

Lucas was returning home from summer football camp, and he saw the scene as he came through the door. All of the blows he'd received from Howard over the years surfaced all at once, and his actions were spontaneous. He grabbed the arm that was holding the belt and yanked back so hard it literally pulled Howard's arm out of its socket.

Howard screamed, but Lucas didn't hear it or care if he did as he kicked Howard between the legs like he was punting a football. Picking up the belt from the floor, he began to very methodically whip Howard. He was holding the belt on the opposite end from the heavy brass buckle. It left far more than welts. It cut Howard to pieces as it ripped his shirt into shreds. Gary and his mom were both so stunned that they could only watch. It was only sheer fatigue that finally caused Lucas to stop his frenzied attack. There was no movement from Howard, who was curled up in a bloody ball.

Lucas finally shook his head as if he were waking up from sleep and knelt down next to his mom and Gary. "Where's your phone?"

Using his mom's phone, Lucas called one of his teammates, Jason Simpson, and asked him to call his dad, Willie. His friend's dad had been a well-known Major League Baseball catcher until a freak accident with a tipped ball fractured his right elbow beyond any hope of repair. Willie Simpson had grown up as a dirt-poor black boy in Columbus, Georgia, where his father had beat him senseless on many occasions when he was a young boy. Baseball had been his ticket out, and he related to Lucas and his situation.

Lucas and Jason had become close friends. Lucas spent more time at Willie's home than his own. Willie was well aware of Howard's abusive history and was quick to respond. When Willie finally arrived, he was accompanied by Jason's older brother, Henry, who was a bouncer in a bar down the river that was well-known to the local authorities as a center of gambling, prostitution, and illegal alcohol. It took either a tough person or a crazy person to ever frequent the premises. It took an even tougher person to work as a bouncer there.

They found Gary with tears running down his cheeks, sitting on the floor and holding his mom. Lucas was still standing over Howard as if he were looking for any excuse to start swinging the belt again. When Willie walked through the door, he paused, taking in the scene before he spoke.

"What happened?" he asked, although he knew exactly what had happened as he took the belt from Lucas's hand.

Lucas was looking down at Howard, who was now trying to sit up in a pool of blood, holding his dislocated shoulder in acute pain. Lucas spoke as if he were in a trance. "He will leave and never come back to this house.

I'll kill him next time he ever tries to lay a hand on my mom or my brother. I don't ever want to see him again."

Willie nodded. He had a sudden flashback of a twelve-year-old black boy in Columbus, Georgia picking up a baseball bat and swinging with all his strength, which he had an ample supply of, and crushing his drunk dad's head as he was about to hit his mother again with his closed fist. He'd dragged his dad's body out onto the nearby highway and left it in the middle of the dark road. The death was later ruled a hit-and-run. He knew Lucas meant what he said about killing Howard, and it wouldn't end well for him.

"Don't worry. You were clearly protecting your family from a crazy drunk. Henry and I'll have a talk with him."

They never saw or heard from Howard again. What they never knew was the encouragement Howard received from Willie and Henry. Together, the two men picked up the semiconscious Howard, supporting him on either side they walked him to Willie's truck, and lifted him into the back seat. When they passed the turn that would have led to the jail, Howard awoke from his stupor, asking, "Where the hell we goin?"

Neither Willie nor Henry spoke a word as they continued to drive west on State Road 20 through Interlachen and past Cowpen Lake before turning right onto state Road 21. They went a short distance on 21 before they slowed and turned onto a narrow unpaved path leading through a thick growth of pines. Soon they entered an open area with a small pond. There were several old live oaks with long branches that almost touched the ground around the edge of the clearing.

Howard had become concerned long before they'd reached this point, but when Willie stepped out of the truck and opened the corrugated steel toolbox in the truck's bed, Howard's apprehension rose several octaves. He tried to see what Willie was doing, but his shoulder was hurting so badly, he couldn't turn around enough to see.

Willie handed something to Henry, and then he could see Henry taking a hemp rope over to a thick branch of the closest oak tree. When Henry started tying a noose in one end, his bladder opened up and he nearly fainted. Henry threw the noose over the tree limb before walking back to the car. By now, Willie was standing next to Henry as they opened the door where Howard was now crying like a baby.

In a quiet and calm voice, Willie said, "Howard, you have a choice to make. You can die now, or you can leave town for good and stay alive. If you do choose to leave, and you ever come back, you'll die then."

Howard immediately realized what Willie was saying. Understanding he was not going to die today, he could only nod his head in acceptance and relief.

As Henry walked back to retrieve the rope, Willie slammed the truck door closed. They drove back to State Road 20 and continued west to the small town of Hawthorne just outside the county line. When they reached 301 South, they stopped at a small twenty-four-hour emergency clinic. Helping Howard out of the truck, they walked him into the door of the clinic. Making sure the two employees of the clinic could see them clearly, Willie said, "We found him by the side of the road. He looked pretty bad and needed help."

Willie then whispered one last time in Howard's ear, "We mean what we say. You're a dead man if you ever come back to Palatka." And they left Howard barely able to stand as they made a swift exit before anyone could ask any questions.

Lucas got a full scholarship to play football out of state and left Gary alone with his mom in Palatka. Gary tried to follow in Lucas's footsteps and play sports, but his size and lack of desire closed that route for him. If anything, it had the effect of hurting whatever little self-esteem he might have had. He was a good-hearted kid. He was happy playing video games and watching others play sports. His intelligence lay dormant. It was only manifest by his high grades, which came without any effort on his part. Although he was a runt, he had a pleasant smile, and he was devoid of any meanness. He did love his mom but worried when they had to move into a small dilapidated mobile home while she waited tables at a local restaurant. He tried a couple of part-time jobs, but his employers seemed to sense a weakness and he was constantly taken advantage of.

He was becoming desperate when he and his mom were about to be evicted from their trailer. Dot was working long hours as a waitress and had no other way to increase her income. Gary was afraid of what his mom might do to make more money. He couldn't find a part-time job anywhere. His brother Lucas was away at school and had no way to help them.

Gary first met Curt Lawsen in a local video arcade. Gary's social circle was so small, he was easily taken in by anyone who was friendly toward him. So, when Curt took Gary under his wing, he was happy to have someone who was outgoing, confident, and popular treat him as a friend. Curt's girlfriend, Shela James, was another matter.

One afternoon after playing video games, the three of them went into a convenience store next door to the arcade to get a soda. Gary saw a sign above the cashier advertising for help needed. While he was in the process of questioning the clerk about the job, Shela casually walked out with an armload of chips and a six-pack of beer as if she owned the store. Gary was upset because he knew he might be associated with the theft, and later he tried to explain to Curt why he needed the job.

Curt only laughed at him. "If you need money, I know a much better way to get some."

"How?" Gary asked.

Curt went on to explain that all Gary would have to do would be a lookout while he stole a car. The car could be sold for a lot more than Gary could ever make as a store clerk. Gary was an honest person who had never done a dishonest thing in his life. But he was desperate, and the fear of his mother being evicted or worse was overwhelming. He knew she was close to the edge of her sanity. So, he agreed to help Curt. Now he was driving away from a rest stop on I-95, living in a nightmare he couldn't escape.

Chapter 5

When Mark returned home from the hospital, Roe, Angel, and Al were all waiting anxiously in the great room. Roe had not been able to sleep after Mark's call. She had gone straight to the coffeepot and made coffee for everyone. They could all tell by the haggard look on Mark's face, he didn't bring good news.

"Let me get you coffee," Roe said as she headed for the kitchen.

After Mark had a large steaming cup of coffee in his hand, he collapsed into a large soft chair and told the others what he'd learned. "There's not a lot I can tell you at this point. I'm still not sure how badly Keri's hurt. I just know it's not good. The two detectives didn't reveal much other than the fact that someone killed the security guard, seriously injured Keri, and beat an old man senseless. Car theft seems to be the motive. The only thing they can't account for is Keri's car. They didn't even know that until they talked to me, and I told them what car Keri was driving."

Angel, who had been listening intently, said, "Mark, I know the guy who is sheriff of the county. I worked with him on a couple of drug cases when I was working for the state DEA. Let me contact him and see if I can learn more. It's unusual to see so much violence associated with a simple car theft. It sounds like someone hyped up on drugs looking for a joyride."

Al chimed in, "My firm is defending a man right now who killed a fourteen-year-old kid who tried to take his car at gunpoint. Another boy a little older was shot as well. Two other kids got away but were arrested later. The people who steal cars for profit commonly use kids under the legal age because the penalties are so lax. What has amazed me about this case is that the press has made the man we're defending out to be the villain. Even though the kids had handguns and the man's wife and three-year-old were in the car with him, he was supposed to let them take his car as if it were their right to do so. I'm hoping the DA isn't going to charge him, but it's Atlanta, and God only knows what a grand jury may do. I agree with Angel though—this is strange. If the people who did this were looking for a joyride, you'd think they'd have been looking for a hot car like a Mustang or a Charger. If they took Keri's car for profit, then why the violence?"

After talking with the group, Mark agreed with Angel that speaking with the county sheriff would be the logical first step. Without more information, there was nothing they could do.

On the outside, Mark appeared to be calm and collected. Only Roe understood what was going on in his mind. It had been years since Mark's only daughter Kim, who also happened to be Roe's best friend, had been brutally murdered. Roe had been by Mark's side as he'd methodically tracked her killers. She was only too familiar with the way Mark was able to commit violent acts while showing little outward emotion or remorse. She sometimes wondered how he was capable of such raw aggression at times and then continue afterward as if nothing had ever happened.

Although she knew he could be a violent and cruel man at times, he could also be a kind and loving person. He could have easily blamed her for the events leading up to his daughter's death, but he hadn't. It had been his understanding and compassion that had led her out of her descent into darkness and enabled her to become the person she was today. So, she knew that Mark's calm demeanor was only a thin cover for what was really fermenting inside.

Just as Roe had observed, Mark's conversation with the group was controlled and thoughtful. He listened to the opinions offered by everyone present. Although everyone agreed that Angel should try to meet with the sheriff as soon as possible, the main question was whether Angel should go alone or if they should all go with him.

Angel's suggestion was a good one. "Let me call him first and talk to him. He is a real by the book type of guy, but he is also a real ballbuster when it comes to law enforcement. I don't mean in a bad way. He just has very little tolerance for criminals, especially crimes involving physical violence."

"I agree," Mark said. "Go ahead and reach out to him and see how he responds. Knowing how she happened to be at that rest stop just after leaving here should give him reason to want talk to us anyway."

Angel stood up. "I'll call now and see if I can get through to him," he said as he walked out onto the patio to make the call. Mark, Roe, and Al waited inside and watched Angel outside as he walked in a circle while occasionally making arm movements as if he were directing an orchestra. He remained outside for almost half an hour before he came back inside.

"He'll meet with us. I'm sure he would have wanted to question us at some point anyway. He was hesitant with having a lawyer present, but I was able to convince him that Al wouldn't be any litigious threat. He said he'd meet us late this afternoon at his office."

Roe had been listening quietly before she spoke. "Guys, I'll stay here. Having all three of you, me, and another lawyer at once may be a bridge too far. You can fill me in after you meet him."

Not wanting to take any chances with traffic, Mark, Angel, and Al left Mark's compound by 3:30, taking I-295 to I-95 South and exited on State Road 16 into heavy traffic from the numerous outlet malls. They reached the sheriff's office well before they were due. After going through a thorough inspection, including walking through metal detectors and wands, they were finally seated in a small waiting room outside the sheriff's office. They didn't have to wait long after watching several uniformed deputies enter and leave the office before the sheriff came out of the door to greet them.

Sheriff Lewis Norten was not elected sheriff of the county because of political affiliation and most especially not by kissing ass. He had earned his position the hard way. He had worked for it. Surprisingly, becoming sheriff had not been his ambition. He simply loved law enforcement, having started out as a local game warden, followed by the police department and then a deputy sheriff. He was a product of the county, having grown up the son of a local fishing guide. He knew the county—every nook, cranny, and waterway—like the back of his hand. He never aspired for rank or promotions. He simply did his job well and the promotions came.

When he was approached about running for sheriff, he refused at first, but his wife and children tried to encourage him by reminding him of the good he could continue to do for the county he loved. When he realized that his opponent would be a lady from another county who was deeply involved in national politics and was being financed by big money from outside the state, he was concerned. He had always felt that politics should never be a part of law enforcement. That finally tipped the scales, and he agreed to run.

It was a nasty campaign where his opponent tried to brand him as a renegade because he'd killed a man when he was working as a game warden. Lewis chose to completely ignore her and her accusations that he fired first at a poacher. In time, the real story came out. He only drew his gun and fired back in self-defense after the poacher had fired three shots and missed all three times. Lewis only fired a single shot. The facts were well-documented by the dead man's accomplice. The frightened man had panicked and fallen out of the boat when the shooting started. The man couldn't swim, but without any hesitation, Lewis dove into the dark lagoon and pulled him out.

The man was now working as a trustee and janitor at the jail and would walk over coals to support Lewis. As it turned out, Lewis's reputation was good enough to enable him to win the election decisively. This was now his eighth year as sheriff, and he'd not yet had to face an opponent in an election. This was the man who now greeted them and ushered them into his office.

Chapter 6

Chicago, Februrary 14, 1929

It was St. Valentine's Day, and Paulus Graziano could not believe how anyone could be so unlucky. He'd worked his ass off to get this job. After dropping out of school when he was fifteen, he got a job working in an auto repair garage. When he was nineteen, he was busted for stealing a car and was given a choice by the judge of going to prison or enlisting in the Army. In 1917, the US had already entered the war and needed warm bodies for cannon fodder. Because of his experience as a mechanic, he was attached to a transportation company and was able to avoid the trenches. His training did expose him to use of small arms, which he hoped to never have to use.

The closest he'd come to injury was during the Somme offensive in August 1918. He was driving a truckload of munitions toward the front lines when the German artillery began dropping shells of chlorine gas directly in front of his truck. Fortunately for Paulus, the winds shifted and blew the gas away from him. After his Mack Truck's cargo had been unloaded, it was reloaded again, but this time, it was with American soldiers who'd been unable to get their gas masks on fast enough to avoid inhaling the gas. It was not a pretty sight, and the memory of the poor men gasping for air was something he tried to forget.

When he returned home, he continued working as a mechanic. By now, Paulus was street-smart, and he was a hard worker. His ability to work on cars, trucks, or anything propelled by a gasoline engine helped him to work his way up the ladder. He knew as much about the workings of an automobile as any mechanic in Chicago.

Eventually, as he gained the confidence of the owners, he was moved to another business that worked on repairing cars in the front part of a garage. Its main purpose was to conceal a chop shop in the rear. Over time, his duties were expanded to enforcing payments by reluctant auto dealers and salvage yards. Because of his understanding of the business, there were few tricks that he was not familiar with. Even so, Paulus was not by nature a violent man, and this immersion into the shady side of the automotive business eventually led him to his current position as Bugs's full-time driver. Now he was changing a flat tire while his boss sat in the rear seat and fumed.

Earlier that morning, just as he'd always done, Paulus had checked everything—tire pressure, gas. and oil, in addition to polishing every square inch of the big car. One of the perks of driving Bugs was that he was able to keep the car at his house when he wasn't driving him. Having a Rolls-Royce Phantom II sitting in his driveway was an impressive status symbol.

In spite of the cold biting wind, he was covered in sweat by the time he had the spare tire mounted, and they were moving again. He was supposed to pick Bugs up at eight sharp. But as usual, Bugs was operating on his own time, and Paulus was left shivering while waiting outside until Bugs walked out around ten.

Paulus jumped out of the car took the suitcase that Bugs was carrying. It was a large leather one with straps that buckled across both ends. And it was heavy. Paulus opened the rear door for Bugs to get into the car before he carried the suitcase to the rear of the car, opened the trunk, and grunted as he hefted the heavy case in. He was glad Bugs hadn't seen the wrapped Valentine's Day present that he'd left in the car's trunk. He only hoped that whatever they were doing would be finished so he could give it to his wife Rita before Valentine's Day was over.

Once they were on their way again, Bugs seemed to relax a little. At 10:45, they were on Clark Street, only three blocks away from the garage where the meeting had been arranged. Paulus was not included in the details of the meeting, but he had ears and common sense. He had been acutely aware of the friction that existed between Bugs and Capone, and he assumed this meeting involved some sort of deal that Bugs was making with Capone's organization.

They had to stop at a light at Webster when a black Cadillac going north ran through the intersection without even slowing down. As the black car passed them, the driver of the speeding car seemed to recognize the Phantom Paulus was driving, and he could see brake lights light up after it passed them at a high rate of speed. At the same time, he saw the commotion ahead. He'd never seen so many flashing lights. Mostly, he saw police cars, but there were ambulances as well. Rolling down his window, he pulled over to the curb. There was a group of people staring toward the commotion ahead.

"What's going on up there?" he asked.

A woman with eyes as wide as saucers replied, "I heard that a whole lot of people got killed. It must be some kind of gang thing."

From the back seat, Bugs was quick to order him to make a quick turn down a side street and drive away from the bedlam ahead. Paulus had grown up on the streets of Chicago and had a keen instinct for survival. He had no idea what was happening, but it couldn't be good. Turning to look at Bugs, who was white as a sheet, he asked, "Where to?"

Bugs was quiet for a minute and seemed to be weighing his options before replying, "Just get us out of here fast. I think whoever was driving that Cadillac recognized this car. Take me to the safehouse."

Paulus understood and took a circuitous route, avoiding main roads, to a quiet middle-class neighborhood before stopping in front of a nondescript townhouse.

A group of kids playing stickball stopped and watched the Rolls pull up to the curb. Not wanting to attract any more attention than necessary, Bugs decided not to make a show of removing the big suitcase out of the car's trunk. As he got out of the car, he leaned into the driver's side window and told Paulus, "Listen carefully to me. I want you to drive down to Joliet. Several blocks past the courthouse, there's a small motel. Take the car there and wait for me to contact you. I need to sort out what the fuck's happening. If you want, you can pick up your wife and kids. Tell them it's a vacation." Without another word, Bugs waved him away.

Driving back to his small home located on the outskirts of town, he told his wife that they had to leave the area immediately. His wife, Rita, had been a nightclub stripper and shared the same street-smart savvy as Paulus. Through his relationship with Bugs, he was able to get Rita out of her bar life and become a full-time wife and mother.

She recognized the urgency in Paulus's voice. She asked no questions as she quickly gathered some clothing for herself and their two young sons. Jamming their suitcases into the trunk next to the other big one, Paulus and Rita Graziano drove south with their two boys as Chicago disappeared in the rearview window. Little did they know that they'd never see Chicago again.

They didn't stop until they reached Joliet, where they checked into the motel that Bugs had described. They waited nervously through the rest of the day and into the night. The valentine gift, along with the large suitcase, remained forgotten in the trunk of the car. When it was dark, Paulus walked over to a small diner next to the motel and picked up some food for his family.

Before he left the diner, he could see the headlines of the Chicago newspaper sitting in the dispenser. With a shaking hand, he dropped a nickel into the box and bought a paper, taking it back to the motel room along with the food while looking over his shoulder the entire way.

The headline *ST. VALENTINE'S MASSACRE* covered most of the front page and grisly details filled the rest. Paulus realized that the flat tire had probably saved Bugs's life as well as his own.

Neither Paulus nor Rita was able to sleep as they continually peeked out of the room's window. The Rolls was conspicuous sitting next to the Fords and Dodges. At one point, they saw two large black cars cruise slowly through in the parking lot in front of their room.

As the night progressed, Paulus began to understand why Bugs had sent him away. If Bugs was a target, his Roll-Royce would stand out like a sore thumb. Before the night was over, Paulus and Rita made a decision that would change their lives forever. Turning off all the lights in their room, and each one carrying a child, they slipped back into the Rolls, which was parked directly in front of the room. Without turning on the car's lights, they drove away from the motel and headed south. Fortunately, Paulus had filled up the gas tank earlier before they'd checked into the motel. With a full tank of gas, they were able to drive well into the morning.

Although they'd left Chicago far behind, Paulus knew they needed to ditch the Rolls. Out in the hinterlands, the car attracted even more attention. Checking into a motel in Indianapolis, Paulus left Rita and the two boys while he looked for the right kind of auto dealer. He knew the right questions to ask and the right words to use when he approached a large dealership.

When he returned to the motel, he was driving a 1929 Chevy series AC International sedan with the new six-cylinder engine. The dealer had salivated at the prospect of the trade, and Paulus wanted to get in and get out as fast as possible, so he didn't care that the dealer was getting the better of the trade. He didn't bother to tell the dealer anything about the real owner of the car. He knew the dealer was well aware of the car's questionable ownership, but there were ways around that.

Anyway, it was his problem now. Paulus knew the first thing the owner of the dealership would do would be to secure a new registration, papers, and tag. Then he would sell the car at a bargain price to some unsuspecting buyer who thought he was getting the deal of a lifetime.

The unsuspecting buyer was a dentist who called himself "Painless Marty Molar." When Marty arrived home with his new prize, he left it parked in front of his house overnight so the neighbors could see it. The next morning, when he was only a block from his office, a modified Ford sedan pulled up next to him and a Thompson submachine gun materialized out of a window. The shooter emptied the entire drum magazine, which held a hundred rounds, shredding the Rolls with lead.

Painless slammed on the brake and dropped low in his seat. It was the luckiest day of his life when he realized he was still alive. It was a miracle considering the number of rounds that had riddled the Rolls. He left the car sitting in the middle of the street, oil and gas dripping onto the pavement and smoke pouring out from under the hood. After walking away from the car and on to his office, he lost a few patients that day because his hands wouldn't stop shaking. He never knew what became of the Rolls, nor did he want to know.

By now Paulus and Rita had seen the contents of the suitcase that Bugs had given him to place in the trunk. It was filled with cash that Bugs was bringing to the meeting. They didn't even try to count it, but they knew it was far more than enough to set them up in a new life. But where? That was the question.

Three years earlier, Paulus had been sent to Florida to pick up a load of illegal liquor that was being smuggled into a god-forgotten place called Cedar Key. Paulus remembered how desolate and removed from civilization the place had been. He'd told one of guys in the garage back in Chicago that if someone wanted to disappear, then Cedar Key would be the place to go.

As they drove south, only wanting to put as much distance as possible between themselves and Chicago, he remembered his previous trip to Cedar Key. Realizing that since they needed a place to hide, that might be a good place to start. They never reached Cedar Key. After driving through an endless Florida wilderness without seeing any sign of life, they coasted on fumes into the small town of

Chiefland. It was located a few miles just east and inland of Cedar Key. Wanting to stay near civilization for a while, they checked into a motel in the town. After eating in a nearby diner, Paulus left Rita and the boys at the motel. He started driving around the small town until he found what he was looking for.

A faded sign with the name *Rufus Ray Whitmer* hung in front of a small office building that looked like it had seen better days. Paulus parked in the dirt lot in front of the office and walked in. There was no receptionist, and the man sitting at a desk inside looked as decrepit as the building. He had a bulbous nose and ruddy complexion that was a side effect of the copious amounts of alcohol that he obviously used. His white dress shirt's collar was frayed, and his narrow mustache contained more hair than the top of his head.

When Paulus walked through the front door, a ringing bell caused the lawyer to hide something in a desk drawer. Before the man could rise up, Paulus introduced himself as Larry Moreno and reached across the cluttered desk to shake his hand. Paulus then asked the million-dollar question. "Would you like to make some easy money?"

The only thing Paulus told Ray, as he was called, about himself, was that he had sold his previous business back up north and some people were unhappy with the deal. But the only thing that Ray heard were the words "easy money." With that handshake, a profitable, ongoing, symbiotic relationship was created between the two men.

Ray Whitmer helped Paulus, now known as Larry Moreno, buy a tract of land that was located several miles outside Chiefland next to an area called the Waccasassa Flats. It was indeed remote, and the swampy terrain surrounding the area guaranteed no likelihood of future development.

Although the thousand-acre property fronted on the narrow, poorly maintained state road, the main entrance was off a dirt road leading from the state road. The dirt road was lined on both sides with ancient live oak trees. The massive branches stretching across the road created the illusion of traveling through a green tunnel. The road ended at the entrance to a large wooden farmhouse. It was the only road in and the only way out.

The first thing Paulus did after moving his family into the farmhouse was to erect a heavy iron gate where the dirt road ended in front of the house. High above the gate, he hung a sign across the entrance. And just as the sign advertised, Moreno and Sons Salvage was born.

Chapter 7

Leaving the rest stop, Curt drove his own car and had Gary drive the Camry they'd stolen. Shela rode with Gary, who was still shaking from the violence he'd just witnessed. She'd calmly walked up behind the guard while Curt was talking to him. Without any hesitation, she'd put the barrel of the revolver up behind his head and pulled the trigger. It even shook Curt up as he shouted at her, "What the hell did you do that for?" while twisting the gun out of her hand. "I told you we would leave the gun in the car."

"He got a good look at us, that's why."

At the same moment, an elderly man came out of the men's restroom. He was not even looking at the three teens as he walked toward the entrance to the women's restrooms. Curt walked up behind him and delivered a vicious blow to the side of his head. The man just folded into a heap on the concrete floor.

Gary was standing off to the side watching helplessly as the events unfolded seemingly in slow motion. A woman who had just parked was running out of the rain and into the covered area. A blinding flash of lightning and thunder blew out all of the lights, causing her to stumble over the security guard's body and fall face forward. When she tried to stand up, Shela kicked her in the head so hard, she collapsed back onto the concrete floor. But Shela was just getting started, as she continued to kick the poor woman.

Finally, Curt said, "Okay, Shela, that's enough. Pick up her keys and let's get the hell out of here before someone else comes up. Her car looks like it's new. Now you're going to earn your way, Gary. You drive the woman's car and follow me close. You can have the privilege of Shela's company as well."

As they drove away, Shela sat in the passenger seat with a big smile on her face. "Gary, didn't I tell you we were going to have fun?"

Shela James had been born with a silver spoon. She had loving parents who were strongly inclined toward the religious side of life. Both her parents had received a generous inheritance and they had parlayed it into ownership of several successful franchises. It would have been hard to pinpoint why or when Shela went rogue. But she did go to the dark side at an early age. You might argue that she fell in with the wrong crowd, but conversely, you could argue that she herself was the wrong crowd. She was drinking and using pot before she'd reached puberty. Her parents tried everything to help her, but the harder they prayed, the worse she became.

In spite of her errant behavior, Shela was brilliant. At some point during her second year in high school, she was tested, and her IQ was off the charts. It was her intelligence that enabled her to stay in school and out of jail. Her parents finally gave up and basically told her to get out. Shela went to live with a spinster aunt who was oblivious to anything she did. At that point, Shela had the best of all worlds. She had a safe place to sleep if she needed it, plus she could come and go as she pleased. As her body art progressed, her aunt didn't even notice the changes. If she was aware of Shela staying out all night, she never said anything.

The high school sent numerous messages to Shela's parents advising them of her attendance, or lack thereof, but by this time, her parents had given up even though they prayed for her on a daily basis. The surprising thing was that in spite of missing so many classes and being under the influence of some form of pharmaceuticals even when she was present, Shela's grades kept her at the top of her class. As she approached her high school graduation in a couple of months, this alone kept her from being kicked out of school, and she was on course to graduate with honors.

What friends Shela had made as she was growing up in Palatka abandoned her one by one as her behavior became more and more reckless. Palatka was a rural town, and a large portion of the population maintained a strong religious affiliation. Simply put, her behavior scared the hell out of her friends. Even the pediatric physician that her family used was afraid to go into an examining room with Shela unless he was accompanied by one of his nurses. If Shela had been diagnosed by a psychiatrist, her behavior would have been considered hedonistic, amoral, and totally devoid of any ability to feel empathy for anyone or anything. She was like a sociopath savant who only craved excitement as she moved from one high to the next with very little in between.

Shela met Curt at the same video arcade where they found Gary. Curt had graduated from high school three years earlier and had started attending a junior college in Gainesville. His academic career had been shortened after he'd been arrested for selling pot to other students. He came back to Palatka and just hung out looking for any way to support himself without having to actually work.

Curt was initiated into the car theft business by an older man who had seen him hanging out around the arcade. He needed a lookout for his business, which involved the opportunistic theft of nice cars. They had gone into an underground parking garage in downtown Jacksonville in the middle of the day. Curt's new mentor, Otis Morphet, focused on a new Lexus sedan that was parked in a dark secluded corner of the lower level. It was the perfect setup. They parked near the elevators, with Curt sitting in the driver's seat of Otis's car, engine running and facing the exit.

Otis walked toward the corner of the garage where the Lexus was parked, holding the tools he needed close by his side. He crouched low as he approached the Lexus. Remaining low, he inserted a thin piece of metal into the seal of the driver's side window, and in less time than it would take to use a key to open the door, it swung open. As he started to slide into the driver's seat, three shots in quick succession rang out and reverberated loudly through the garage.

Otis sank to the garage floor next to the open door, with blood seeping through his shirt and pouring out of the back of his head. The security guard, who was caught in an awkward position in the back seat of the Lexus between the legs of a secretary from an office in the building above with his pants wrapped around his ankles, had reached down, drawn his revolver, and put three 38 Special +P rounds into the hapless Otis, abruptly ending his automotive career.

From a distance across the garage, Curt had jumped at the shots and could see someone get out of the car and reach down as if he were trying to pull something up. Curt made a quick decision, and while the guard was frantically trying to pull up his pants, Curt headed for the exit with tires screeching. In an instant, Curt became his own boss. He'd been a good student and was able to parlay what he'd learned from Otis in order to continue stealing cars on his own.

Curt thought he was the cool one seducing the good-looking high school girl, but it was actually the other way around. Shela had been watching Curt before he ever saw her. She was looking for an older guy who had a car and was old enough to buy alcohol. Curt checked off all the right boxes for her interest. She only had to bump into him, drop her sunglasses, hike up the back of her dress, and bend down to pick them up while giving him a view of the motherlode. It worked. Like a female black widow spider, she pulled him into her web. Curt was soon controlled by Shela without ever realizing that she was the one pulling the strings.

Now Gary was fighting to keep up with Curt even though Curt was staying within the speed limit as he drove south on the interstate. He couldn't shut out the image of Shela shooting the guard point-blank in the head, and his entire body was shaking. Shela was bouncing in the passenger seat, trying to find a music station on the car radio. When the first song she dialed up was something about a highway to hell, Gary could only think to himself that it was a message meant only for him. She swayed to the song until she suddenly realized that Gary was not appreciative of the great music. He was still shaking slightly, and his hands were white from his tight grip on the wheel.

"Come on, Gary. Loosen up. Didn't I tell you we'd have a blast?"

Gary didn't reply, but only stared straight ahead and gripped the steering wheel even tighter.

Shela seemed to think for a minute before she unfastened her seat belt, reached over the center console, and with both hands began to search for his zipper with a big grin on her face. "Gary, you're too uptight. I'm going to help you relax."

Chapter 8

Sheriff Norton

Lewis Norten first greeted Angel warmly before he directed his attention to Mark and Al, shaking their hands as Angel introduced them. Norten was a tall, thin black man with close-cropped light gray hair, almost gaunt in appearance, and skin that showed signs of heavy exposure to the elements. He was wearing wrinkled blue jeans and a faded checkered shirt. A belt with a wide silver buckle was keeping his jeans from falling. His eyes were red from lack of sleep.

"Fellows, you'll have to excuse the way I look. I'd just got home from fishing with my two boys last night and was in the middle of cleaning fish when I first got the call from the highway patrol. I haven't had time to go home since. We have our share of crime in this county, but when something as violent and senseless as this happens, it's all hands on deck. Let me make sure I understand where you all fit in here. Angel told me that Ms. Smith had spent the weekend at Mr. Price's home along with himself, Mr. Price, and your son." He nodded toward Al. "Anyone else there?"

Mark answered, "The only other person there was Roe Estes, who also lives there. She's an attorney who works for the state."

Angel quickly followed with, "Lewis, Roe is a good friend of mine. She works for the state ATF out of Tallahassee. That's how I happened to be spending the weekend there."

"What led Ms. Smith to be at the rest stop?"

Mark answered, "I'm partially responsible for why. She was supposed to leave Sunday morning to return to her home in Orlando. She needed to prepare something for a podcast on Monday. I'd managed to get tickets for a Jaguar game, and I convinced her to stay for the game and leave later. I hadn't expected the weather to be a factor."

Al spoke up, "Mark, you can't blame yourself for any of this. Keri was as excited about going to the game as any of us."

Lewis was thoughtful when he spoke again, "The timeline from when she left your house and ended up at the rest stop would align with the time the storm came through. The storm was bad enough, I could imagine her stopping to let it pass."

Mark asked, "Is there any possibility someone might have just randomly followed her?"

"No, Mark. All the evidence at the crime scene indicates that whoever did this was already there and had already killed the security guard. It looks as if Ms. Smith actually tripped over the guard and fell before she was assaulted. Her injuries were not the result of a simple trip and fall. They were far more severe. By the way, did Ms. Smith have a cell phone?"

Mark quickly answered, "Yes. It was not with her when she was found?"

"No, it was not."

"Give me her number and carrier."

After writing it down, he said, "I'll be right back," and left the office. He was back after a couple of minutes. "We'll see if we can track it and locate it. If Ms. Smith left it in her car, we may get a break on locating her car.

Al asked, "So her car is still missing?"

"Yes, the minute we were aware that it was missing, we put out an alert. Unfortunately, enough time had elapsed, so the car could have been a couple hundred miles away with a different tag."

Mark responded, "That's assuming the car was taken by professionals. If it was taken by kids looking for a joyride, it would probably be somewhere nearby."

"Mark, you're right. That's the part that's so unusual. Professional car thieves are rarely violent. They want to draw as little attention as possible. Let's hope the cell phone will give us something."

Angel asked, "Lewis, have there been any other similar crimes anywhere in the area?"

"Angel, we've had a rash of car thefts locally, but not with this kind of violence. We're in the process of checking statewide for anything that might be related."

"Any witnesses?" Mark asked.

"Not really. The older man who was knocked out can't seem to remember anything. His wife is visually impaired, and she only remembers seeing shadows. The trucker who pulled into the rest stop only saw two cars leaving at a high rate of speed. We now believe one of the cars was Ms. Smith's car. The other car appeared to be some kind of souped-up project car.

"Listen, guys, I'm talking to you all partly as a part of the investigation and partly because of Angel here. You may be approached by reporters if they know how you're connected. I'd appreciate it if you wouldn't discuss any of this yet. I can only promise that we're doing all we can to find the killers. The security guard who was killed was supposed to celebrate his fiftieth wedding anniversary this week. In the meantime, we are pulling for Ms. Smith to make a full recovery as well."

Mark asked, "You used the word 'killers.' Any idea how many?"

"Only that the two cars left together and the wife with poor vision kept referring to two shadows."

"What about security cameras?" Mark asked.

The sheriff shook his head. "The cameras had been going off and on since Friday. The storm didn't help, and nothing was recorded during the timeline of the murder. A crew was scheduled to work on them today."

Norten had nothing else to tell them, or he didn't want to tell them anymore.

As they all stood up to leave, Angel thanked the sheriff and said, "Lewis, will you please let me know if anything develops? You do need to get some sleep."

Chapter 9

When Shela leaned over and started unbuckling his belt and working on his zipper, Gary almost ran off the road. He was so focused on keeping up with Curt that although he was driving within the posted speed limits, the rain and dark made it difficult for him to stay close. Add to it the fact that Gary didn't have a lot of driving experience and he was manning an unfamiliar car that required all of his attention.

If Gary could have read Curt's mind, he would have understood that the last thing they needed was being pulled over for some driving infraction. They had sped out of the rest stop because a sixteen-wheeler was entering the rest stop and Curt wanted the driver to see as little of them as possible.

Once they were back on I-95 South, he stayed under seventy. Leaving I-95 at the next exit onto US 1, Gary was vaguely aware that Curt was leading them on a westerly course. The route was through the most desolate countryside Gary had ever seen. The darkness and rain made it seem even more isolated.

By the time they reached East Palatka, Shela had her hands well into his jeans. Even though he imagined that Curt in his car just ahead of them could see every detail of her movements, he responded to Shela's skillful manipulation as he achieved the hardest erection of his young life.

Shela looked up at Gary with a big smile on her face. "Gary, you are a surprise. You've been hiding this from me. I'm going to call you 'Big Boy' from now on."

Up to this point in his life, Gary's sexual experience had been limited to a few pornographic magazines that he'd found when they were cleaning out Howard's belongings. The second that Shela leaned over the center console and lowered her head toward his lap, he exploded, almost running off the road again.

Shela started laughing and bouncing to the music again. "Gary, I can see that you need some lessons on the birds and bees. We'll work on this again later."

By the time his breathing had returned to normal, Gary could see that they were entering East Palatka and crossing the St. Johns River. There were only two options for crossing the river from where the rest stop was located. Either Green Cove Springs, which was well to the north, or Palatka, which was almost due west.

They drove very slowly through Palatka, and once through, they stayed on back roads, avoiding Gainesville by winding around more two-lane roads and towns with names like Micanopy and Wacahoota.

Just west of Gainesville, Shela let out an, "Oh, shit!"

Startled, Gary asked, "What's wrong?"

"It's her cell phone. It must have fallen on the floor," she said as she lowered her window. After looking to be sure there wasn't a car behind them, she threw it out of the window toward the ditch.

"Don't mention this to Curt. He'd just act pissed and blow shit for a while."

After passing through the hamlet of Bronson, they were again in a desolate area before they turned off the main highway and drove a short distance on a well-maintained gravel road.

Curt finally stopped in front of a tall, heavy iron gate with a sign above that read, *Moreno and Sons Salvage.*

Chapter 10

West Central Florida, 1930

Many months had passed since Paulus and Rita Graziano had fled from Chicago with only the clothes on their backs and a stolen suitcase full of money. Paulus and Rita Graziano ceased to exist the moment Paulus walked into Ray Whitmer's office. Although neither Paulus, now Larry Moreno, nor Rita, who adopted the last name of Moreno but retained Rita, had completed high school, they each had a PhD in the art of survival. A lack of formal education was offset by a high level of street smarts and a hefty dose of common sense. They had been immersed in the criminal world as it existed in the big city. Before they would attempt anything remotely illegal, they recognized they were now living in a vastly different environment from what they'd experienced in Chicago. That realization was the smartest decision they ever made.

Larry remembered the time he had to visit a dentist in Chicago to have an infected wisdom tooth removed. He'd mentioned to the dentist how lucky he was to have such beautiful girls working in his office. The doctor had only smiled and said, "Son, remember this, never shit where you eat." Larry had been breathing in the gas when the dentist made the comment, and it was only much later before he understood what the dentist had meant. It applied perfectly to their current situation. There would be no use of violence, robberies, or car theft within a hundred miles of their business. They would be good, benevolent, churchgoing, law-abiding, neighbors. If there were to be questions about their obsession with privacy, they would compensate by their civic generosity.

Larry and Rita stayed true to their plan. They imported twenty plains buffalos on the pretext of raising them for the meat. It gave them an initial excuse for a fencing system that resembled a prison enclosure as well as a system of very large, enclosed barns. There was a natural system of shallow lakes that extended halfway around the portion of the property where the main ranch house was located. At the time, there were no regulations requiring permits to dig or dredge lakes or waterways, so the shallow lakes were expanded and deepened so that several high dry areas containing the house and barns were almost totally surrounded and protected by water heavily populated by alligators and water moccasins.

Ray Whitmer helped Larry by introducing him to a limited number of workers who were well paid for their efforts. Workers for building barns, fencing, and dredging were necessary, but Larry knew he needed to find a few people he could trust in order to proceed with the business that he and Rita were planning. Working with his new clients seemed to bring out whatever positive qualities had lain dormant in Ray Whitmer. He seemed energized by the new couple, and he could sense that bigger and better things lay ahead.

When Larry explained to Ray that he needed a few full-time workers for the future salvage yard business who might be willing to ignore a few issues of legality but would be compensated well beyond what any normal employers might pay, Ray understood immediately what he meant. After all, hadn't he turned a blind eye when he helped "Larry Moreno" to establish a new identity, never knowing what Larry's real name was or where he had come from with such a large amount of money?

A few days later, Ray drove up to the ranch house with someone for Larry to meet. Ray walked to the front door and left the individual waiting in the car.

"Larry, I've got someone I want you to meet. Before you form any opinions, let me explain. The man sitting in my car, Abraham Jackson, was just released from the chain gang from over in Alachua County. He had a good job working for the school district repairing buses and anything else with an engine. He and his wife and young boy were leaving a grocery store in a small town outside Gainesville when a white guy reached out, grabbed his wife's ass, and asked, 'How much for a piece of this?'

"Abe only hit the man one time, but it was enough to break his jaw in two places and leave him with a concussion that lasted for weeks. Unluckily for Abe, the idiot he hit happened to be the son of a state senator. Abe lost his job and his home. His wife and son had to live with relatives until he was released.

"So, you ask, how I knew all this, and I'm sorry to say that I was the lawyer who represented him, but I was just spitting into the wind. No one locally would touch his case, but his aunt had worked for my parents, and when she came and asked me for help, I couldn't say no. I'm amazed that he's out after only five years of working on the chain gang. I know Abe is one bitter and angry man, but he was raised in a God-fearing home and his only run-in with the law was when he punched the wrong person."

Larry listened to Ray without making any comments, but his respect for Ray increased when he heard the story.

He was well aware there were still differences in the way blacks were treated in some places in both the North and the South, but he still had a problem with it regardless of where it occurred. The best mechanic he'd ever known was black. He had not only been a mentor, but he was also a trusted friend as well. Treating someone differently only because of the color of their skin was something he'd never understood.

"Go ahead and bring him up to the porch, Ray, and let me talk to him."

Ray walked back to his car, spoke to the person inside, and opened the passenger side door. The man who got out seemed to dwarf the car. He was one of the largest men Larry had ever seen. He had to be six foot four or five with wide shoulders. His biceps were so large they threatened to bust the sleeves of his shirt. His skin was jet-black, as was his long hair, which reached down to his shoulders. His face was expressionless as he walked up onto the front porch and accepted a chair as Larry indicated.

Larry could only imagine what it would be like to be hit with the man's huge hands. Larry thought he was probably lucky he hadn't killed the guy as Ray introduced him to Larry.

"I understand that you know a little about working on automobile engines."

"Yes, sir, I do," Abe replied in a measured tone while his face still showed no expression.

"Ray here tells me you're looking for work."

"Yes, sir, I am. He probably also told you why I lost my last job."

"He did. And I don't hold that against you. I think most any man with any degree of self respect would have done the same. Abe, I'm looking for someone to work for me here on a full-time basis. If it works out, it could be a very profitable position. I'm only looking to hire a very few people, but they must be people I can trust explicitly."

"Sir, Mr. Ray here has told me that I can trust you and that you'll be fair. That's all I can ask. If you hire me, you won't regret it."

Larry stood up and put out his hand. "Abe, you have a job." As Abe's hand engulfed Larry's, Moreno and Sons Salvage had its first full-time employee.

The next person that Ray recruited was an ex-deputy sheriff from an adjacent county who had the audacity to challenge the current sheriff for election. The sheriff had paid a local prostitute to swear that the deputy had demanded sex from her and had threatened her life when she'd refused. By the time the deputy had cleared his name, the election was history, and he was out of a job as well. He was now desperate for work with a new wife and a child on the way. Roger had grown up in the area, and Ray knew he could be trusted. Thus, Roger Graham became the second hire for the salvage yard.

For the first several months after they had stopped in Chiefland, Florida, both Larry and Rita were looking over their shoulders in fear of retribution from Bugs. They were just beginning to relax a bit when their past suddenly caught up with them.

Chapter 11

After meeting the sheriff, Mark, Angel, and Al returned to Mark's home. During the drive, they considered their options. It was painfully obvious that for the moment, there wasn't a lot they could do. Angel and Al, as well as Roe, would have to return to their respective jobs.

After they reached Mark's home, Angel suggested that since he had a good relationship with the sheriff, he would be advised of any progress on the case. Roe was currently working out of Tallahassee with a drug task force, so she would be able to monitor any statewide criminal activity, and Al said he would search the legal databases for any information that might help. Since Mark was retired from the university, he had the time to follow up on any lead that might develop.

As he was about to leave Mark's house, Angel received a call from Sheriff Norten.

"Angel, I just wanted you to know that we were able to track Ms. Smith's cell phone to an area outside Gainesville. We'll work with the local people and try to find the phone. At the very least, we now know which direction they were headed. The thinking here is that the car was headed toward US-19 and then down to Tampa, where it would disappear into a container on a freighter ship headed south. We're not aware of any chop shops in or west of Gainesville. I'll let you know if we learn any more."

"Thanks, Lewis. I appreciate it."

As soon as he'd closed the call, Angel told the group what he'd learned from Norten. They all agreed that it only created more unanswered questions.

Roe was the last to leave. She intentionally waited until Al and Angel had left so she could talk to Mark in private.

"Mark, make yourself a drink and come out onto the patio. I need to talk to you before I leave."

After they were both comfortably seated on the patio—Mark with a cup of coffee and Roe with a soda—Roe looked directly at Mark and asked, "Mark, I want to know what you plan to do next." Roe was the only living person who could address Mark so directly. What they had experienced together had created a bond of trust but also dependency on each other. Although Roe was not his biological daughter, she was emotionally attached to Mark as he was to her. It was a mutually symbiotic relationship. "I know what you're capable of doing when you've been hurt, and I know you're hiding the hurt and anger you're feeling right now."

Mark listened to Roe's words and was quiet for a few moments before he spoke. "Roe, I have to be honest. I'm not sure what I'll do next. I keep asking myself, why do those I care for come to such violent endings? My daughter, my wife, Al's mother, and now Keri—all are victims of violence. If anything ever happened to you, I think it would be the end for me."

"Mark, I feel the same. That's why I'm concerned."

"Roe, for the time being, I'm going to give Vera support and remain optimistic about Keri. Anyway, unless something else turns up, there's really nothing else I can do. How about I promise you that I'll let you know if and when I'm going to do anything stupid? That way you can tell me I'm crazy to do it."

"That sounds good, Mark. Just promise me you'll let me know before you do."

As Roe left, she felt some relief, but she was still uneasy about Mark's state of mind. After she was gone, Mark drove back to the hospital to check on Keri's condition and give Vera some relief.

Keri's mom was sitting in the same position next to Keri's bed where Mark had left her earlier in the day.

Mark finally convinced her to take a long break. He promised he'd stay by Keri's side until she returned. "Vera, I'll call you if there's any change in Keri's condition."

After Vera had left, Mark settled into the chair next to Keri's bed. Seeing Keri in her condition was painful, so he turned the chair so that he was staring at a blank hospital wall. This also gave him time to think about what he'd learned so far, which wasn't much. He felt that what differentiated this from traditional car thieves was the brutality associated with the crime. This person or persons was over the edge and out of control. Either they had done this before, or even if they hadn't, they would do it again. He knew that the sheriff would cast a wide net searching for anything similar. If nothing came up, they may have to wait for the assailants to brutalize another innocent person. He was concerned about how fast the sheriff would let any of them know if he found anything.

Mark understood. The sheriff had to follow protocol, and keeping civilians informed of every piece of information they gathered was not a responsible way to solve a case. Knowing that Roe would have access to maybe even more search tools than even the sheriff, he used his cell phone and called Roe, who was still driving toward

Tallahassee. Mark explained what he wanted her to look for.

"I'm ahead of you, Mark. I'd already figured that out. Tomorrow I'll start looking. You'll be the first to know. Any change in Keri's condition?"

"No. I'm sitting here with her now. It doesn't look good though."

"Mark, get a good night's sleep and start fresh tomorrow."

"Thanks, Roe. I hope you know how much I appreciate your concern for my well-being. I'll talk to you later."

As soon as Vera returned to resume her vigil, Mark returned home and got a needed night's sleep.

The first thing Mark did the next morning was to go for a short but fast run along the river. After he'd cooled off, he took a mug of hot black coffee out onto his deck and watched the sun rise over the river. He desperately wanted to do something. But what? It was simply not in his nature to wait for something to happen. Finally, frustrated, he showered and drove back down I-95 to the hospital.

After reaching the hospital, he convinced Vera to go with him to the hospital cafeteria and get something to eat. The nurse assured her that it would be okay. As soon as they were sitting at a table with their food, Vera pointed to an older white-haired lady who'd just walked into the cafeteria. "That's Mrs. Lounds. She and her husband were the couple at the rest stop where Kari was hurt."

She appeared to be alone, and Mark quickly said, "Why don't you invite her over to sit with us?"

"All right," Vera said as she quickly stood up and went over to the lady and pointed to where Mark was sitting. The lady nodded and looked in Mark's direction.

After she'd put food on a tray, she started walking in the general direction where they were sitting. Aware that the lady was having trouble locating them, Vera went back up to her, took her elbow, and guided her to the table where Mark was sitting. Vera introduced Mark to Clara as she sat down.

"I'm sorry. I can't see very well anymore."

Mark asked, "Do you have anyone here helping you?"

"Yes. My son dropped me off on his way to work. He'll pick me up tonight. I can see well enough to find my way around the hospital."

"How is your husband doing?"

"Ralph is getting better. He's still gets dizzy every time he tries to stand up, but at least he knows who I am now. I was really scared at first. They tell me that his symptoms are what you'd expect from a severe concussion."

"Does he remember any more about what happened?"

"Not much. It was so unexpected, and it happened so fast. He did tell me that he has an image of a young man about normal height. Oh, and the man was smiling. That's the last thing he remembered. I think the police want him to tell them more. But that's all he can tell them."

"I understand that you only saw the images of two people."

"Yes. I wish I could have seen more than I did, but it was dark, and I only saw shadows. I think my poor eyesight is what made my husband get a dashcam for the car."

Mark almost choked himself when he heard what Clara said. He had to take a long drink of water before he could say another word. Trying to remain calm, he simply repeated, "*Dashcam?*"

"Yes, Ralph is a little paranoid ever since we almost got hit by a car that ran a red light. He said there were too many crazies in the world, and it would be a smart thing to have."

"What happened to the dashcam?"

"It's probably still in the glove box of the Mercury where Ralph put it when we parked. Ralph always takes it off the dash and puts it in there whenever we leave the car. He was always afraid that someone might break into the car and steal it."

Mark realized that Clare still had not picked up on the possibility that the cam might be a valuable tool in identifying the assailants. Vera, though, was much quicker, but looked at Mark as she asked Clare, "What happened to your car after they brought you and your husband to the hospital?"

"Oh, our son who lives in St. Augustine came and got it. He's keeping it at his house until Ralph is able to drive again."

Mark gave Vera a slight nod before she asked, "Clare, do you think your son would mind if Mark here took a look at your dashcam? Maybe it would show whether my daughter's car was there before you."

"No, I'm sure he won't mind. I do need to call him and let him know what you want to do."

"Thank you, Clare. It would mean a lot to me."

Mark was almost hyperventilating as Clare fumbled around in her large purse trying to find her phone. She eventually pushed a large preset number on the phone. Her son answered immediately, and Clare replied, "No, Ben, there's no problem. Your dad is okay. I just wanted to ask you if it would be okay if a friend of the girl who was almost killed could take a look at Ralph's dashcam.

It's in the glove compartment. He wants to find out if she was already at the rest stop when we got there. His name is Mark Price. The girl's mom is here with us, and she says it's important to know."

Clare looked up at Mark and said, "He won't be home until five this afternoon. How about five-thirty?"

Mark nodded. "That will be great. Tell him I'll see him then."

Clare gave Mark Ben's address and phone number, which he entered into his phone.

When they went back toward Keri's room, Vera asked Mark, "Do you really think the dashcam will show anything?"

"Vera, I really don't know. It was raining hard, but it's worth checking."

With some time to kill before he was to meet Ben, Mark drove onto I-95 South and stopped at the rest stop. It was indeed located in the middle of a long-deserted stretch of highway. Even in daytime, there were only six or eight cars in the front and a couple of eighteen-wheelers parked in the rear. He walked around and tried to visualize how it happened. A crew of state workers were packing up equipment and leaving after completing repair work on the surveillance system.

The actual spot where the guard had been killed and Keri was assaulted had been power-washed, but Mark could still see small cracks in the concrete surface that were stained black from remaining traces of blood. He still couldn't shake the feeling that he was partially responsible. Forcing himself to keep moving, he returned to his car and drove south to the first exit and doubled back toward St. Augustine and his meeting with Ben Lounds.

Chapter 12

West Central Florida,1930

Following the St. Valentine's Day Massacre, Bugs had maintained a low profile. With the loss of so many of his men, his cash flow had been seriously curtailed. Not to mention the fact that he'd drawn down his cash reserves to almost zero in order to fill a suitcase with cash. He was now painfully aware that any deal he had hoped to make was no longer an option. He desperately needed that cash back. If the money was anywhere in the vicinity, it would be known on the underworld grapevine. He could only assume that Paulus had taken the money and hauled ass out of there. Bugs had a criminal mind, but he didn't have a violent disposition. But this was different. He fanaticized what he would do to Paulus if he could get his hands on him.

Although he hated to admit to anyone that he'd lost a lot of money, he finally began to call in favors. He even made it clear to the people in his garages that he'd pay a good bonus to anyone who could lead him to Paulus. He'd tracked the Phantom as far as Indianapolis and knew Paulus had traded it for a new high-powered Chevrolet. Bugs went out of his way to ensure that if he couldn't enjoy the Phantom, then no one else would either. At that point, the trail dried up. That was, until a mechanic in a garage told him what Paulus had told him about disappearing in Cedar Key, Florida.

Two men associated with his organization volunteered to travel to Cedar Key to look for Paulus. If that was where he went, he should be easy to find.

Rocco Aiello was a small, skinny man with a thin mustache and thick glasses who was also an accounting genius. Unfortunately for him, he was caught skimming money from the bank where he worked. After he'd served his time in prison, he was never going to be trusted handling anyone's money. But he was good at ferreting out other cheaters, and his services were available to any person or business that suspected someone to be taking cash from the till. He would be the brains of the search party.

The muscle would be delegated to Gianni "The Hammer" Barone. Gianni was wider than he was tall, his neck wider than his head, and he was bald with tiny beady eyes. He had developed a reputation for beating people to death with his bare hands. And he was dumb as a stump. He was simply told that he was to do whatever Rocco told him to do.

The odd couple wasted no time in traveling to Cedar Key. As they traveled from Chiefland to Cedar Key, Rocco wondered how anyone had ever found this place. Having lived all his life in the city, he felt as if he were on another planet. Gianni wasn't even noticing their surroundings. He was only dreaming of the next person he'd get to hammer with his fists.

Rocco would have been more interested in the town if he'd been aware of its rich history. Cedar Key had been a major Florida port during the mid-1800s and through the Civil War but was now a mere shell of its previous self.

The couple checked into the Cedar Key Hotel, which happened to be the only hotel in the town. The hotel bar was the hub of the town, and after spending the evening conversing with many of the residents, Rocco was convinced that Paulus had never made it to the town. He'd been smart enough to search Paulus and Rita's home before he left Chicago. He carried with him a wedding picture that had been left in a drawer in their house. No one he met in Cedar Key recognized the photo.

Working backward, Rocco and Gianni returned to the closest town of Chiefland the next morning. They checked into the best-looking motel before going to the diner next door. He showed the photograph to several people in the diner including the woman behind the counter, who immediately recognized Paulus and Rita.

"Yes. That's Rita and Larry Moreno. They just moved here recently."

Rocco felt a rush of adrenaline similar to the rush he always felt when he'd redirected a bank's money into his own account.

"Do you know where they live?"

"They live somewhere out in the country. I'm not sure where, but I'm sure Ray Whitmer would know. I think he's their lawyer. His office is just down the street that way." She pointed down the main street.

Ray Whitmer was sitting at his desk as he watched the car park in front of his office. Alarm bells started to go off the minute he saw the two men get out of their car and approach his door. They were what natives would call "Suede Shoe Boys." But one look at Gianni Barone and he knew these men were not coming here to sell real estate. They each wore long black overcoats, expensive black hats, and the sunlight reflected off the shine on their shoes. No, these men were not from anywhere around here, and they were not bringing good news.

Fortunately, Ray was well into his transformation and was totally sober. He took a deep breath and braced himself for whatever was coming.

Rocco did all the talking. "I was told that you might be able to help us." He handed the photograph of Rita and Paulus to Ray. "The woman is my sister. When she married this man, our father went off the rails. Like most fathers, nobody was good enough for his only daughter. He told her he never wanted to see her again. Now he's about to die and he wants to make up. He wants to give them his blessing and to see his grandchildren before he leaves this world. I'd like to see my sister as well."

Ray knew from his recent association with Rita and Paulus that Rita was an only child, and both her parents had died in the influenza epidemic in 1918, leaving her at the mercy of an abusive orphan home. He tried to remain calm and not let his apprehension show. He also knew that he couldn't claim ignorance.

"That's Rita and Larry Moreno. They just recently settled here. They're fine folks."

Rocco smiled a Cheshire cat smile and replied, "Yes, they are. I'm anxious to see them again. Can you tell me where they live?"

"It would be my pleasure. I'm sure Rita will be overjoyed to see you. They live outside town over on the Flats."

"Flats?"

"Sorry, I should know you aren't familiar with the local geography. I mean the Waccasassa Flats. They bought a ranch out there."

"How can we find it?"

"Let me give you the address. It's off 339, not more than twenty to thirty minutes from here. If you have a map, it's easy to find."

"Mr. Whitmer, you don't know what a help you've been."

The door hadn't finished closing behind them before Ray was dialing Larry's phone number. Now Ray understood why Larry had gone to so much effort to have a phone installed in his house. Never mind that it was a line he had to share with both the church and the school down the road. He breathed a sigh of relief when two female voices answered hello at the same time.

"I'm calling Rita Moreno," Ray said.

One voice said, "Yes, this is Rita," just as another chimed in with, "Hello, this is Amanda at the school. I'll hang up now."

"Rita, this is Ray. Is Larry there?"

"Hold on a minute. He's in the barn."

"This is urgent, Rita. Get 'em quick."

In less than two minutes, Paulus was on the phone. "Yes, Ray, what's so urgent?"

Ray quickly told Larry about the two men.

When he gave him a description of the two men, Larry let out a breath. "I know exactly who they are. What kind of car were they driving?"

"It was a newer model black Packard. I'm pretty sure it was a 640 Custom Eight."

"Good job, Ray. You just earned another bonus. I need you to do one more thing for me. Get a state auto title transfer form and have it ready for me. Put a fictitious seller's name on it and leave the buyer's name blank. Also get me a driver's license for the fabricated name as well. I'll be in touch later."

"Do you want me to come out to your house?"

"No. You stay in town and give yourself a good alibi. Rita and I will be okay."

Since settling into his new life, Larry had armed himself well. In 1930, if you had the cash, you could buy any firearm you wanted. He'd found a World War I 30-06 Browning automatic rifle, commonly known as a BAR, a 12-gauge Winchester Model 1897 trench shotgun, and two .45 caliber Colt M1911 handguns. Although Larry and Rita intended to avoid any violence, if at all possible, they had no choice in this instance. Now it was a matter of survival.

The road leading up to the main gate was lined by trees and thick underbrush that provided ample cover for any potential ambush. Larry put a loaded M1911 pistol in a large jacket pocket before shoving a twenty-round clip of 30-06 rifle rounds into the BAR and another loaded clip in his jacket pocket. Rita kept the shotgun and the second M1911 inside the house, where she stayed close to the two boys.

Larry climbed over the fence some distance away from the gate before hiding behind a fallen tree. From this position, he could see a distance down the length of the road as it approached the gate.

It was late in the afternoon before the last of the people who had been working on the lakes and barns were leaving. As soon as he'd gotten into position, a large black car turned onto the road in front of him. Larry had the BAR resting across the tree trunk, aimed toward the approaching car. But as he'd anticipated, the car slowed and stopped. He knew the occupants were planning their approach while they got a feeling for the surroundings.

As the last of the workers left through the gate, heading toward the main highway, the large Packard backed up to let the workers pass before turning around and disappearing. Returning to the house, Larry explained to Rita what he planned to do. Rita understood and was ready to get it over with as quickly as possible.

The hit men waited until after midnight to make their move. In the still of the night, Larry heard the faint rumble of a large V8 engine. He saw a flash of headlights, which were quickly turned off. They had left the car parked back toward the main highway and were quietly walking toward the gate.

There was some momentary hesitation, but they were soon climbing over the fence adjacent to the gate itself. *That's an issue I'll deal with later*, Larry thought to himself. There was an open expanse of maybe forty-five yards between the gate and the house itself. The two men were so sure of themselves as they moved toward the dark house, they were walking almost shoulder-to-shoulder when Rita switched on the floodlights.

The blinding floodlights lit up the entire area between the gate and the front of the house, brighter than day. Larry was stretched out flat on the ground under a dark blanket thirty yards away with the BAR aimed point-blank toward the two startled men. The BAR was set to fire on full automatic, and the twenty rounds of surplus full metal jacket, 30-06 rounds tore through the hapless men. Both men were carrying Thompson submachine guns with drum magazines.

As he was being hit with rounds from the BAR, Rocco reflexively squeezed the trigger of his Thompson. Firing toward the ground as the bullets from the BAR spun him around, the .45 caliber rounds from his Thompson nearly cut off one of Gianni Barone's legs.

And just as quickly as it had started, it was over. Rita switched off the floodlights, and as a slight breeze blew the smoke from the gunpowder away, the frogs and crickets resumed their nighttime chorus. When Larry walked over to look closely at the two mutilated bodies, there was no need to feel for a pulse. They were dead.

He couldn't help but think it ironic that he'd made it through the World War I meat grinder in France and never once fired a shot at another man. Now, he'd killed two men in his own front yard. He checked their pockets for the car keys but found none. They were apparently not afraid of it being stolen out here in the boondocks.

Larry looked up towards Rita, who had come out onto the front porch. "Are the boys still asleep?"

"They never moved an inch."

"Good. Now, if I open the gate, do you think you can drive their car back up here while I start moving them?"

"I think so."

As Rita took a flashlight and walked toward the road to get the men's car, Larry used a wheelbarrow to carry each man to a woodpile behind a barn. After Rita had driven the car up to the house, she closed and locked the gate.

"Rita, why don't you stay inside with the boys? There's no need for you to see what I'm going to do."

After watching the two men being massacred, Rita had her fill of violence for the night. It was a smart choice because even Larry was challenged by what he did next. Using a large, round, flat stump that was used as a chopping block to cut up kindling, he methodically chopped off both men's hands with an axe. He let them finish bleeding out, but after the damage done by the BAR, there was little blood left in either of the two very dead men. Bringing the Packard around to the woodpile, he placed a large tarpaulin in the trunk and wrapped the bodies in it. Telling Rita what he was doing before he left, he drove the Packard several miles toward the Suwannee River crossing at Fanning Springs.

There was no traffic this time of the morning. Finding a deserted spot on the riverbank, Larry pushed the bodies into the strong river current flowing toward the Gulf of Mexico. Returning to the ranch, he wrapped up the severed hands before he packed them in an old shoebox. He wrote a note on a piece of notebook paper and stuffed it into the box along with the hands. Then and only then did Larry and Rita allow themselves a well-earned nightcap of a strong drink.

Larry drove into Chiefland the next morning in the Packard and met Ray in his office. Ray had the fake title and driver's license ready. Paulus left Chiefland and drove south on US 19. Driving very carefully, it took almost three hours for Larry to reach Tampa. Placing the shoebox in a proper shipping box, he mailed it as first-class mail. He hoped it would arrive at its destination before it started to reek.

Larry was now able to execute the first of the many transactions that he and his descendants would complete over the coming years. With the aid of the fake driver's license and the Florida automobile title, he was able to sell the Packard Custom Eight for a tidy sum. With cash in his pocket, he bought a seat on a bus and slept all the way back to Chiefland, where Ray met him and drove him the rest of the way home.

Ray knew better than to ask any questions. It was best that he never knew what had happened to the two men. Whatever it was it could not have been good. He was thankful that he was Larry Moreno's friend and not his enemy.

A package arrived at Bugs's safehouse three days later. When he brought it in, he grimaced at the foul odor coming out of the package. When he opened it and realized what he was looking at, he threw up on the floor. He had planned to leave town and lie low for a while anyway. Now, between the note and the contents of the package, he had no doubt that it was time to leave Chicago for a spell.

For the rest of his life, Bugs would get severe heartburn every time he was reminded of Paulus Graziano.

Chapter 13

Moreno and Sons Salvage

Driving the stolen car, Gary was stunned when he first saw the imposing gate—supported by huge pillars built from Florida lime rock—that towered above them. The current gate bore no resemblance to the simple iron gate that Larry had initially erected years earlier. When they first stopped in front of the gate, the entire area had lit up like a football field. He watched as Curt got out of his car and approached a box on the left tower and took a phone out of the box. After a brief conversation, he got back in his car and waited. Shela had suddenly become visibly subdued compared to her previous hyper state.

Before he got back into his car, Curt told Gary, "Gary, you want to keep your mouth shut from here on. Only speak if someone is talking to you. These are some dangerous people. We've heard stories of people going through these gates and never coming out."

Curt's words did nothing to help Gary's depression. Not only was Gary scared shitless and feeling like he was drowning, but he was also dead tired and wanted to close his eyes and go to sleep. Maybe then he would wake up and remember that all this was only a bad dream. But the noise created by the gate opening assured him that this was no dream.

The huge gates didn't swing open. Instead, they seemed to slide into the limestone pillars on either side. Just inside the gate, standing next to a golf cart was one of the largest men Gary had ever seen. His skin was jet-black and his totally bald head glistened under the glare of the bright floodlights. He walked out to meet Curt, and after a brief conversation, Curt walked back to where Gary and Shela were waiting in the Camry. "Stay behind me and just do as you're told."

As they passed through the gate, they passed an edifice on their right that looked like an office building. A driveway led off toward the right and curved toward the rear of the building and ended in a parking lot. The main driveway they were on continued on for a short distance before it forked again with one part curving toward the right and the other one continuing straight between bodies of water visible in the moonlight.

They followed the golf cart as it took the right fork and soon entered a fenced compound. The size of the building in front of them took Gary's breath away. The parking area was at least a hundred yards long and fifty yards in width. Gary could make out a couple of semitrailers and at least two empty trailers made for transporting cars. On the far end of the building, it looked as if there were endless lines of cars. Had there had been enough light, Gary would have recognized it as a junkyard covering many acres filled with vehicles in all states of damage. There was a loading dock with a wide-open door. On either side of the dock were large sliding doors that were also open. Gary could only catch a glimpse of the cavernous interior.

The man in the cart motioned for Curt to park in front of the loading dock. He pointed for Gary to park the

Camry directly in front of one of the open doors. Curt got out of his Mustang and motioned for Shela and Gary to exit the Camry and get into his car. Gary watched as Curt walked just inside the large open door.

The huge black man disappeared and instead a man wearing jeans and a tight-fitting T-shirt appeared. His dark black hair was pulled up into a tight ponytail that seemed to accentuate his lean browned face and narrow nose. He was of medium height, but his muscular body indicated serious use of weights. Most obvious was a .45 caliber M1911 pistol he carried in a holster hanging from his belt. While watching the man converse with Curt, Gary didn't expect the man to invite them in for a drink. He couldn't explain what it was, but even if he hadn't been carrying a gun, the man projected a demeanor of violence.

The man's name was Leonardo Moreno, or Leon, the grandson of Larry and Rita Moreno. Leon and his younger sister now operated Moreno and Sons Salvage. Larry and Rita had done well with the business. They made wise decisions over the years by capturing a large part of the salvage business, covering a wide geographical area. They developed a reputation for paying top dollar for wrecked and damaged vehicles.

Over time, they developed a network of buyers in the salvage auctions across the state. When metal was in such high demand during the wars, they had profited. Because the business was so isolated, and since it only had a small group of reliable employees who could be trusted, they were able to operate a very discreet chop shop. The disassembled parts were easily absorbed by the legitimate salvage parts, which added to a sizable profit margin.

Early on, Larry Moreno made the right connections so that he was able to send out many stolen high-end autos to South America, where the demand was always high and the questions were few. Besides shipping out parts to auto repair shops, they became adept at assembling complete cars from wrecked ones. By shipping these cars out of the country, the VIN numbers, including the CON VINS, were largely ignored.

Larry's first hire, Abraham Jackson, turned out to be an automotive savant. He was a genius at dismantling cars in record time and leaving no trace of the vehicle. He instinctively had known how to find all vehicle registration numbers as well as how to alter them, so the changes were undetectable. The large black man, Ethan Jackson, who had ushered the trio into the yard, was Abraham's grandson and had either learned or inherited Abe's automotive skills.

The Paulus descendants had all been able to maintain a booming open salvage business while keeping the illegal side of the business well hidden. The original plan to become pillars of their community had paid off. They made generous contributions to local charities and were members of a local church. Over time, the Morenos became pillars of the surrounding communities. They were even able to use both money and influence to have the ex-deputy, Roger Graham, elected sheriff for a neighboring county.

Over time, as the salvage parts business became so profitable, the need to process stolen cars dwindled to only a vestige of what it had originally been. By the time Leon was running the salvage business, a stolen car was either immediately chopped up and sold as parts, or if the car was a very high-end auto, it would be shipped to South America.

Larry Moreno lived to the age of eighty-five, passing away only weeks after Rita's death. They had lived a good life, with the only heartbreak occurring during the Korean War. Their two sons, Tory and Cletus, grew up in rural West Central Florida. They attended local schools and were good kids with problems only related to the early teenage years.

Cletus became fixated on the military at a young age from watching the events of World War II as a child. As soon as he finished high school, he enrolled in the Marines over the objections of both of his parents. Larry had seen firsthand the horror of war in Europe during World War I, and he wanted his son to never have to experience the same thing.

After he'd completed basic training, Cletus qualified for flight training for the emerging new aviation division of helicopters. Without ever realizing the dangers he would be facing, Cletus found himself engaged in what would be known as the "The Forgotten War" on the other side of the world in the most desolate place he'd ever seen.

The Korean War never achieved the notoriety that the Vietnam War did. It started in 1950 and followed closely on the heels of World War II. With the memories of the Second World War so still so painful, America was in no mood for another war. Only the soldiers who fought and survived could convey the circumstances and the brutality they endured. Because of the poor decisions and lack of understanding of conditions the Army faced, many hapless American soldiers were left in impossible situations. That's where Cletus found himself in 1950.

The helicopter Cletus was piloting was an HTL-4. It was one of the earliest designs that would evolve into the more sophisticated modern versions. The maximum capacity was five people. At the outset of the war, its potential for evacuating wounded soldiers was realized. It could carry two walking wounded plus the pilot inside the tiny bubble-shaped cockpit in addition to two seriously wounded soldiers on an outside stretcher, one on each side. A thick plexiglass shield had been designed to cover the head of the outside stretchers.

Cletus had left his operational base and was flying over a snow-covered white landscape on his way to evacuate more wounded men near the Chosin Reservoir. Yi Ming was a conscript in the Chinese Communist forces who had no understanding of why he was almost totally covered in snow, tired, hungry, and freezing. He was a long way from his home in China, where he'd been taken from his parents' modest home, loaded into a truck, and driven away. His white outer garment made him virtually invisible as he huddled next to his friends.

The Chinese forces moved only at night as they slowly encircled the Americans, who were moving north trying to reach the Yalu River and decimate the North Korean Army. The Chinese soldiers were instructed to remain motionless during the day in order to avoid detection. They only moved under cover of darkness.

As Cletus's helicopter passed directly over Yi Ming, he was startled, inadvertently causing his finger to depress the trigger of his rifle. The shot caused many other soldiers to immediately begin firing at the helicopter as it passed close overhead. One of the tracer rounds hit the helicopter's gas tank, causing it to explode. The helicopter went down in a ball of fire. Total silence followed, and the Chinese soldiers disappeared into the snow again.

After dark, when the Chinese officers determined who had fired the first shot, they had Ji Ming kneel on the snow in front of his comrades while they gave a speech before they shot him in the back of his head.

Cletus's body was never recovered. His name joined the long list of soldiers from the Forgotten War who were never accounted for.

When Larry reached eighty, the surviving son, Tory, who had been a good student of the business and had taken over the daily responsibility for running it, convinced Rita and Larry to enjoy the fruits of their labors. And they did by traveling all over the world. The one place they avoided like the plague was Chicago. Tory continued to grow the business until he died young from a coronary event. It was his two children, Leon and his sister, who now owned and ran the business.

The only time an employee had tried to turn on Moreno and Sons happened somewhere in the Fifties. A federal agent who was convinced that the company was involved in the drug trade had bribed an employee of Moreno and Sons, Jimmy Crompton, to disclose everything he knew about the salvage business. They were supposed to secretly meet on the water near Fowlers Bluff on the Suwannee River while supposedly fishing. When neither Jimmy nor the agent returned from their trips, a search was mounted.

Both their boats were found drifting out into the Gulf of Mexico. One of the peculiar aspects was the fat water moccasin found curled up in each of the boats. No trace of either man was ever found.

After a brief conversation, it was Larry's grandson, Leon, who disappeared into the depths of the massive warehouse with Curt. When they reappeared, Curt was smiling as he approached his Mustang. "Okay, both of you need to come with me."

Gary and Shela followed Curt into the building. Curt went toward the left and into a small office with large glass windows. Leon Moreno looked carefully at Gary and Shela. He looked back at Gary, and a faint smile crossed his face. "Son, did you pee in your pants?"

Gary only stuttered and blushed as he realized that his pants were still wet from his encounter with Shela, who turned her head to hide the grin on her face.

"Uh-huh, yes, sir. Curt never stopped all the way here."

"Curt tells me this is the first time you've helped him."

"Yes, sir."

"Let me see your driver's license."

Not knowing what to expect, Gary took his wallet out of his pocket and handed Leon his license.

He took it over to a copy machine and made a copy.

Handing the license back to Gary, he leaned in close to him. "Gary, if I ever have the slightest doubt about you, just know that I can and *will* find you. It will not be good. I'm also assuming that you took the Camry with no trouble."

Both Curt and Shela were silent, knowing that what Leon was saying to Gary applied to them as well. They were also aware that what they'd done earlier was not going to turn out well.

Ethan, who had driven the Camry into the depths of the building, returned to the small office and handed Leon a piece of paper.

"What year is it?" Leon asked.

"This year. It has just under 10K miles.

Leon nodded while looking at Curt. "Wait in your car."

Curt, Shela, and Gary went back outside and waited in Curt's Mustang until Leon came out of the door with an envelope in his hand. Leaning down without saying a word, he handed Curt a bulging envelope. Ethan approached on the golf cart and said, "Follow me."

The gate had opened by the time they reached it, so they didn't have to slow down. Curt suddenly wanted to get as far away as possible before anyone at Moreno and Son's Salvage heard the morning news.

Chapter 14

Ben Lounds lived in a gated subdivision a short distance off US 1 in St. Augustine. Turning off US 1 onto Wildwood Drive, Mark went from a crowded business district into what seemed to be a jungle. When he entered Ben's subdivision, he was immediately stopped at a guardhouse. Ben had already called the guardhouse, giving Mark permission to enter. Mark had to smile at the guard, an elderly white-haired gentleman who wanted to have a conversation about whether the fish were biting and seemed reluctant to let Mark go.

Continuing up the road on Osceola Trail, he drove through a green tunnel where the vegetation was so thick that Mark still couldn't see any of the homes. He came to a sudden stop as a group of white-tailed deer stood in the road blocking his way. He was able to continue on after they had leisurely crossed the road and vanished into the thick foliage. Finally, he was able to see houses set back in the trees. The homes all were located on large lots which gave them an increased sense of privacy.

When Mark reached Ben's house, he parked in a circular driveway in front of the house. He could see an older model Mercury sedan sitting in a separate driveway that led to the garage area toward one end of the house. Before he could ring the doorbell, Ben opened the door and invited him inside.

"Mr. Price, this has been a huge clusterfuck. How is your friend doing?"

"Not well, Ben. Please drop the mister and call me Mark. I'm reminded enough that I'm becoming a senior citizen. And thank you for letting me look at the dashcam."

"Mark, I can't believe that none of us thought about it until now. It's been a couple years since my dad bought it, and with all that's happened, it was forgotten until my mom mentioned it to you. I just now finished downloading it. Let's go see what we've got. I'm not that optimistic, because it was the cheapest one my dad could find back when he bought it. Come on back and let's see what we've got."

Ben's study was located toward the back of his house. Even though Mark's home provided a spectacular view of the St. Johns River, he had to admire the view from the room he entered. The glass windows revealed a stone patio, which ran along the rear of the house with a wooden deck supported by salvaged railroad crossties hanging out over a virtual jungle. A small creek flowing through the rear of the property created a wild and natural visage that no landscape artist could ever equal.

The computer was up and running, as Ben simply hit the play button and quickly fast-forwarded it until it began to show the highway and a heavy storm.

"It's pretty obvious why they wanted to get off the road," Ben said as they both watched a large tractor trailer blow by on the left, throwing water across the windshield of the car. Soon they watched as Ben's dad slowed and entered the rest stop. As he approached the car parking area, the view improved slightly. Mark was looking for Keri's Camry, but he didn't see it. What he did see instead was a modified pony car, probably a Mustang. The windows were darkly tinted and the bulge in the center of the hood indicated the engine had seen serious modification. The car had been painted in a dark color, but with the heavy rain and the poor quality of the recording Mark couldn't tell what it was.

"Hold it. Can you back up a bit and slow it down?" When the car came in view again, this time, he had time to take a mental picture of the souped-up Mustang. Unfortunately, Ralph parked before he reached the Mustang so the tag couldn't be seen, but Mark knew he wouldn't forget the car. As Ralph pulled into the parking spot, the recording continued to play in slow motion.

Suddenly, two figures appeared as they ran through the rain and into the shelter of the building. The two figures were visible for only a split second, but Mark could see a long flowing dress and dark boots. As she disappeared into the covered area, she turned her head as if looking for someone behind her. In the mist of the rain and the still-working lights, Mark could see her hair reflecting a rainbow of bright colors. He wouldn't forget that either. At the same time, the security guard stepped into view, and as he did, Ralph turned the car's engine off and the recording abruptly ended.

Both men huddled close to the screen as Ben rewound the recording.

"Did you see your friend's car?"

"No, but I'm sure we saw the killer's car and them as well. I have a thumb drive. Do you mind if I record the last couple of minutes of this? Then you'll need to take this to the sheriff. It's not much, but the sheriff will have the resources to follow up on the car in the recording."

"Not at all, Mark. I don't see how this can help you very much, but maybe it will answer the question about your friend's car."

"Ben, you've been a great help. I hope your dad continues to improve. I'll leave my phone number with you. If he is able to remember anything else that might help me, please give me a call."

Mark stopped by the hospital after he left Ben's home and checked on Vera and Keri. As he'd expected, there had been no change in Keri's condition. After he told Vera what he'd learned from Ben Lounds, he drove back to his home in Jacksonville.

Mark filled a highball glass with ice, cut a Persian lime in half, squeezed the juice over the ice, and poured a generous amount of Tanqueray gin over the ice. Sitting down at his computer, he inserted the thumb drive and paused the play when the image of the Mustang appeared. Working back and forth until he'd found the clearest image. He then enlarged the image and printed it. He did the same for the view of the girl.

His cell phone rang, and he saw on caller ID that it was Ben Lounds. Curious, he answered, "Yes, Ben?"

"Mark, you wanted me to call if my dad remembered anything more. I'm calling from his hospital room, and he just told me he remembers that when they stopped at the rest stop, it was raining hard, but he desperately needed to pee. Mom wanted to go to the restroom as well, and my dad realized that the umbrella was in the trunk of the car. He said he got out of the car and quickly opened the trunk to get the umbrella. When he opened it, he was looking toward the rear of the Mustang, and although he doesn't remember any tag numbers, the Florida tag and the first letter of the county name somehow stuck in his mind. It was a *P*. He's not going to talk to the sheriff's people until tomorrow. I'm going to give them the dashcam then as well."

"Ben, thanks again for the heads-up. It sounds like your dad is going to be okay. Let me know if you learn more."

Before he'd even hung up, Mark was online looking up names of Florida counties. He found five counties whose names started with a *P*.

Chapter 15

After leaving the stolen Camry at Moreno and Sons, Gary Anders sat in the cramped rear seat of Curt's Mustang. Curt drove and Shela sat in the front passenger seat. He held up the envelope stuffed with cash and handed it to Shela.

"Count it. Let's see what we made."

Shela eagerly started counting the hundred-dollar bills from the envelope. Gary had said nothing, but he finally asked Curt, "What do you think that guy will say when he hears the news about what happened at the rest stop? Will he know it was us?"

"Duh! No shit, Sherlock. He'll know. Screw him. He doesn't run the only chop shop in the state. We got away clean. What's he going to do anyway? He'll forget about it. That Camry will be broken down into parts, sitting in bins, waiting to be shipped out to repair shops all over the country before we get home. How much we got there, Shela?"

"So far, I'm up to three thousand, and I still have more to count."

"See what I told you, Gary? This beats working at the gas station any day."

Gary remained silent as he was thinking. *How do I get out of this? There's not enough money in that envelope for me to do this again.*

"Okay, I've finished counting. We've got forty-five hundred here."

Looking at Curt, she asked, "How much for Gary?"

"Gary gets a cool thousand. How about that, Gary? That good with you?"

"Yeah, that's all right."

Curt used the main roads on the return trip to Palatka. He stopped at a twenty-four-hour convenience store outside Gainesville and bought two six-packs of beer and a big bag of pork rinds. Shela had the radio blasting at an earsplitting volume, which was okay with Gary because there was no way he wanted to engage in any conversation.

Just outside Palatka, Curt suddenly slapped the dashboard and turned off the music. Shela frowned at Curt. "What the fuck? That was a good song."

"It's my goddammed radiator. It's leaking again. I can tell by the way the engine is running hotter. This time, I've got to replace the whole damn thing."

By this time, they were pulling into Gary's mobile home park.

"Gary, I'll see you tomorrow. I'll be in a different car. I'll have to put this one in the garage until I have time to fix it. Now I'm glad I kept Otis's car."

As Curt and Shela drove away, Gary walked toward the entrance to the run-down mobile home he shared with his mom. He was preoccupied with finding a way to cut all ties with Curt and Shela as he walked into the door. There were no lights on, but he was aware that there was someone else in the room. He fumbled for the light switch, and when the light came on, he saw his mom huddled on the worn sofa, rocking back and forth and sobbing uncontrollably. He instinctively knelt on the floor next to her and put his arms around her.

"Mom, tell me what's wrong?"

It took her a couple minutes before she could speak, but she was finally able to blurt out, "I got fired today. All because I refused to sleep with the manager."

Gary Anders had been pushed, bullied, and put down his entire life. Tonight, he'd experienced the most turbulent event of his young life. Some would have been beaten down and never gotten up. But this was the moment little Gary chose to get up and become a man. Seeing and hearing his mom's pain and anguish coupled with the events of the past evening, he was filled with the same rage that had triggered his older brother to assault his mother's boyfriend. He didn't realize that he was shaking and crying himself as he continued to hold his mom. "I promise you, Mom. It's going to be okay."

After they had both cried until they were exhausted, Gary sat next to her on the sofa and began to explain, "I've found a part-time job that will get us by for now. You can look for a job somewhere else. That's not the only restaurant in Palatka. You might even find a lawyer who'd help you sue the asshole for harassment unless he rehires you or gives you a really good recommendation."

His mom had calmed down and nodded her head. "Gary, you're right. He wouldn't want that kind of publicity."

When Gary showed her the ten hundred-dollar bills, she had a hard time believing what she was looking at.

"Gary, are you sure this is okay? How did you get it?"

"Yes, Mom, it's okay," he said, but his mind was racing to plan his next move, realizing that from this point forward, he would be using Curt and Shela for his own benefit and not for theirs.

It was at this time that Gary, without realizing it, began to use his superior intellect to his advantage.

Chapter 16

Mark Gomez Jr., now known as Al to his new family, used his computer on his flight back to Atlanta to look at the subject of carjacking in a much broader context than he'd previously been doing. Before the events in Florida, the carjacking case he was involved in was focused only on defending the man who had effectively defended his family. The reasons or motivations for the carjacker's actions were largely immaterial. Now he was looking at the case through a different lens.

He had only known his dad now for a little over a year. During that time, he had developed a great amount of respect and admiration for Mark. He could tell that the assault on Keri had affected him deeply. He knew there were many details about his dad's past that he didn't know. How would he respond to Keri being hurt after having lost his wife, daughter, and finally Al's mother to violence? Al could only guess from the few comments he'd heard Roe make during the times they had been together. He knew that Mark, along with his mother Rosa, had been a part of some military action that neither his mom, Rosa, and now Mark would ever talk about. The same for Roe, who obviously knew a lot more about things Mark had done following the deaths of his wife and daughter.

After his mother Rosa's violent death in Tampico, he knew that he'd never return to Mexico. Mark was the only family he had left now, and this was his home. Now more than ever, he felt drawn to his new family, and he wanted to help any way he could. But at this point, he wasn't quite sure how.

Al's law firm was located in a towering office complex near Lennox Square and occupied most of the fourteenth floor. He lived on the third floor in a luxury condominium complex literally within walking distance of his office. It had a gated parking garage underneath and a twenty-four-hour guard on duty in the lobby. As a junior member of the firm, there was no way he could have afforded his condo, but his family's immense wealth had left him lifestyle options most of his peers couldn't yet dream of affording. Al tried to keep his affluence very low-key, but some of his coworkers couldn't help but notice. Even so, Al was driven to succeed on his own merits, and his secret ambition was to one day own his own law firm.

When he entered his firm's office after being out for several days, he knew he would be facing a huge backload of work. When his assigned paralegal met him with a stack of folders the minute he walked in, he was prepared.

Kelly Ellis was barely five feet tall with blond frizzy hair that made her look like she'd just stuck her finger into a light socket. She'd come to Atlanta from Moultrie, Georgia the day after she graduated from high school. Her parents were good people but dirt-poor. She broke the heart of her boyfriend, the high school star athlete, when she gave him a peck on his cheek as she said a final goodbye and climbed onto a Greyhound bus bound for Atlanta. He was a good guy, but his dream for her was to be a baby machine like so many of her peers. She did want to have children one day, but she knew she was capable of doing far more things in addition to being a mother. Kelly was a poster child for speaking slow Southern drawl. But behind the drawl, she was smarter than most of the attorneys in the office. She was working her way through school and fully intended to practice law one day.

As she handed the stack of files to Al, she asked, "Where have y'all been? I hope it was a good time. This place has been crazier 'an a fox in a henhouse."

"Good morning to you, too, Kelly. And yes, I had a good time, but I can tell that you're going to make me forget it. Let's get a cup of coffee. Before I start to look at all this, you can give me an update on what I've missed."

Once they were seated in Al's cubicle, Kelly began to update Al on what had been happening in the office.

After listening to the update, Al was relieved to know that nothing of any great importance had transpired. "Kelly, you haven't mentioned the carjacking case with Mr. Evans."

"Oh, that's in one o' the files I gave you. The grand jury still idn't finished. I know that they're supposed to be so secret, but people talk, especially after a couple martinis. We've heard that the prosecutor is tryin' like hell to charge Evans with murder, but he's not getting' the cooperation he was expecting from the grand jury people. I think people are fed up with the crime in the city and they're hittin' back. Anyway, there's a good chance this case is gonna be dead on the vine."

"Good, I hope for Evan's sake that it is. He should be given a medal for protecting his family instead. Thanks for the summaries. I'll dive in now and get caught up."

He worked nonstop, totally immersed in his work, forgetting lunch and finally taking a break midafternoon. He had purposely saved the Evans file for last. The only thing that had changed appeared at the very end of the file. There was an addendum that included new information relating to the assailants. The second teen whom Evans had shot was recovering but still in the hospital. He'd made a formal confession to the police naming the two other boys involved as well as the person they intended to sell the car to.

After what he'd learned while he was researching carjacking, this information suddenly commanded his attention. Reading further, he learned that the police had brought the named buyer in for questioning but were not able to make any formal charges, nor could they hold him since they couldn't prove that he'd committed any crime. He was just another person suspected of dealing in stolen property, and his name was added to a long list of possible offenders.

Writing the man's name on a piece of paper, he went out to Kelly's desk and gave her the name. "I'd like for you to find out everything you can about this guy."

Kelly gave Al a curious look and nodded. "By quittin' time, I'll tell you what kind of rubbers he uses."

Al had to turn his head to hide his smiling but blushing face from Kelly. "Great, I'll look forward to knowing that."

Kelly had a way of making the most offhand comments that often left Al scratching his head. But in the end, he knew she just might follow through. She'd already developed a reputation in the office for her ability to find the most intimate details about anyone. He watched as she retreated into a world of her own as she seemed to climb into her computer, her blond frizzy hair standing on end.

For the rest of the afternoon, Al did some research of his own by looking up the history of Keri and her sister, Tanya, who had been brutally murdered. He was fascinated to learn how her sister's accused killer, Jim Herbert, had only been days away from execution in Florida's electric chair when new evidence had emerged that had eventually led to proof of his innocence.

By now, his curiosity was aroused to the point that he picked up the phone and called the office of the criminal defense lawyer who'd defended Jim Herbert. He really didn't know why he was making the call except for the fact that when he'd pulled up the visitor logs at Raiford Prison for the period before Herbert was scheduled to be executed, one name jumped out at him like a flashing neon sign. The name was Mark Price.

It was past 4:00 PM, but after he'd identified himself, he was put on hold until a female voice said, "This is Karin Stills."

"Ms. Stills, my name is Mark Gomez. I'm an attorney in Atlanta. I work in the firm of Goldman, Chapman & Harper."

"Stop right there. I'll call you right back."

As soon as she'd looked up the firm's phone number, she called Al's office right back. "Sorry about that. I just wanted to be sure who I was talking to."

"Not a problem. I happened to be acquainted with Keri Smith. She was assaulted at a rest stop near St. Augustine a couple days ago."

"Yes, I know. I represent the family. I've been trying to reach her mother, but she's not answering her phone."

"Keri's mom is with her at the hospital, and I'm sure she's focused on Keri."

"How is she?"

"Not good, I'm afraid. Actually, I'm calling you because after reading the transcripts of Jim Herbert's trial,

I happened to see that a man named Mark Price had visited Herbert in prison. I know Mark Price, and I couldn't help but wonder why he would have been visiting him."

"Al, I only know that Price and Herbert had been friends before Herbert's conviction. Mark Price happens to be the biggest enigma I've ever come across. He was responsible for proving Herbert's innocence. I still don't know how he did what he did, and I'm sure I don't want to know everything. He had help from some very questionable people."

Stills went on to explain how Keri was the sister of the girl Herbert was accused of killing. "I only know he saved a man's life and then he went back to his home in Jacksonville as if nothing had happened. What's your connection to Mark Price?"

"He is my father. I won't bore you with details, but we only recently learned about our relationship. We're still learning about each other. That's one of the reasons I'm calling."

There was a long pause before Karin spoke, "Well, Al, you've only added to the mystery of your dad, but I will tell you that from everything I witnessed, you come from good stock. If you're ever in Orlando, please look me up. Maybe by then you'll be able to reveal more about the perplexing Mark Price."

"Thanks, Karin, at least I now understand the connection between my dad and Keri. I'll be sure Keri's mom knows you want to be updated about her condition."

He was ending the conversation with Stills when Kelly walked into his cubicle with a huge smile plastered on her face.

"This guy is a real toad. It's scary to know that pissants like him are walking the streets. See for yourself," she said as she handed Al a stack of papers and went back out the door.

Al quickly started reading the information that Kelly had given him. He didn't stop reading until the office had almost emptied out, and even then, he sat still, deep in thought, wondering if he had the courage to do what he was thinking of doing.

Chapter 17

Mark discovered there were five counties in the state of Florida that started with a *P*. The closest county by far was Putnam County. It was a landlocked county bordered on the east by St. Johns and Flagler County. Since Keri's assault had occurred in St. Johns County, it would be reasonable to begin his search in Putnam County. The bulk of the population of the county resided in and around the town of Palatka, which was on the St. Johns River.

Using his computer to search, he made a list of all the auto repair shops and garages in and around Palatka. The automobile dealers were crossed off the list because he didn't think whoever was driving the Mustang would be using a new car dealer for service. Mark was well aware that what he was doing was only a shot in the dark, but at least he was doing something. Realizing it was too late to do anything tonight, he refreshed his drink and watched a Johnny Carson rerun before getting a good night's sleep.

The next morning, he was having coffee, bagel, and fruit on his veranda when his cell phone rang.

"Good morning, Roe. What gets a government worker up so early?"

"Bite me, Mark. I've actually been here in my office since five looking at recent carjacking cases. I found one that's interesting. A couple of months back, a businessman was driving from Mobile to Jacksonville. He'd stopped at a rest stop at least fifty miles west of Tallahassee to sleep for a few minutes, but he dozed off and slept longer than he'd planned. The rest stop is an unusual one because one complex serves both east and westbound traffic. I've stopped there myself. It's in the middle of nowhere, and during the daytime, it really is a beautiful location, but it can be a little bit intimidating at night. It's guarded at night, but the entire area is so large, there are isolated areas that are not well lit. It's a popular place for truckers and drivers who want to catch a little sleep because it's removed enough from the highway so that it's quiet.

"Anyway, the guy had intentionally parked in an isolated spot. When he woke up, he decided he needed to use the restroom before he headed out. As he got out of his car, he was hit across the back of his head and fell flat on his face. Someone kicked him at least once, and he heard a voice say, 'Stop, just get his wallet and keys.' He was coming to, and he rolled over and tried to stand up but couldn't. As his car disappeared toward the exit road, another car was following right behind. Guess how he described it?"

"A souped-up Mustang."

"Bingo. Also, the man was driving a new full-size Lexus sedan. It took him a long time before he could stand up, walk, and track down the security guard. No telling how long it took before authorities arrived, interviewed him, and finally put out an alert for his car. The assailants only had to go a couple miles in either direction before they could exit I-10 and head in any direction on secondary roads. The only other word on the case was a footnote. Early in the morning, a state trooper was having breakfast in a diner in Cross City, Florida. He watched a shiny new Lexus sedan that matched the description pass on US 19 heading south. A souped-up Mustang was right behind. He remembers because it seemed to be an odd combination. But he hadn't received any alert to look out for them at that time. There hasn't been any record of the Lexus since. It's probably on a slow boat to some South American country by now."

"I agree. The Lexus wasn't stolen for a joyride. The other interesting question is where was the car being taken? Maybe the Port of Tampa? It will be interesting to see if the sheriff in St. Augustine connects it to Keri's case."

Mark then told Roe about what he'd learned from the dashcam.

"Be careful, Mark. Don't go running off the reservation. I'd give Norten a little time to follow up on whatever information they've picked up before you get too involved. He's a good sheriff, and I'm sure he's doing everything he can. These are obviously some bad people."

"Don't worry, Roe. I'm just going to be looking. Anything I find out, I'll be sure the sheriff knows as well."

"Roe, thanks for calling. Just keep looking when you have time to do it."

"Mark, you know I will. I'm with you. I want these people to be caught."

Mark was soon driving south on I-95 and turned off onto State Road 207 to Palatka. He passed through East Palatka and crossed the bridge spanning the St. Johns River. He was always impressed at how wide the river had already become at this point.

Since he lived on the northern part of the river in Jacksonville, he knew some things about the river. For starters, it was one of the few rivers that flowed north. It was a slow-flowing river since its descent from its origin further south all the way to the point it emptied into the Atlantic Ocean at Jacksonville was no more than an inch per mile. The river's currents were even affected by the ocean's tides.

He had carefully planned out the location of the auto garages on a map, and he had a rough plan to work through them. He didn't spend a lot of time at any of the places he visited. He only tried to identify the person in charge and show them a picture of the Mustang. He'd stopped at all of the garages he had on his list and was beginning to think that his search was pointless. In such a small town, surely a car like the Mustang would stand out, especially to a mechanic.

He slowed as he passed a run-down-looking shop in an old concrete block building. The shop wasn't on his list, but he decided to ask anyway. As he walked toward the open bay door, a man in coveralls covered in grease that hadn't seen a washing machine for a long time—or maybe even never—walked out to meet him.

"Can I help ya?"

Mark couldn't identify the man's ethnic origin because his skin could have been natural or the result of exposure to any combination of fossil fluids. Based on the smell alone, Mark could imagine the man bursting in flames if anyone struck a match nearby.

"I wonder if you might recognize this car?"

Turning his head to the side, the man spit out a load of dark tobacco juice. He followed up by wiping his mouth as the drops dribbled down his chin with his bare arm. This added additional possibilities for his brown skin coloring.

"I don't think I ever seen that one. Most of them cars come out of Taros. That's where they hang out and try to make hot rods outta perfectly good cars."

"They?"

"Teenagers. I think Taro lets 'em drink beer and smoke weed."

"Can you give me an address?"

"It's over on Crest. That's off 100. Aren't no sign last time I went by. You'll know it by the cars and the loud music."

Mark handed the man a fifty-dollar bill and thanked him. Maybe he might use it to wash his overalls, but Mark doubted that would ever happen.

Mark had no trouble finding the place. The man's descriptions were spot-on. It was in an area comprised of warehouses with a few run-down houses randomly located between. There were several newer cars parked in an open field next to two large Quonset-type huts inside a compound enclosed by a chain-link fence. Barbed wire was stretched across the top. A large entrance wide enough to allow vehicles to enter between the two metal buildings was wide-open.

After Mark parked on the street, he approached the entrance, where he could hear loud music and laughter. As he entered between the buildings, he could see a couple of car lifts under a corrugated steel roof. A drum being used as a trash can, overflowing with beer cans, sat between the two lifts. The cars sitting on the lifts were clearly hot rods in the making judging by the colorful paint. A dozen young kids who appeared to be teenagers were standing or sitting around the lifts laughing and drinking. Once he'd passed between the buildings, the volume of the music really hit him. As soon as the group saw him approaching, they froze and stared at him.

Mark approached the nearest kid and had to yell over the music, "Where's Taro?"

The boy pointed to a door in one of the buildings and then turned away as if he'd never seen Mark. Walking up to the door, Mark started to knock, but the door opened before he did. The figure indicated for Mark to enter, and closed the door as soon as Mark was inside.

The room must have been soundproofed, because the drop in decibels was dramatic. The figure standing in front of him was a small Oriental man who looked as if he were about to tee off on a golf course. He was as well groomed, whereas the proprietor of the previous garage was not.

"I'm assuming that you're Taro?"

"That's correct. And you are?" Taro replied in a voice that reminded Mark of an English professor he once worked with during the years he was a university professor himself.

Handing Taro the photo of the Mustang, Mark replied, "My name is Mark Price. I'm only looking for someone who can identify this car."

Taro looked at the photo for a moment before handing it back to Mark. "What is your interest in this car, Mr. Price?"

"So, you do recognize it?"

"Again, I ask you, why are you looking for this car?"

"Whoever was driving this car might have been a witness to an assault that left a friend in a hospital intensive care room. If you haven't been questioned by the police or sheriff, I can guarantee you that you soon will be. I just happened to be a little bit faster."

"I'm sorry for your friend. Yes, I do recognize the car. It was modified and even painted here at my shop. Let me first explain to you what happens here. I'm well aware of the rumors that I deal in stolen cars, and the kids come here to drink and use dope. One of the three may be true. I don't deal in stolen cars, and drugs are not allowed. I'll admit that there may be occasional consumption of beer. This garage is the go-to place for kids who want to customize cars. They come from as far away as Orlando and Jacksonville. I've developed an underground reputation for helping kids create their dream cars and letting them participate in the process. It's not cheap. In fact, what I charge is beyond exorbitant, but there are those who can and will pay. It affords me a great lifestyle. I just got back from the local country club where I played golf with the mayor. I only supervise the work. I let the kids themselves do the hands-on work. It's part of the mystique. They are able to form a bond with the car, which they wouldn't have if they just bought it."

"Who paid for you to build this car?"

"It does have a rather interesting history. A man by the name of Gerald Wilson made it big with a line of fast food franchises just as they were starting out. He built a big house on Crescent Beach and one near here on the east side of the river. His teenage son wanted a hot Mustang, and after he'd researched the topic, he convinced his dad to let me help him build it. We did build it, but the kid got two speeding tickets, and soon after that, he was arrested for drunk driving. This all happened within a month. His dad took away the car and sent the kid off to a military school.

"Gerald called me and asked if I had anyone who might want to buy it. I told him I'd look around and I'd call him back. Actually, I did have someone who'd watched it being modified and was willing to buy it. I called Gerald back a couple days later, and he thanked me but said he'd already found a buyer. I didn't ask who, and I have no idea who owns it now.

"I know your next question will be, 'How do I find Gerald Wilson?' Well, here's the rub. At the same time the events with the car were taking place, Gerald's main store manager or overseer was arrested for using the franchises for distributing drugs. Gerald was not charged with anything, but he still lost everything. I heard that he started drinking heavy and maybe even using drugs himself."

"So where is he now?"

"He's now running off-the-radar, unlicensed bars. He also adds gambling and prostitution to the mix. There are some secluded spots on the St. Johns River. He'll use a fishing shack off some creek and turn it into a highly profitable business. It may only operate for a few months before it's raided and shut down. He's had a remarkable sense of anticipating any impending shutdown or raid. The spots are so secluded that it only takes one lookout on the road into the place. One phone call and anything illegal goes into the river. By the time the law gets there, they're holding a Bible study class and drinking lemonade. So far, he's not been arrested a single time or connected to anything illegal. You might say he's taken the franchising concept to a new level.

"'How do I find him?' you ask. Word of mouth is the way. Most liquor stores will pass the word. Sometimes it will be posted online. I do know the places are dangerous. There are shootings, knifings, assaults, and robberies associated with them. If you decide to go, don't go alone."

But true to his nature, Mark was already thinking of how he would do it alone.

Chapter 18

Because his work as a defense attorney had opened his eyes to the dirty underbelly of the city, Mark Alberto Gomez was determined to never become a victim himself. During his younger years growing up in Mexico, he had been surrounded by cartel members with guns. His uncle, Andre, had insisted that he learn to shoot as soon as he was strong enough to hold a gun. He knew his mother Rosa didn't approve, but at the time, it hadn't been her most important issue to draw a line in the sand over. Getting him to the US to be educated was her primary goal, and she'd succeeded in doing that. Over time, she had increased her level of influence in the cartel hierarchy even to the point of eclipsing her brother, Andre.

Al was sent to an exclusive boarding school in New York when he was twelve and had only gone home to Mexico for short visits since then. By the time he graduated from a prestigious law school in Virginia, he had obtained his citizenship, and he knew he'd never return to Mexico. His English had lost all traces of a Spanish accent, and he was able to switch from one language to the other with ease.

When he obtained his concealed carry permit, he fired a gun for the first time in years and realized that he enjoyed shooting. In fact, he was pretty good at it. His handgun of choice was a .45 caliber Colt Commander with a lightweight alloy frame. Al was well aware that there were many good semiautomatic pistols that could carry fifteen or more rounds, but he reasoned that if he needed more than eight rounds the Commander carried, he'd probably be dead anyway. Plus, he liked the stopping power of the heavy .45 ACP round. His large size made carrying a concealed gun easy to do. But he also knew that talking about using a gun and using it were two different things. He'd not yet had to point a gun at a live person. What would he do when put under pressure to actually use it? The jury was still out on that question.

The file that Kelly had made for him was the life story of a small-time criminal named Dennis Swilley. Dennis was a little man with multiple tattoos and a little-man complex. In addition to not being very attractive, his face had severe acne scars. His criminal history consisted of theft in all of its different permutations. He started his career at the tender age of eight when he snatched the penny jar off the counter at the local convenience market and ran like hell. His grandfather had been a deputy sheriff before he began working for a security firm in West Florida. His dad had a managerial position working at the Port of Tampa. They were both reputable men, but Dennis was always looking for the easy way. Although he was a dishonest person through and through, none of his criminal activity involved violence on his part. He just lacked the concept of ownership. Whatever you had, was also his, if only he could take it from you.

Dennis would never have the courage to hijack a car himself. That was not his style. But if someone offered to sell him a vehicle and he could buy it for a few dollars cash and sell it for a lot more, who was he to refuse? Thus, he developed a reputation for paying quick cash for a nice automobile with no questions asked. He could make a car disappear in a New York minute. Because he was able to remain so low-key, he had remained under the radar of the authorities for a long time. Dennis had finally found a sweet spot in his (up to now) lackluster criminal career. That was why, when the teenage carjacker in Al's case gave his name to the police, they found no evidence of any current criminal activity.

Al's plan was simple. He only wanted to follow Dennis out of curiosity and see what he was doing. The Atlanta police certainly didn't have the manpower to do it even if they'd been interested in doing it. He didn't really have any reason to think that Dennis was connected in any way to the people who attacked Keri. But in some way that he couldn't totally understand, just like Mark, at least he was doing something.

With every day that passed, Al felt a greater and greater respect and connection to his dad, Mark Price. He knew that the death of his mother had been a blow to Mark as it had been for himself. Even though Al spent many years living away from her, they'd remained close and talked at least once a week. Only now did he realize how much she must have loved his dad. During the time he was in law school, she had been open about the family business and her brother's plan to bring him into it after he'd graduated. She didn't want him to become involved with the cartel. The more he learned about the business, the more determined he was to never be a part of it.

Rosa discreetly planned ahead and set up trusts for Al in the US. Over time, she moved huge sums of money into them without the cartel ever realizing what she'd done until after her death. She even had the foresight to set up a trigger mechanism that would release damaging information about the cartel if anything happened to either him or his dad, Mark. The only thing that propelled him to work at his current firm was to gain experience and learn the business aspects of running a highly successful law firm. What Al didn't know was the leverage his mother had used to have him hired by Chatam Bulger and Welker. Rosa had used her influence over one or more of the partners to secure him a job with the firm that was known for its limited hires. But even if he were fired or resigned tomorrow, he was financially secure for life.

Kelly had listed the address as well as the bars and restaurants that Dennis frequented. Dennis had an on-again, off-again girlfriend that he sometimes stayed with. One thing in Kelly's report that was peculiar were the car rentals he'd made in Florida. They'd been made in Tampa. Was Swilley visiting relatives in Tampa? There was no mention of living relatives.

Since Al was between significant others, he had his evenings free to do as he pleased. His most recent paramour, Valeria Rosario, had finished her post grad studies at Oglethorpe University and returned home to South America. Both she and Al had agreed from the start the relationship was for convenience and would only be temporary, especially since Valeria was engaged to the prime minister of her country.

Before he left his office, he printed out the latest photo of Dennis Swilley as well as a couple of the addresses of the places Kelly had listed. After he left his office, he stopped at a small deli on the main floor of his office building. He ate a couple cheeseburgers before he walked to his apartment, where he changed into jeans, an oversize Falcon sweatshirt, and running shoes. The last thing he did before he left was to make certain his Colt was locked and loaded before tucking it inside his belt in a soft clip-on holster.

Al was allowed two parking spaces in the basement garage of his condo. One spot held a 911 Porsche Carrera convertible. An older model Toyota 4Runner sat next to it in the second spot. It was the last model year Toyota produced the 4Runner with their eight-cylinder engine, and it was the car Al drove ninety percent of the time. He'd kept it in immaculate condition. He only kept the Porsche because it had been a graduation gift from his mom. Before leaving his condo, he looked at the map showing the addresses Kelly had listed for Dennis and picked the closest one.

The Purple Rose Tavern was located just off Peters Street in an older part of Atlanta that Al had never seen until now. The streets were lined with one story businesses that had changed many times over the years. Some of the buildings were covered in graffiti—or art, depending on your point of view. Looking north toward downtown, the towering stone, glass, and steel towers seemed to be looking down on the quiet neighborhood of one- and two-story buildings as if to say, "I'm coming."

The Purple Rose Tavern had been whitewashed in a weak attempt to cover the Confederate flag that had once been a prominent feature painted on the outside wall. There was one entrance door in the middle of the building. The only available parking was on the street. There was very little traffic, and he had no problem parking directly across the street from the bar's entrance.

When Al walked through the door, he was expecting to be hit with loud music but instead he could barely hear Hank Snow singing a song about a railroad. Even though it was dark outside, it was even darker inside. All suggestions from the American Cancer Society had not yet reached this establishment with the thick smoke adding to the low visibility. Al had to stand still for a few moments before he could orient himself and locate the bar, which ran across the entire length of the back wall. Most of the rest of the room was lined by booths with seats covered by dry, red, and cracked Naugahyde. A couple of doors on the right end must have been the bathrooms.

As soon as he was confident that he could safely reach the bar without hitting something, he walked on in and sat on a stool at the bar. He could tell there were only three others sitting at the bar, but he still couldn't see if the booths were occupied.

When the bartender approached him, Al had to stifle a laugh. He was maybe five foot ten and very wide, but what seemed out of place to Al was his appearance. He was wearing a red-and-white striped shirt with a red bow tie and a pair of red suspenders. His full head of black hair was parted down the center of his head. His overall appearance seemed to be massive overkill for this place.

"I'm Mac. What's your poison tonight, sir?" he asked in a baritone voice that seemed more like a rumble than a question.

"Surprise me with a cold draft," Al answered with a smile.

"I see that this is the first time you've visited this establishment. You had to stop inside the door and let your eyes adjust before you walked to the bar."

"You're very observant. And yes, it is my first time here."

"Let me guess. You're either meeting someone here or you're looking for someone. People don't just accidently wander into this fine place."

"Right again," Al replied as someone toward the end of the bar waved his mug asking for a refill. As the bartender walked away to draw another beer, Al quickly tried to look around the room hoping he'd recognize Dennis Swilley if he happened to be sitting in one of the booths.

Feeling confident that Dennis wasn't in the bar, when the bartender returned, Al took the photo of Dennis Swilley out of his pocket. Trying to not make it obvious, he pushed it across the bar toward Mac. Mac had obviously played this game before, as he made no motion to pick up the photo. Instead, he leaned across the polished bar surface, and while using a bar towel to wipe up a drop of beer he'd spilled with Al's beer, he looked down at the picture of Dennis.

Smiling, he looked at Al and said in a quiet voice, "Might be someone I've seen. I'm not sure. Why are you looking for him?"

"I'm not a threat to Dennis. I know who he is and where he lives as well. I'm not looking to bust his balls. He may be able to help me find someone," Al replied as he slid two fifty-dollar bills under his cell phone across the bar.

Mac was good. He picked up Al's cell phone and looked at the screen and laughed loudly, palming the two fifties and magically making them disappear.

"That's amazing. I've never seen anyone do that before," he said as he handed the phone back to Al. "I'd really be careful if I were you. I don't think Dennis is a violent man, but he runs with some pretty nasty people. He does come in here pretty frequently. He usually meets up with a big, bald black dude that would scare Godzilla. I have no idea what their business is, but they are usually talking about automobiles."

Out of the corner of his eye, Al saw the person sitting alone in a dark spot at the far end of the bar stand up and walk toward where he was sitting.

"Well, here comes Mimi, right on cue. Be careful mister. This woman will slit your throat after she picks your pocket. She's one of the slickest I've seen, and believe me, I've seen a lot."

"Thanks for the heads-up, Mac."

It was hard to tell the age of the dark-haired woman who approached Al. Makeup and a dark room could hide a lot, so she could have been anywhere between eighteen and forty plus. Still, she was very attractive, and the tight low-cut dress she wore accentuated a shapely body. She didn't wait to be invited. She just took a seat next to Al and smiled a bright smile.

"I'm Mimi."

Al laughed and answered, "I'm Alfred E. Neuman."

"Well, Alfred, it's nice to meet you," Mimi said as Mac had to turn his head away, nearly choking as he tried not to laugh out loud. "How about buying me a drink?"

"Sure. Mac, bring the lady a beer like mine."

Thrown off her game, Mimi started shaking her head, "No, sweetheart, I can't drink beer. A lady needs champagne. Then we can go over to one of the booths and drink in private."

"I'll make you a proposition before you proposition me. Mac, is that a deck of cards under the register?"

Mac nodded and brought the deck over to Al with a curious look on his face.

"This is what we'll do, Mimi. I'm going to shuffle this deck, and we'll each draw one card. The lowest card will buy the one with the highest a hundred-dollar bottle of champagne. How does that sound to you?"

By now, Mimi realized that she was the brunt of a joke, and she didn't take it well. She swung her right hand with long sharp nails toward Al's face. With his left hand, Al caught her wrist and just held it stranded in midair. At the same time, his right hand deftly removed Mimi's wallet from the handbag she was carrying over her left shoulder. There were some things he'd learned as a kid while growing up with cartel members that he'd not forgotten.

Standing up, Mimi screamed at Al, "You fucking asshole!" She headed toward the front door.

She'd almost reached the door when Al said loudly, "You forgot something."

When she turned around, Al threw her wallet toward her. She had to bend down and pick it up before going out of the bar, leaving a stream of obscene invectives in her wake.

Mac was now bent over in laughter as the other two patrons at the bar joined in the show, laughing as well.

"I don't know who you are, buddy, but you don't know what a favor you've done for me. I'm actually the owner of this place, and I've been trying to get rid of her for a long time. She's bad for business. I think she met her match tonight."

"Mac, you can do me a favor as well. If Dennis comes in, don't mention that anyone was looking for him."

"You got it, my friend. By the way, you're welcome anytime. A free beer is waiting for you."

As Al left the bar, he should have been more vigilant. Mimi was standing behind a wooden construction fence only feet from where Al's car was parked. And she was not alone.

Chapter 19

Both Gary and Shela returned to school the day after stealing the car. As they passed in a hallway between classes, Shela approached Gary and said, "Meet me in the parking lot after class."

Shela was standing in the parking lot next to a newer model blue Honda sedan. "This was Otis Morphet's car. Curt kept it hidden after Otis was killed. Curt hates to drive it because it's not as fast or as flashy as his Mustang."

Gary was surprised at Shela's lack of concern for the events of the previous evening. She seemed to have totally forgotten it all.

"Where's Curt?"

"He's taking the Mustang apart trying to replace the radiator. Get in the car. Let's have some fun before we see Curt."

Before now, Gary would have run from Shela, but for some reason, she didn't scare him anymore. The truth was, he'd enjoyed what had happened with her in the car when they were driving it to the salvage yard. So, without hesitation, he slipped into the passenger seat. "I'm up for fun as long as it doesn't involve shooting anyone."

Shela was out of the parking lot before Gary could even get his seat belt buckled up. She knew where they were headed and didn't say a word as she drove. Gary knew they were headed for the river as they passed through a neighborhood of older and restored homes and the road became a one lane paved road that passed several mobile homes before the road abruptly ended in a dirt cul-de-sac. Two dirt trails led off the turnaround and Shela never slowed as she took one of the trails without slowing down. They passed through thick vegetation for a short distance and suddenly stopped on a high bank overlooking the river. It was obvious Shela was quite familiar with the spot as she turned toward Gary. "Nobody ever comes here in the daytime."

It only took a moment for Shela to get out of the car and move into the back seat. "What are you waiting for, Gary?"

Gary thought to himself, *Why the hell not? Screw Curt,* as he moved into the back seat where Shela was already undressed down to her panties and granny boots. The boots didn't bother Gary in the least. There was a moment's hesitation on Gary's part as his eyes tried to register the multiple tattoos on different parts of Shela's body. As she pulled her panties off, he couldn't help but focus on the coiled cobra on her abdomen. Its tail stretched out of sight, disappearing into her pubic area.

Shela noticed Gary's momentary hesitation and asked, "You're a virgin, aren't you, Gary?"

Gary could only nod. "Yes."

"Well, I can tell from looking that you're ready to lose it."

And Gary was ready and willing. He must have done okay, because in a short time, Shela was exhausted and grinning. After smoking a cigarette, Shela realized that there was going to be an encore for which she had no objection.

They drove back into town in silence, and as Shela entered one of the poorer neighborhoods, Gary asked, "Where are we going now?"

Before Shela answered, she'd already turned into a driveway next to an old run-down frame house. The driveway extended to the rear of the house where a cracked and moldy concrete structure stood as a reminder of better days. It had originally functioned as a garage for a motor home. One of the two sagging wooden doors was partially open, and Gary could see Curt leaning into the engine compartment of the Mustang.

Gary had a momentary sense of dread the minute he recognized Curt. Would Curt know what Gary had just done, and if so, how would he react? Knowing how volatile Shela could be, he had no idea what she might say. Fortunately, what they'd just done had left Shela in a good mood, and she wasn't ready to spoil a good thing. Curt was not in a good mood as he slammed a wrench down on the concrete floor.

"Goddammed car. That fucking Taro changed everything from stock when he built this car. Nothing fits like it should."

Gary was confused, "Why don't you take it back to Taro and let him fix it?"

"Are you shitting me? That son of a bitch charges too goddam much. I could probably buy a new Mustang from a dealer for less than what he'd charge for a new radiator."

After his experience with Shela, Gary was gaining more and more confidence. He was also starting to see the bigger picture of the carjacking business. He knew that what he was going to say next would probably piss Curt off, but he no longer cared what Curt thought. "Curt, you know that it might be better if you didn't drive the

Mustang when you're stealing a car? That Honda would be a lot less obvious?"

Curt's face was turning red as he walked up toward Gary.

"And when did you suddenly become the expert on stealing cars?"

"Curt, I'm not an expert, but some things are just common sense. And sometimes it might be a good idea to look at something with a different perspective. While I'm pissing you off, I'd also suggest that you and Shela just steal cars without shooting or beating someone up. Just suppose someone or a surveillance camera saw this Mustang. How long do you really think it'll take for the authorities to track it down? I'm telling you both right now, if you're going to keep using violence just to steal a car, then don't count on me to help you."

Emboldened by his newly found courage, Gary turned his back on Curt and Shela, who had a surprised look on her face, and started walking back up the driveway toward the street.

"Okay, Gary, hold on. You may be right. Before you go, let's talk about it. I'm open to listening to whatever smart-ass idea you've got. You agree, Shela?"

Shela didn't want to lose her new boytoy. She'd like to keep Gary around for a little while longer as she carefully replied, "I'm good with that. If he starts to get on our nerves, we'll fuck him over good." She looked directly at Gary with a grin on her face.

Curt carefully wiped his greasy hands on a dirty rag and asked, "So, wise guy, how do you think we should steal a car?"

"I'd go where the most expensive cars are located, and I don't mean here. I'd look for unlocked cars especially at night, so you'd remain invisible. Maybe high-end gated communities would be a good place to start. If you could find a way to sneak in at night, I'll bet you could find cars sitting in driveways, unlocked, with the keys just sitting there waiting to be driven away. A lot of people in those places have an entitled sense of security. You could be a long way from there before anyone realized their Mercedes was missing."

"Will Moreno and Sons Salvage take high-end cars or are they just looking for cars to chop up?"

"They'll take high-end cars as well."

"Then let's look for a good place to find high-end cars."

Chapter 20

After Mark left Taro's garage, he passed a convenience store, and on a hunch, stopped and went in. To his right just inside the door were the dispensers for a local newspaper as well as other cheap papers advertising cars, trucks, and boats sold mostly by private citizens. On the wall was a bulletin board with numerous pieces of paper advertising pets, four-wheelers, grills, and almost any piece of unwanted item you could possibly think of. Mark looked closely at the many ads until he saw what he was looking for.

Pinned to the board and almost invisible among all the flotsam ads was a pad with tear-off sections. Mark tore one off and looked closer. It was a small crude map with an *X* marking a spot. Under the map was one word: *Party*. He thought it might be what he was looking for. He took a bottle of water to the counter, where he paid the young man behind the counter. Holding up the piece of paper with the map, he asked the clerk, "Would this be a good party?"

The clerk had a frightened look as he answered in a heavy accent, "I'd be careful, man. I know some rough people who go to those parties. I wouldn't go by myself."

He didn't say anything else, and Mark didn't push him any further. It was obvious he wanted to avoid any conversation regarding the "party." Mark was more certain than ever that this was a Gerald Wilson franchise that he was looking for. It was well past five and Mark knew he needed to do some research before he attempted to attend the "party."

Returning home to Jacksonville, Mark rechecked all his messages. Having heard nothing from Vera, he knew there was no change in Keri's condition. He called her anyway. She answered immediately, "There's been no change, Mark."

Mark could hear the weariness and despair in her voice. "I'll come by in the morning, Vera. Hang in there. Remember what the doctor said—it's going to take time."

He put a frozen dinner in the oven before pouring himself a generous portion of Tanqueray over ice with lime. While the dinner heated, he used an online service to locate the spot marked X on the map from the convenience store. It was on a secluded part of the river several miles south of town. A two-lane road ran in a convoluted path from US 19 toward the river. At first, there were scattered homes, but they soon ended until there were only cow pastures dotted with cabbage palms on either side of the road. The pavement ended abruptly, and a well used dirt road entered thick trees for the rest of the distance to the river.

Because there was no street view from the pavement to the river, Mark could only see the faint outlines of a building next to the water. A long dock extending well out into the river was visible. He understood what Ralph had meant when he said that a couple of sentries posted on the approaching road could protect the occupants from any surprise raiding party.

Mark couldn't even be certain the bar was owned by Gerald Wilson. Would he be there? Even if he were, would he be willing to talk? But Mark had to admit that his curiosity had been aroused, and if he were honest with himself, he would acknowledge that he was looking forward to going to the party marked *X*.

The next morning after a quick run, he showered and dressed in old jeans, a well-worn, loose-fitting Cuban shirt, and a pair of beat-up running shoes. Driving down I-95, he stopped at the hospital in St. Augustine and relieved Vera for a couple of hours. She appeared to be a little more optimistic today. "They took her off the ventilator, and she's breathing well on her own. Dr. Goldblatt says it's a good sign."

"One step at a time, Vera. Why don't you go back to your hotel for a while? I'll stay here until you get back."

"Okay, I'll take you up on it. There's a bookstore next to the hospital, and I'd like to get a couple books to read. I've got my phone so you can call if anything changes."

After Vera left, Mark sat and stared at Keri lying in the hospital bed. With the ventilator removed, as well as a few of the wires and electrodes, she was beginning to look human again. Only the heavy bandages covering her head and the purple bruising evident on her face were obvious signs of the brutality of her assault.

Sitting there watching her created a torrent of conflicting emotions. On one hand, he was overcome with anger toward whoever did this to her. On the other, he was feeling waves of guilt. Why were the people close to him the ones who suffered—his wife, his daughter, Rosa, and now Keri—but he was untouched? Roe was still okay even though she had endured a lot. Maybe he should never have connected with his son, Al. If anything happened to him as well, he wasn't sure he'd be able to handle it. But at least he was safe in his work in Atlanta, and he hoped he'd stay there out of harm's way.

When Vera returned, she was carrying a bag bulging with several books. Thanks for relieving me, Mark. I'll be okay."

"Vera, if you don't hear from me for a day or so, don't worry. I'm going to follow up on a few things that will take me out of town."

"Mark, if you ever find out who did this, please shoot 'em once for me."

"Vera, if I find out who did this before the sheriff does, shooting would be an act of kindness compared to what I'll do to them."

Vera only smiled and nodded her head as Mark left.

It was late afternoon when Mark turned onto the county road off US 19. He followed the winding route until the pavement ended at a large dirt cul-de-sac. The only vehicle he saw was a beer truck that passed him heading back toward the main highway. It was evidence of just how brazen the owners were to have a beer company deliver to their door.

He assumed that the activities were mostly nocturnal, so he turned around in the cul-de-sac and drove a short distance back toward the main highway. He quickly found what he was looking for in a small turnoff without a gate. The dirt track led into an empty pasture. There was enough growth along the roadside fence to provide some cover as he parked behind the myrtle and palmettos. This position still allowed him a good view of the road. He made himself comfortable in his seat and waited for dark. As soon as darkness descended, he realized he'd have to roll his windows up as the mosquitoes found him and came in for blood.

It wasn't long after dark that the first car passed, headed toward the river. By 9:00 PM, the traffic picked up. The vehicles were an indication of the diversity of the bar's clientele. Everything from jacked-up Bubba trucks to high-end foreign makes passed by.

Assuming the party must have started, Mark drove toward the river. By now, all of the available parking along the dirt road was filled and the line of parked cars extended back as far as the cul-de-sac. Mark was actually happy to park so that he was not locked in on the narrow dirt trail. He parked in the cul-de-sac with his car pointed toward the paved road instead.

As he walked along the dirt road, he could hear the bar well before it was visible. It was a weathered wooden structure set well above the ground on old, thick pilings. A wide wooden staircase led from the ground up to a small, open deck. A double door opened into the interior. Sitting on the deck was a huge black man who stood up as Mark walked up the steps.

"I haven't ever seen you before. How did you find this place?"

Mark was caught off guard by the unexpected question. He hesitated a moment before replying, "Taro told me about the place."

"Are you carrying a gun?" the doorman asked.

"No." Mark was glad he'd left his gun in his car."

"Then you don't mind if I check then." He performed a cursory pat-down. "Wait here," he said as he disappeared into the building. He was back in only a minute, accompanied by a man with a thin pencil mustache.

He was well dressed in pleated slacks and a polo shirt, but he was overweight and reminded Mark of an old-time snake oil salesman. He looked closely at Mark and said, "What did Taro tell you about this place?"

"Well, he told me two things about it. First, he said I might find out about a Mustang that was for sale, and second, he told me it was a good place for a game of cards."

"I thought I told Taro that the car had been sold."

"Yes, that's what Taro said. I was just hoping maybe the sale didn't work out and it might still be available."

The man seemed to debate with himself for a minute before he made a decision. "Henry, let him through. I'll talk to him some more inside."

The doorman remained expressionless as he nodded and stood to one side to let Mark pass. Mark followed the man into a large room. The music was coming from an old-time jukebox in one corner. A bar extended the length of one wall. A huge TV screen was mounted behind it but had not yet been turned on. Mark could see a wide deck extending out over the river. A couple of the tables on the deck were already occupied. There was no ceiling inside the main room, but instead the room opened up to high rafters holding the roof. The wall opposite the bar had two doors that led off the main room. They finally sat at a table, well away from the jukebox.

"My name's Gerald Wilson. Yours is?"

"Mark Price."

"Mark, most everybody that comes here are regulars, or they come with regulars. Not many people walk in here alone."

"Well, Taro didn't volunteer to come with me."

"I don't suppose he would. He's too much of a pussy. He wouldn't do anything to tarnish his name at the country club."

"I understand that he's pretty good at taking people's money."

"No shit. Did he tell you that I had that Mustang made for my son? If I told you how much it cost, it would make you gag."

"Why did you get rid of it?"

"My son just fucked up. He had three different chances. I had to put him in a structured school before he killed himself or worse—someone else. Do you have children, Mark?"

"Once upon a time, I did."

The way Mark said it made Gerald realize that it was not a topic that Mark wanted to talk about, so instead he asked, "So why are you interested in the Mustang?"

"I have a favorite nephew who wants it. He saw it while it was being built, and it got in his head. He claims there's nothing even close to it in the world of modified cars."

"Your nephew is right. It's one of a kind. But after I sent my boy away to school, I had some temporary business setbacks. I didn't need the car, but I needed the money. I asked Taro if he might have a buyer that would be interested. By the time he called me back, I'd had someone make me an offer. It didn't even begin to cover what I'd spent, but a bird in the hand is better than ten birds in a tree. So, I sold it."

"Who bought it?"

"It was some rich doctor from Gainesville. From what little I learned, it was to keep his stepson happy. Or maybe it was to keep the boy's mama happy. Anyway, it was a quick cash deal, and it made everyone feel good except for the doctor who was paying for it."

"What was his name?"

"Bloomquist. But his name isn't important. They put the car's title in the kid's name. It was Layman, Layson, Lawson, or something like that. Now that I think about it, I believe it was Lawson. I was too busy counting the money to give a shit."

"Does the kid live in Gainesville?"

"I've got no idea where he lives. So, do you want to play some cards? We've got a game starting around twelve."

While they were talking, Mark couldn't help but watch two girls who were already well on their way to being shit-faced, dancing in front of the jukebox. One was already topless, and the second one soon joined her. The few people present were starting to gather around to cheer them on.

By now, Gerald was watching as well. "Things are starting to warm up. By one or two, this place will be rocking. Go on over to the bar and get a drink. Tell the bartender that the first one is on me," he said as he stood up and walked away.

Mark used the opportunity to head for the door. He figured he'd gotten all the information he was going to get from Gerald. As he walked out onto the small deck at the entrance, the big doorman asked, "Leaving early? The place hasn't warmed up yet."

"I guess I'm getting too old for this much fun."

"Maybe a little wisdom with age?"

As Mark started to walk down the stairs, two men and a woman were coming up the stairs toward him. His eyes were drawn to the woman, who might have once been attractive, but her heavily wrinkled face was hard to ignore. She was wearing the tightest pair of shorts Mark had ever seen. Her top was covered with a fishnet blouse that could have only trapped a very large fish.

The man looked vaguely familiar, and when he spoke, Mark recognized him as the mechanic who had given him directions to Taro's place. He had only partially cleaned up. The wifebeater T-shirt he was wearing couldn't hide the belly that was hanging over his jeans. It was hard to look at him without imagining oil, grease, and tobacco juice on his arms. The other man was thin and short, with pig eyes and big ears. Mark was sure he remembered him from the movie *Deliverance*.

The mechanic recognized Mark at the same time. "You're the guy come by asking questions. Why are you leaving when the fun hasn't even started yet?"

"I'll leave all the fun for you," Mark replied with a smile.

It was obvious that the mechanic and his friends had already been hitting the bottle pretty hard, and they took Mark's reply as an insult.

"The hell you are. You're going to come back in with us. I'll bet Lula Belle here would like to spend some quality time with you, too. Right, Belle?"

She then proceeded to step up toward Mark like a robot with open arms and blank eyes.

"Easy there," Mark said as he held up an arm to stop her.

Enraged, the mechanic reached behind his back with his right hand. As the hand reappeared, a blade flashed in the light. Mark was standing on the step above him. As the knife moved forward, Mark simply stepped to the side and used his right hand to grab him behind the neck using the force of the man's momentum, slamming him into the stairs. The knife harmlessly fell down the steps.

The *Deliverance* man started to move toward Mark, but was stopped in his track by the doorman, who grabbed him by the neck, lifting him up into the air. Still holding onto the little man, he reached down and helped the mechanic up to his feet.

"Leroy, you and RG need to calm down. Go on inside. If I hear either of you causing any more trouble, I'm going to throw you both in the river."

"Thanks," Mark said as the trio tucked tail and disappeared inside the bar. He reached out his hand. "I'm Mark."

"I'm Henry. I should thank you. I don't think you needed my help. You handled him very efficiently. Really, I think he should be thanking me for saving him. Anyway, sorry about that. We get a lot of that kind of shit here."

"I can only imagine."

"Listen Mark, if you're ever interested in some part-time work, Gerald pays well. I'm working too many hours anyway."

"I appreciate it, Henry, but I've got all the scars I need."

"There's that wisdom thing again."

Mark didn't realize it, but he still had room for more scars.

Chapter 21

When Al left the Purple Rose Tavern, he had his keys in his hand as he approached his car. Before he could unlock it, he heard a cold voice behind him.

"Not so fast, dickhead. You and I aren't finished. I think you owe me at least a hundred dollars for a bottle of champagne. Why don't you just throw in your wallet and car keys as well?"

Mimi was flanked by two true gangbangers. They had facial tattoos, and even in the weak streetlights, Al recognized the teardrops—one for each kill—identifying them as hardcore gang members. A long, heavy chain dangled from the hand of one, and the other carried a machete cradled in his arm.

Al was just about to take out his Colt when another voice barked a hard command. "If either of you punks even breath hard, I'm going to blow your dicks off with a three-inch Magnum 12-gauge."

The two bangers began to back up very slowly. Mimi was filled with rage as she realized she'd lost again. Realizing there was nothing she could do, she walked away with her two soldiers.

"Mac, you just saved my butt."

"Not really. I could see that you were about to pull the gun out of your pants. I didn't want the publicity in front of my place of business. I don't think you need it either."

"Right again."

"I suspected Mimi might do something like this. Anyway, I wanted to talk to you outside the bar in private. I want to make you an offer."

"Offer?"

"I can let you know when Dennis comes in and point him out to you if you can promise me that you only want to talk to him."

"I can promise that. What I might do at a later date, I won't promise anything. A lot will depend on how cooperative Dennis will be when I finally talk to him."

"Fair enough. Just as long as nothing comes back on me."

"One question, why are you doing this?"

"I'm not exactly sure why. I consider myself to be a good judge of character, and I think you're an upright guy. A man can never go wrong by having the right friends. Plus, Dennis has been a good customer for years, and he's never caused me any trouble. There's no need for the guy to get hurt."

"Mac, I'm flattered. I'll try to not let you down."

Al gave Mac enough information so he could reach him without divulging his occupation or employer.

Shaking like a leaf, Al got into his car and drove home. Maybe he was out of his league in trying to follow up on Swilley. It was beginning to dawn on him that this was not a game like an argument in a courtroom. This could be life or death. Was it worth it to continue what he was doing? But then he thought about what the lawyer in Florida had told him about his dad, Mark Price. True, his dad was an enigma. There was so much about him he didn't know, but one thing was for certain: He didn't shy away from danger. So why should he?

The next morning, Kelly came to Al's cubicle to tell him that so far, she'd found that Swilley's grandparents had lived in a county adjacent to Chiefland, but his parents had moved to Tampa when he was still young. She still couldn't find any of his relatives that lived in Levy County.

After Al left work, he went back to his condo and heated a pizza in his oven, then cracked open a cold beer. He tried to call his dad to check on Keri's condition, but Mark's phone was not accepting calls. He was beginning to think that he was just being stupid to be focusing on Swilley, but there was something about Swilley's Florida connection that didn't make sense.

After the beer and pizza, he dozed off, but his phone woke him with a text message: *Swilley just came into the bar, M.*

Suddenly wide awake, Al dressed as he'd done on the night before and drove to the Purple Rose as fast as possible without being stopped for speeding. He found a parking spot on the street again and entered the bar. This time, he didn't have to wait to for his eyes to focus in the dim lighting but instead walked directly to the bar, where Mac was drawing up a beer. Without saying a word, Mac only nodded toward a booth in the far end of the room. Al went to the end of the bar and sat on a barstool near the booth where Swilley was sitting. The mirrors across the back of the bar provided an easy way for Al to observe Swilley without having to turn around.

Dennis Swilley was a small man wearing a cap with a big *A* on the front. A ponytail hung down behind the cap. Even in the dim lighting, his skin was a pale white, indicating minimal sun exposure. Al assumed that Swilley's profession was mainly nocturnal, which would account for the pale complexion.

Mac brought Al a draft beer and slid it over the bar with a nod. "On the house."

Al studied Swilley for some time, watching him nurse a mixed drink while smoking a cigarette. While he was trying to think of some excuse to walk over to where Dennis was sitting, he watched him pick up his cell phone.

Whoever was calling had energized him, because he closed the call and quickly stood up. He walked over to the bar, put a bill on the counter, and said to Mac, "I gotta go," then walked out.

The minute Swilley walked out the front door, Al followed right behind. Al went straight to his own car while watching Swilley at the same time. Swilley was parked on the opposite side of the street. As he got into his car and drove away, Al had to make a U-turn, almost colliding with an oncoming car. He barely made it and was rewarded with a one-finger salute as he tried to keep Swilley in sight.

Maintaining a tail without being spotted was not something Al had experience with. In doing so, he erred on the side of caution, causing him to almost lose Swilley a couple of times. Fortunately, the direction led away from congested areas and into an older neighborhood with little traffic. When Dennis turned into a driveway next to an older frame home, Al drove on by hoping that he hadn't been noticed. He parked a few houses down and walked back to the drive Swilley had entered. The driveway ran to the rear of the house. The only light showing in the house came from a window toward the back.

There was no lighting on the driveway, so Al moved very slowly, keeping close to the wall of the house. As he got closer to the back, he could see an open carport attached to what must be the garage. There were no garage doors, only a single door to the garage. Swilley's car was parked in the carport, but there was no sign of him. There was a small window in the door entering the garage, and there was a light inside.

As Al moved alongside Swilley's car toward the garage, he heard a door at the back of the house open. With nowhere to go, he dropped to the ground next to the car and gambled that whoever was coming out of the house would walk on the opposite side of the car. He could hear someone coming down wooden steps and walking across the concrete carport. Fortunately, they were on the other side of the car. He could see under the car as the person unlocked and entered the garage door. The person turned on more lights inside the garage but left the door partially open.

As he lay on the cold concrete of the carport, Al knew he had a major decision to make. He could very easily back out of the driveway and leave. If he continued on, it might not turn out well for him. He made his decision by taking out his handkerchief from a back pocket and tying it around his face like the old-time stagecoach robbers. Then he moved toward the garage door.

He saw that it was indeed Dennis Swilley. He was bent over the front bumper of one of the two cars removing a tag. Al quickly came up behind him, wrapping his arm around the little man and putting pressure on his carotid artery. With the blood flow to his brain cut off, Swilley lost consciousness immediately as Al lowered him to the floor. One wall of the two-car garage was lined with a pegboard that held tools. And the one thing common to all garages was a roll of duct tape that Al found hanging on a nail. He used it to bind Swilley up securely.

While he waited for Swilley to wake up, he looked at the rear of the garage. There were wooden double doors that opened onto an alleyway. A fish-eye peephole was set in one of the doors so a person inside the garage could look out into the alleyway without having to open a door. It didn't take long for Swilley to wake up and realize that he couldn't move. When he saw that Al was wearing a mask, beads of sweat began to appear on his brow.

"What the fuck are you doing?"

"Dennis, I only want answers to a few questions. First, I want to know who you sell your cars to? And don't tell me you don't know what I'm talking about. I know kids bring cars to you and you make the cars disappear. The cars are going somewhere for resale or to a chop shop. I'm sure this car right here is stolen. That's why you're changing the tags. Who and where?"

"Man, you are crazy. I'm not telling you shit."

"Dennis, I don't have time to argue with you. It's obvious that we aren't going to be able to communicate. I'll have to find someone else to work with."

Al was a little frightened of himself with what he was doing. It seemed to be a natural reaction and far too easy. When he was growing up, he heard so many stories of violence from the people who worked for his mother and uncle. His goal had always been to leave it all behind and to wipe it all from his memory. But here he was, acting as if he'd been trained to continue the very traditions he'd run away from.

He dragged Swilley around to the trunk of the car and opened it, lifting him up into the trunk's floor. There was a gas can in one corner of the garage. He brought it over and slowly started to pour some into the car's trunk, where Swilley was watching with wide-open eyes.

"I need a lighter. Remembering that he saw Dennis smoking at the bar, he felt in Swilley's pockets until he found a lighter.

"I found a lighter," Al said.

"No. I'll tell you." At this point, realizing what Al was about to do, Dennis had a sudden come-to-Jesus moment and would have given up his own mother.

"I'm short on time, so you'd better not drag it out. Where do you take the cars?'

"Different places."

"What different places?"

"Sometimes up to Jasper. Sometimes to Albany."

"What about Florida?"

"Only for a real high-end car."

"Where in Florida?"

"Tampa."

"Where in Tampa?"

"A place near the Port."

"Are there any other places in Florida where you've taken a car?"

"I've heard about a place outside Chiefland called Moreno and Sons. It's on an isolated road they call the Iron Road. They have a reputation of paying more than anyone."

"So, you've never taken cars directly to this place in Chiefland?"

"No, the salvage yard near Chiefland is isolated and I'm afraid to go there. I've just heard scary stories about the place, so I've always bypassed it and gone straight to Tampa."

"Who in Tampa buys the cars?"

"I'm not sure, but I think the buyers are connected to Moreno and Sons, because I've heard them refer to the Iron Road plant. That's all I know."

"Why do you have to take a car all the way to Florida? Why not someone locally?"

"They like high-end cars and always pay more than anyone in Georgia."

The conversation was halted abruptly by someone banging loudly on the rear wooden doors.

"Who is that?"

"Some people are supposed to be paid."

Al went to the door and looked through the peephole. There were two young males who couldn't have been more than fifteen or sixteen, but the third person was a huge man with multiple facial piercings and a bald head standing next to the door. He was wearing a T-shirt with *Fuck You* printed across the front.

"They expect me to open the doors so I can give them their money for the cars."

Without any hesitation, Al pulled Swilley out of the trunk of the car and dragged him through the single door and into the carport. A tall fence on either side of the garage separated the alley from the backyard of the house. Running back into the garage, he turned the gas can over so more gas could pour out, running underneath both cars.

Standing just outside the door, he touched off the fumes with the lighter and closed the door quickly as the flames followed the gas into the garage. Picking up the small man, he threw him across his shoulder and carried him back up the driveway toward the street. Leaving him still bound up on the sidewalk, Al ran to his car and quickly drove away, gripping the steering wheel tightly to keep his hands from shaking.

In his rearview mirror, he could see the growing light from the burning garage. He was pretty sure he saw a large black Lincoln exit the alleyway down the next street as he passed by. His hands continued to shake as realized he was guilty of the very thing he'd thought he'd left behind in Mexico.

Chapter 22

It was 1:30 AM. Curt, Shela, and Gary were sitting in the blue Honda sedan that Gary had inherited from Otis Morphet. The car was parked on a deserted street in an upscale neighborhood outside Ocala. One side of the street was bordered by a neighborhood of nice middle-class homes. On the opposite side, a tall thick growth of shrubbery hid a tall wall constructed from native Florida limestone. The wall was intended to ensure that anyone who entered the compound had to go through one of the two guarded entrances manned by armed guards. The main gate was open twenty-four hours. The rear gate entrance was open from 7:00 AM to 10:00 PM and was mainly intended to be used by service and commercial vehicles. But due to some weird reasoning, the association allowed vehicles to exit through the gate at any hour.

The security was essentially a private police force bought and paid for by the very wealthy residents. There were no homes valued at less than three to five million, but some were in excess of twenty million. The homes were on lots varying from two to three acres. They all bordered an eighteen-hole golf course that was built to mimic a famous course in Scotland. Only residents were allowed to play the course, allowing easy access to tee times for the homeowners but also creating an aura of exclusivity.

Once a year, the club sponsored a member guest tournament—one for men and another for women. An invitation to play in one of the tournaments was considered to be worth its weight in gold. Traditionally, the winning pairs of the two tournaments would each receive a new Lexus. It was rumored that a state senator who was invited to play had canceled a meeting with the nation's president in order to participate as a guest.

The trio had picked this spot because Gary remembered seeing something about the club on the news. And Ocala was located close enough to Chiefland so that if they were successful in stealing a car, they would be able to dispose of it before dawn. All three had a cell phone set on vibrate.

Gary and Curt both were dressed in jeans and dark-colored long sleeve shirts. Shela remained in the car as Gary and Curt got out, removed a collapsible ladder from the trunk of the Honda, and headed toward the wall. They had spent the better part of the day cruising around the periphery of the compound looking for an easy point of entry. At this spot, there was little traffic even in daytime. Here, the homes inside the compound backed up to the wall, and most importantly, there was a small tree within the line of shrubs that had a limb reaching out across the top of the wall.

The tall shrubs provided concealment, so they were able to open the ladder and wedge it against the wall. Curt went first by climbing up the ladder and reaching for the tree limb. He was then able to lift himself up and onto the top of the wall. While he tied a rope to the tree limb, Gary struggled to lift himself until Curt took one of his arms and pulled him up while muttering under his breath, "Pussy." They used the rope hanging down the inside of the fence to rappel down to the ground, again finding themselves in dense shrubbery.

As soon as they were safely on the ground, Gary looked at the wall and the rope hanging down and the realization suddenly hit him. There was no way he'd be able to climb back up. This was what true commitment must be as he started to look around at his surroundings. They hadn't considered it when they planned it, but a full moon provided enough visibility to enable movement without using flashlights. Looking at their surroundings, they could tell they were in the backyard of a home. There was a long pool and a guesthouse between them and the main house. The faint light visible inside the rear glass walls of the house were probably night-lights. A large number of the residents were seasonal, but this was the time most residents would be present for golf and especially the equestrian activities, which were a vital part of the local economy.

Curt led them to the side of the property and started moving toward the front of the house. Again, even the side of the property was lined with tall, thick hedges concealing the fence separating the lots. Gary had shown Curt how to use Google Earth to look at the outline of the houses, so he knew they were heading toward the garage side of the house. The four garage doors were closed, and there were no cars parked outside.

They knew that most residents would be parking their cars inside the garages, but not all of them. Some residents used their garage space for things like a recording studio or a full gym. The mindset of the people who lived in this gated community were the same as in all wealthy communities.

"I'm paying for safety and I'm taking it for granted. I'm not concerned about leaving my keys, my purse, or my handgun in my unlocked car. Who would dare to violate my privilege?"

Gary instinctively understood this mindset. And he was right. After moving from the first house to the second and then the third without seeing a single car in a driveway, they saw a car sitting in a portico of a two-story house that looked like a reproduction of a New York hotel.

The minute they moved toward the house, a car's lights materialized in the street and was moving toward them. Both Curt and Gary just dropped to the ground and tried to flatten out like pancakes, hoping their dark clothes would make them invisible. The car was a police car, and it was moving slowly, as if the driver were just killing time as he went through the motions of his job. The second it had passed, they moved to the car parked in the portico.

Two hours earlier, Dr. Walter Hawkins had been playing cards and downing shots at the clubhouse. After he'd lost nearly twenty thousand dollars in a card game, he had the presence of mind to know it was time to fold and go home. After downing one more shot, knowing he was only driving inside the compound, he'd headed home. Not wanting to wake up the maid who had a room off the garage, he just drove into the portico and entered the house through the unlocked front door, not bothering to take the car keys or to lock the Maybach Mercedes. He knew he lived in a safe place.

When Curt tried the driver's side door of the Maybach and it opened, he was surprised. Then when he realized that the keys were still inside, he started the car, and the big engine gave a deep throaty growl.

Curt smiled a huge smile. "Bingo."

Gary climbed into the front passenger seat while Curt slowly drove out of the driveway and headed toward the rear gate. Although there was no guard at this hour at the back gate, the resident code on the car automatically opened the gate, allowing them to drive out unchallenged. There would be a video recording of the vehicles that exited after-hours, but it would be hours more before anyone had reason to look at the video.

Curt drove back to the side street where Shela was waiting. He rolled his window down and simply said, "Follow us."

While he had to stop at a red light while leaving Ocala, Curt punched a speed dial on his phone. Gary could hear an automated voice: "Leave a message."

Curt only replied, "Delivery in estimated hour and half."

Curt stayed on US 27 through Williston and Bronson before turning off on State Road 339 and crossing the Waccasassa Flats. When he reached the graded road turnoff that led to the salvage yard, he stopped by the side of the road and got out of the Mercedes.

"Okay, Gary, get behind the wheel. It's your turn to be the big man. Shela and I want to see how you do with a delivery."

What Gary didn't realize was that both Curt and Shela were still concerned about what Leon might do to them if he had connected them to the murder at the rest stop. If Leon were to do anything, they wanted to send Gary in first as the sacrificial lamb. Maybe it would give them a chance to run if anything went south.

Gary led in the Maybach with Curt and Shela following in the Honda. This time, the lights came on, flooding the cars with bright light. There was no time or need to use the outside call box, as the gates started opening the minute the lights came on.

The same huge man called Ethan came out through the gates in a golf cart, stopping in front of the Maybach. Getting out of the cart, he approached the driver's side window of the first car and carefully looked inside at Gary.

Moving back to the Honda, he directed a flashlight beam onto the car. Curt was in the driver's seat and had his window rolled down. "We got a good one this time."

Ethan took a cell phone out of his pocket and punched in a quick dial number. Turning his back, he walked away from the two cars. After a brief conversation, he put the phone back in his pocket and returned to where Curt and Shela were waiting.

Leaving no room for discussion, Ethan said, "You two wait out here." Getting back into the golf cart, he motioned for Gary to follow him in the Mercedes.

As they passed through, the gates closed behind them and the floodlights were turned off, leaving Curt and Shela sitting in the dark, wondering what the fuck had just happened.

Chapter 23

By the time Mark left the riverfront bar and returned to his home in Jacksonville, it was too late to call Roe. He fixed himself a strong Tanqueray over ice with lime juice and finally fell asleep watching Al Bundy dig himself out of a hole with his wife Peggy.

The next morning, after a short hard run, he took a pot of coffee out onto the patio and sent a text to Roe asking her to call back. Roe was in a meeting when he called, but she left it to call him back.

"Morning, Mark, any change with Keri?"

"Nothing significant. She is off the ventilator and breathing on her own, which is good."

"Every time you call, I'm holding my breath."

"Roe, the frustrating part is not being able to do anything to help her."

"I understand. Just remember that Keri's a strong woman."

"I was wrong in saying there was nothing I could do." He continued to explain what he'd learned about the car the hijackers were driving. "What I'd like for you to do is to use the state's database and see if you can find out any details related to the sale of the Mustang. The owner told me he sold it to a doctor in Gainesville named Bloomquist who then put the title in his stepson's name.

"Not a problem, Mark. Give me a few minutes and I'll call you back."

Roe soon called Mark back. "Mark, it's a little bit confusing. From what I'm seeing, a Gerald Wilson sold the car to Joseph Bloomquist, who immediately transferred the title to Curtis Lawson. The address for Lawson is the same as the address for Bloomquist in Gainesville. That's all I can find out about the car. Mark, before you do anything else, call my mom in Gainesville and see if she knows anything about Bloomquist or Lawson. Gainesville's not that big, and my mom has big ears."

"Good idea, Roe. I'll call her now. I'll keep you updated."

Roe's mom, Sid Estes, and Mark had met during the time Roe was in over her head with some very bad people. It was shortly after Mark's daughter Kim had been brutally murdered. Both Sid and Mark were burdened with the events they were both facing. Sid and her husband never knew any of the details of Roe and Mark's relationship.

They had no idea of the things that Mark—with Roe's help—had done to avenge Kim's death. The only thing they knew with certainty was that Mark was largely responsible for bringing Roe back from the brink of destruction and becoming a positive influence in her life. For this, they would be eternally grateful.

Sid answered on the third ring. "Hello, Mark, are you in Gainesville?"

"No, Sid, I'm calling from Jacksonville. I just got off the phone with Roe, and she said you might know something about a doctor in Gainesville."

Sid laughed. "And I'll bet she told you I have big ears."

Mark couldn't help but laugh as well. "You both know each other too well. I'm trying to find out something about a Dr. Bloomquist. Have you heard anything about him?"

"Wow, you picked a hot one. He and his wife happen to be the current club champions at the tennis club my husband and I belong to. They are both nice people."

"Do you know anything about her son, Curtis?"

"Oh, yes. Curt went to school with our son up until the tenth grade. He was nothing but trouble. Bloomquist and Curt's mom finally gave up on him and let him go live full-time with his dad in Palatka. I guess his dad didn't care what the kid did and let him run free. Curt was a smart boy, but he never was able to reconcile his mom and dad's divorce. I really don't know anything about the dad, only rumors."

"Such as?"

"Big drinker, gambler, and no qualms about hitting a woman."

"Does Curt still live with him?"

"I really don't know. I can give you the phone number listed in our club directory, and you could call her. She might be willing to talk to you."

"Thanks, Sid, I'd appreciate it."

When Mark called the number Sid gave him, the voice that answered sounded out of breath. "Yes?"

Mark answered, "Mrs. Bloomquist?"

"How can I help you?"

"My name is Elton Graham with Equity Insurance Group. I'm trying to reach Curtis Lawson. This is the number he listed on the application."

"Application?"

"For car insurance."

"Mr. Graham, you're calling the wrong person. My husband and I are not providing insurance for Curt. The car is in his name, and he is fully responsible for insuring it. Maybe you should talk to either Curt or his dad."

"I apologize, Mrs. Bloomquist. Curtis had indicated that you and your husband would be buying coverage for him."

"Mr. Graham, I'm biting my tongue to refrain from using the words I'd like to use. We did buy the car for Curt but with the clear understanding that he'd be responsible for everything related to the car. I'm not even going to mention your call to my husband. I'm afraid he'd have a heart attack."

"I'm so sorry, Mrs. Bloomquist. Could you at least tell me how I could contact Curtis?"

"I can only tell you that Curt lives with his dad in Palatka. I don't have a street address. I just know that it's close to the Palatka water plant."

"Where do they work?"

Mark heard a loud laugh. "I don't think Curt has ever had a full-time job, and his dad keeps getting either fired or arrested. A friend who lives in Palatka told me that he's working for a man named Wilson helping him run a riverfront bar. That's all I know."

Mark almost dropped his phone when he heard what the mom was saying. "You did say Wilson?"

"Yes, that's all I can tell you Mr. Graham. Good luck," was the last thing Mark heard before she hung up.

Mark now realized that Wilson had been holding out on him. He obviously knew a lot more than he was telling. Why?

He knew he would have to make another trip to the river bar.

At the same time he was making the decision to go back to the bar, his phone rang.

"Mark, this is Al. I have some interesting information."

Chapter 24

Driving the stolen Maybach, Gary followed Ethan along the same route at the salvage yard they'd followed before. Gary was apprehensive, but at the same time he was curious. Why was he coming in alone? Anyway, he knew he'd soon find out as they approached the same huge building just as they'd done before.

He parked, and Ethan opened the door for him. "Come with me."

Gary followed Ethan into the same small office where Leon sat waiting behind a desk. Ethan left and Gary sat and waited for Leon to speak.

Leon was holding a newspaper in his hands. He laid the paper onto the desk and spoke. "Gary, right?"

"Yes, sir."

"Gary, tell me what happened at the rest stop outside St. Augustine when you all took the Camry."

At that moment, Gary knew that he'd rather have Leon as a friend than either Curt or Shela. It was obvious that Leon had connected them to the incident at the rest stop. Taking a deep breath, he started telling Leon how he met Curt and had told him how badly he needed money. Curt had promised him an easy way to make some. He left nothing out, including how Shela had killed the security guard and brutally assaulted the woman.

Leon sat listening without showing any expression. He only spoke once to ask, "Was Curt driving his Mustang at the rest stop?"

By the time Gary had finished his confession, Ethan came into the office and handed Leon a slip of paper, plus something wrapped in a towel.

Leon looked toward Ethan, who only nodded as he said, "Tampa."

"Gary, the car you brought in is a top-of-the-line Mercedes Maybach. It's a V12 dual turbo that will do zero to sixty in 4.5 seconds. It cost maybe two hundred fifty thousand dollars here in the US, but will bring five hundred thousand cash in a Third World country, which is where it's heading. Tell me how you got it."

Gary explained how he'd given Curt and Shela an ultimatum and then how he'd engineered the plan to steal a car from a gated community.

Leon listened and sat silent for so long that Gary began to worry. "Gary, do you think you could bring in another car like you did this time?"

"Yes, I just may have to go further away to find a similar community. I certainly wouldn't go anywhere near the same place again."

"Gary, have you heard the term, *Never judge a book by the cover*?"

"Yes, sir."

"Well, I think a lot of people are misjudging you. You were right to threaten to walk away from them. Their predilection toward violence is the sort of thing that brings all sorts of unnecessary attention. They've done this once before, and they were warned. They're both ticking time bombs. I haven't yet decided how I'm going to handle the situation, but I'll be doing something. In the meantime,

I'm going to give you money for the Mercedes. I'll leave it up to you how you want to split it up. What Curt won't know is that I'm giving you another envelope that you'll need to stuff into a pocket. You were the mastermind for this job, and it'll contain your bonus."

Leon took the towel Ethan had left on the desk and unwrapped it. "Gary, this was inside the glove compartment of the Mercedes." He held up a small, short barrel revolver. It's a light weight 357 Magnum. It's loaded with five rounds. I'd recommend that you hide it in your pocket. Even if you know nothing about guns, all you have to do is to point it and pull the trigger. My advice to you is not to trust either Curt or Shela any further than you could throw them.

"Furthermore, I'd recommend that you put some distance between yourself and the two of them. The more I think about it, I think we just may be able to help each other out. Gary, I'm going to give you this piece of paper. I'm writing a phone number on it. If you can bring in another car with them, you need to contact me and give me a heads-up. Maybe I can help you divorce Curt and Shela. Only send a text and never—and I mean *never*, for the sake of your health—mention names or places. And remember, I know where you live with your mom. I make it a point to learn everything I can about the people I'm dealing with. Understand?"

"Yes, sir, I got it. And thank you."

As he walked back outside the building, he saw the Maybach was already being driven up a ramp into the back of a tractor trailer. Ethan was outside waiting by the golf cart and took him back outside the main gate where Curt and Shela sat fuming while they waited. At this point, they didn't know whether to be pissed off or scared, but they were relieved to see only Gary and Ethan returning. Ethan motioned for Curt to roll down the window.

"The kids got your money. Now go!"

Gary got into the back seat of the Honda as a relieved Curt quickly drove away from Moreno and Sons. While Curt was driving, Gary was counting the money in the envelope Leon had given him. Gary could tell by the way Curt was driving that he was getting angrier by the minute. Shela had turned up the volume on the radio and was bouncing to the music having probably just consumed something illegal.

Curt finally spoke. "What was that all about?"

Gary remained calm and answered, "What do you mean?"

"Why the hell did you go in alone? What happened?"

Again, in a measured tone, Gary answered, "I may have just saved both your dumb asses. Leon was not happy with what you did at the rest stop. He knew everything about it. I assured him that you wouldn't do anything like that again. He promised me that any more violence connected to any of us would result in us being fed to the alligators in his lakes. Why he used me to deliver the message, I don't know. Although, when I went into the building, I saw several men just standing there like they were waiting for an order from him. I'll admit it. I was scared shitless. Oh, I forgot. He also said that you'd better hide your Mustang in a deep hole, and under no circumstance should you ever drive it back here again."

The last part seemed to inflame Curt even more.

"Okay, goddammit, how much is in the envelope?"

"Ten thousand."

"That's all?"

"Leon went to great lengths to explain that the risk associated with a car like that was much greater than one that could be disassembled and made to disappear. Ten thousand's not bad."

Curt continued to drive for a while without saying anything else. As they passed through Bronson, he pulled off the road into the parking lot of a deserted tractor supply and turned around to look at Gary.

"Okay, Gary, take your thousand out of the envelope and give me the rest."

Gary only laughed. "I'll tell you what I'll do. I'm going to cut you two in for a half." He handed the envelope up to Curt. "I'm keeping my part, which is half. Here's your half."

Even in the dark car, Gary could sense Curt's temper rise over the boiling point just as he'd anticipated it would. And again as Gary predicted, after he'd taken the envelope from Gary, Curt's hand came up with his gun and he started to turn back toward Gary.

Gary was well ahead of him. He had already taken the gun from his pocket. He put the barrel up against Curt's ear, cocking the hammer back with a big click as he did. "Curt, if you even fart, I'm going to scatter your brains across the dash. Very slowly, hand me your gun."

After Gary had Curt's gun in his hand, he said, "Now drive." Curt drove through Bronson toward Williston. He stayed on State Road 318 and 310 across the middle of the state, bypassing Gainesville and Ocala. When they approached a bridge crossing a feeder creek running into the Ocklawaha River, Gary told Curt to stop. At this early hour of the morning, there was no traffic on the desolate highway.

"Turn off the car and give me the keys, Curt." Gary took the keys and got out of the car and carried the gun he'd taken from Curt, carefully holding it by the barrel over to the edge of the water. It was dark, and he couldn't be clearly seen by either Curt or Shela. He made a throwing motion, as if he were throwing the gun out into the water. Slipping the gun into his back pocket, he returned to the car and handed the keys back to Curt as he got into the car. "I can't believe you were stupid enough to keep a gun you used to murder someone. If we try to steal another car, we won't be carrying any guns."

When Curt finally stopped in front of his trailer, he told a subdued Curt—Shela being in a different universe—"I'll talk to Shela later at school."

As he entered his mom's trailer with two small revolvers and a shit pile of money, he realized that he'd never felt as empowered as he did at this moment.

But even so, he knew he had to find a way out. There was no way this could end well. He knew he was going to take Leon up on his suggestion and hope he meant what he'd said about helping him end his relationship with Curt and Shela.

Gary was not alone in thinking that something had to change.

Ethan returned to Leon's office after taking Gary back outside the main gate of Moreno and Sons. Leon was sitting in the same position at his desk, and he appeared to be deep in thought. Ethan knew not to interrupt his thoughts, so he patiently waited until Leon spoke.

"Ethan, this business has profited and survived because of the wise decisions both my grandparents and parents have made. I think the time has come for us to make another decision. I'll be talking to Carmen in the next day or so. I want her opinion, and yours as well. This has been on my mind for a while, and the events of the last few days have only made it more urgent. Your instincts are good, and you are a part of the business. Let me tell you what I'm thinking."

Chapter 25

"Good morning, Mark. I have some interesting information. But first, how is Keri doing?"

"Morning, Al. Outwardly, she is healing well, but the doctors are still reluctant to say much. I think they're not very optimistic. Have you caught up from taking time off?"

"Yes, Mark, and then some. Listen, the reason I'm calling is to tell you some interesting things I've learned. Remember I told you all about a case where I'm defending a carjacking victim?"

"Yes, you said the man killed one of the teenagers."

"Right. Well, here's what I've learned." Al continued to tell Mark about what he'd done. But he didn't tell Mark how it had affected him emotionally.

When he finished, Mark was silent for a minute before he replied, "Al, you are scaring the hell out of me. You can't put your career—and possibly your life—in danger like this."

After what Al said next, Mark had to wipe his eyes with the sleeve of the sweatshirt he was wearing. Al had up until now called him by his name—Mark—but for the first time, he used a different term.

"Dad, I saw the visitor logs at Raiford Prison. You visited Jim Herbert while he was on death row. I even called Karin Stills and talked to her about the Herbert case. I wanted to know who my father really is. I know that neither Roe nor Keri will ever betray you by telling me anything about your past. I respect their confidence. But just from my conversation with Karin Stills, I know that you are capable of doing whatever it might take to protect those you love. If I'm a son of Mark Price and Rosa Gomez, I'm not afraid to do anything they would do."

After he'd regained his composure, Mark took a deep breath. "You don't know how much it's meant to me to discover I had you as a son. You also can't understand what it would do to me if I lost you after losing the other three people I loved. I feel the same about Roe. You and Roe are my life now."

"And I am glad you feel that way, but at the same time, I think you know that life is filled with uncertainties, and neither you nor I can run from doing the right thing. I am enjoying practicing law, but the last couple of days, I've suddenly become aware that it's a boring existence. I actually think I can do more than one thing at the same time. Anyway, what I'm saying is that my relationship with the firm I'm working with will allow me the freedom to pick and choose my cases and to come and go as I please. Money is not a question. Rosa made sure that if I never worked another day, I'd be okay. So, in essence, what I'm saying is, let me help you look for the lowlifes who hurt Keri."

"If I agreed to let you, what would you do next?" Mark already suspected what Al's answer would be.

"I'd go to Florida and just snoop around the salvage yard Swilley mentioned. Remember what the sheriff said about Keri's cellphone's last signal being just south of Gainesville. He thought maybe they were taking the car to

Tampa. But what if there is another chop shop option and it happens to be this Moreno place?"

Mark then told Al about what Roe had learned about another carjacking west of Tallahassee where violence was involved. It had occurred late at night in another rest stop west of Tallahassee. The car was later spotted going south on US 19.

"Maybe it was headed to Tampa, but if this Swilley was telling you the truth, maybe there is something to this Moreno place."

"Dad, I'd bet the farm that Swilley was telling the truth. I've never seen anyone as frightened as he was at the moment I pulled the lighter out of his pocket and started to close the trunk on him."

As Al was speaking, Mark was shaking his head and thinking that although Al had grown up with no knowledge of Mark or his existence, the similarity between the two was frightening. He also knew the smart thing to do would be to go to Sheriff Norton in St. Augustine with what they'd learned. But since everything was only speculative at this point, he couldn't see a problem with waiting a little longer. Until they had more definite proof, there was no reason to waste the sheriff's time.

"Al, you've got to promise me that you won't start any more fires or go into another dive bar alone."

"I promise. We'll go in together."

Chapter 26

After ending the call with Al, Mark was filled with mixed emotions. On one hand, he was overflowing with pride that Al had actually called him, "dad." But he was also filled with misgivings about agreeing to let him get involved in his search for Keri's assailants. His own life had been a rollercoaster of violence. Maybe he could speed up his own search and spare Al any exposure to further danger. With that thought in mind he knew he'd go back to the river bar and try to find the father of the Mustang's owner.

With his plan fixed in his mind, he stopped by the hospital to check on Keri while on his way toward Palatka. Vera looked as if she hadn't moved from the same spot where she'd been sitting the last time he left the room.

"Mark, anything new?"

"Vera, we have a lot of new possibilities, but no one has been arrested yet. Don't waste your energy on that. Just keep focusing on Keri. Has there been any change? I can tell that some of the bruising is not so obvious. What are the doctors telling you?"

"Dr. Goldblatt is optimistic. She says they'll start to bring her out of the induced coma today. We really won't know what the long-term effects will be until then. She says that all of her systems are functioning well. The big questions are all related to her head injury."

"Vera, who's taking care of Brutus?"

"My brother in Lakeland. Remember? He's the retired cop. He and Brutus have always gotten along well since Brutus was a puppy."

"The only reason I thought about him was the possibility of having him here when Keri starts to wake up."

"Mark, I hadn't even thought about it, but that's a good suggestion. I'll mention it to my brother. He'd bring Brutus up here in a heartbeat if he thought it might help."

Mark left the hospital late in the afternoon after giving Keri's mom a break. Just sitting in the room with an unresponsive Keri added to his determination to find the people responsible. He left the hospital with a renewed sense of urgency.

He stopped at a local restaurant in Palatka that advertised *Liver and Onions, All You Can Eat*. He washed it down with supersaturated sweet tea. It was one of Mark's favorites, and he took his time eating. He even treated himself to a slice of homemade coconut cream pie for dessert along with a cup of black, hair-curling coffee that had probably been on a slow boil since breakfast. He knew that just like the previous night, the bar wouldn't be busy until later.

When he reached the end of the pavement that led to the bar, he parked in the cul-de-sac with his car pointing out just as he'd done before. He was sure he saw a figure sitting in a beat-up pickup truck as he got out of his car. He was probably a lookout watching for anything that might be the law.

Mark left his gun and wallet in his car knowing he'd be searched again. He took a couple hundred dollars and stuck them in his pocket for beer money. As he walked down toward the river, the side of the trail was lined with autos, and he imagined that the bar was even louder than the night before. When he walked up the steps toward the entrance, he was greeted by the same bouncer as before.

"Good evening, Henry."

"Mark, right. I guess you decided to walk on the wild side again."

"Henry, I guess I'm a slow learner. Could I ask you a question?"

"You can ask me anything. Whether I'll give you an answer depends on the question."

"Is there a man named Lawson working here?"

"Henry's eyes opened wide. "Mark, you must be a magnet for trouble. What do you want with Frank?"

"I just want to talk to him."

"Most people try to avoid talking to him. I can say that because he knows to leave me alone. I will tell you, he is not a nice man. I've even told Gerald that he's bad news, but he must run a profitable card table for Gerald. I think he has a game going now."

"Do you know anything about his son?"

"Not much. I do know he was hanging out with a man named Otis Morphet, who had a reputation of shady car transactions. At least up until Otis picked the wrong car to steal."

"Where does the son live?"

"I guess he's still living with his dad in Palatka."

"Do you remember the address?"

"No, but I gave Frank a ride home from the bar a while back. His car had some problem. He's renting a house on Myrtle Street. I don't know the house number. It's a big old run-down house with an RV barn in the back. It must have once been used for a business of some sort, because there was a sign in the front that someone had just painted over with black paint."

"You know, Henry, you've told me all I really need to know, but since I'm here, I may as well have a beer and enjoy the entertainment."

"Just be careful that you're not the entertainment, Mark."

Mark laughed and gave Henry a high five as he walked into the bar.

The noise was deafening. Tonight, a DJ was playing the music. There was a rigged-up music system with huge speakers in all four corners of the room blasting out country music. The bartender controlled the choice of music from behind the bar. The songs being played were mostly determined by the suggestions from the patrons, and the bigger the tip, the more likely the requested song would be played. Sometimes the same song would be played over and over due to the size of the tip.

Playing the same song over and over came naturally to the bartender. In addition to bartending, the man behind the bar had once worked as a late-night disk jockey for a small radio station in Gainesville during the short time he matriculated at the university. A friend had warned him that the station manager was going to fire him the next day and replace him with the owner's nephew.

His shift started at midnight, so he brought a cheap bottle of bourbon with him, and as he began to drink, he announced the first song to be "Shake, Rattle and Roll." As soon as it finished playing, he announced the second song to be "Shake, Rattle and Roll." He continued to play the same song for over three hours until someone was able to reach the manager, who came to the station and booted him out. But by then, Julius had become a local legend in Gainesville.

In addition to the loud music, the big-screen TV mounted on the wall behind the bar was turned on. It was playing porn videos. There was standing room only along the bar, and both men and a few hard-looking women were only paying enough attention to occasionally voice an observation as if they were watching a sports event.

Mark edged up to the bar between two men who were discussing the size of different body parts showing on the screen.

He ordered a domestic five-dollar beer before he looked carefully around the room. He finally located Gerald Wilson sitting in a corner talking with two men and a young woman. He walked away from the two men standing at the bar, relieved to not have to listen to the anatomy lecture, and approached the table where Wilson was sitting.

The moment Wilson recognized Mark, a dark expression briefly crossed his face before he smiled. "I'm sorry, I'm not good at remembering names."

"Mark Price."

"So, what brings you back, Mark? Are you looking for that free drink I offered you?"

"Gerald, I guess your memory loss extends to the person you sold your son's Mustang to. You didn't tell me the rest of the story."

"What do you mean by 'rest of the story'?"

"You told me who you sold the car to and that it was for his stepson named Lawson, but you forgot to mention that the boy's dad was working for you."

When Mark made that statement, one of the two men sitting at the table with Wilson turned and looked at him with a disgusted look on his face. The man had a stubble of a beard and long, bushy sideburns. He wore a tight black T-shirt and black jeans. Mark could see that he was muscular, but even sitting down, it was apparent that he was a short man. His lower jaw was recessed, and that along with a prominent nose created a feral countenance.

The feral-looking man stood up, but not before giving Gerald Wilson another long, hard frown and a slight nod. "I'm Frank Lawson. What do you want with my son?"

Mark watched as Lawson stood up. The man was trying to look as threatening as possible, but when he was standing at full height, he was still looking up at Mark, who towered above him.

"I only want to talk to him."

"My son lives with me. Why don't you talk to me?"

"He may have witnessed a carjacking that hurt a friend of mine really bad. Anything he might remember would be a big help in finding out who the carjackers were."

Lawson looked back at Wilson again before he said to Mark. "Let's go out on the dock where it's not so loud."

Later, Mark wondered how he could have been so stupid. But at the moment, he didn't feel intimidated or threatened by Lawson. He replied, "I'll follow you."

Chapter 27

Kelly was waiting with an exasperated look on her face when Al returned to his office.

"How can I get office hours like yours?"

"Kelly, it must be my sparkling personality. I can't think of any other reason."

"You can only dream. By the way, there was an interesting bit of news this morning on a local station. You know that Swilley guy I did the work up on?"

"Yes, What about him?"

"He was found tied up on the sidewalk in front of a house in a quiet neighborhood. The garage in the back of the house was burned to the ground. The fire department spokesperson said if they'd gotten there any later, the whole neighborhood might have gone up. Swilley refused to talk to the authorities and claimed someone hit him from behind, someone he didn't know who'd taped him up."

Smart man, Al thought to himself.

Kelly continued, "The bad news is that the grand jury looking at the hijacking case is being pressured by the DA to indict our client regardless of the evidence. So, you better brace yourself for what's coming."

He was uncomfortable with the way Kelly was looking at him, as if she were waiting for him to say something more. He went on toward his office, but he could feel her eyes burning into his back. When he reached the door, he turned and asked Kelly to follow him.

"Kelly, I want you to do something else for me. First, look up a Florida company called Moreno and Sons Salvage and see what comes up. I'll need an address as well. Then will you do some research on realtors in Florida that cover the area between Gainesville and Cedar Key? I'm specifically looking for someone reputable who deals in large tracts of land."

"Sure, but only if you promise me that nothing bad will happen to um," she said, walking back toward her desk.

For the rest of the morning, Al buried himself in paperwork, making sure there was nothing on his calendar that couldn't be handled on the phone or, better yet, by Kelly. When she entered his office after lunch, she handed him a paper with a name, address, and phone number as well as a hand-drawn map.

"Okay, now I'm an expert in real estate in Florida. I started out by calling all the big box realtors asking for someone who deals in large land tracts in the counties between Gainesville and the coast. They all suggested someone in their own firm. All were different. Then I called a few one- or two-person independent realtors. The ones who only handled homes and smaller properties consistently gave me the same name, Carmen Baker. Then I looked up the offices that handle deeds and real estate transfers in Gilcrest, Levy, and Dixie counties, and talked to people who run and work in the offices. Every time I mentioned Carmen Baker, I got a positive response. Then I looked her up and found that she has an office in Gainesville. When I called her office, I got a recording that only said, 'Leave a message and I'll get back to you as soon as possible.' I didn't leave a message. Apparently, Carmen doesn't have to spend a lot of money on advertising. This is the address and phone number of her office. And that's all I've got to say about realtors in Florida.

"Now, as for Moreno and Sons Salvage, I couldn't find much about the owners. It is privately owned by the family and is a well-known source of automotive body parts all across the US and even South America. As far as I could see, it's a reputable and legitimate company. They file all required reports and pay their taxes. They've been in business since 1930. I made a map showing where it's located. It is unusual for a large and apparently well-known business to be located in such a relatively isolated area."

"Kelly, you did good. I'll try calling Baker myself and see if she'll answer."

Al still couldn't get his client off his mind. He was worried as he sat and wondered to himself how they could have gotten to the point where a man protecting his family could possibly be charged with murder. Especially in this circumstance. But one step at a time as he dialed the number listed for Carmen Baker, realtor.

But surprise, surprise, the phone was answered by a husky female voice who simply said, "This is the second call coming from a law office in Atlanta within a short time. Am I in trouble?"

Al couldn't help but laugh. "Not from this end, you're not. I just had my assistant do some research for me. I'm looking for a realtor who handles land in West Florida. Your name kept coming up. I'm coming down, and I'm interested in a tract of land large enough for hunting and possibly fishing."

"I might be able to help you. Large tracts come and go. Sometimes property might be available that's not listed. It's a delicate dance. Are you coming down anytime soon? If we could meet, I could learn more about what you're looking for and what you are willing to spend."

"You tell me when and where and I'll find the time to meet you."

"I'll be in my office tomorrow morning if that's not too soon. Do you have my office address?"

Al read the address Kelly had given him back to her and replied, "Ten o'clock?"

"That's good. I'll look for you then."

Al walked out to where Kelly was sitting and looking up at him, shaking her head before he even spoke. "Kelly, you're not going to like what I'm going to do, but it's something I need to do. Don't worry, I'll let the big guy know I'll be out for a couple of days. I'll keep my phone close so you can reach me anytime. I really think you're the one in charge anyway."

It didn't take him long to return to his condo, pack a small travel case, and start the drive south on I-75. It was a six-hour drive, and he reached Gainesville well after dark, taking the Archer Road exit. He'd checked ahead and knew there was a courtyard near the exit.

He was able to get a room, and after eating at a hamburger place next door, he tried to relax in his room and think of how he could fake his way through the next day.

Chapter 28

Following Lawson through the door toward the river, Mark realized there were two separate docks. The large open dock toward his left was the patio off the main bar area. It was well lit with several people laughing, drinking, and talking loudly. The part in front of him had no lighting and extended further out into the river. He'd only walked a few feet out onto the dock when the hairs on his neck stood up. At the same moment, he was aware there were other people who had followed Lawson and himself out into the dark area.

Instinctively, he rolled to his right as the blade of a knife in Lawson's hand missed his neck, where it was directed, and instead slashed across his shoulder. As he continued to turn, he could tell there were at least four figures moving toward him. In the dark, he couldn't see any chairs or objects to use for defense, so he instantly made a strategic decision.

Continuing to let his momentum add to his speed, he took two steps toward the end of the dock. Not knowing what was below, he went off feet first. As he left the dock, the crack of a pistol was followed by a noise and pain as a bullet passed so close to his head it made a small indentation in his earlobe. Luck was with him as he landed in deep water. Afraid to surface knowing the gunman might be able to see him, he stayed several feet underwater, and instead of swimming away, he swam back toward and under the dock. He surfaced slowly and silently.

Mark could clearly hear the men on the dock above laughing. "Frank, I'm sure I hit the son of a bitch."

"I think you did, Horace. There's enough moonlight on the water to see that nothing's come up. Plus, I may have missed his carotid, but I'm sure I cut the shit out of something. I want you to stay here for a few minutes and watch. Even if he's alive, he can only hold his breath for so long."

"All right, Frank. But I think he's a goner."

The next voice Mark heard was Gerald Wilson, who was not happy. "Frank, I've told you we can't have this kind of shit. Booze, drugs, and girls are one thing, but this kind of crap is just too much. Our goal has been to stay under the radar of the sheriff as much as possible. This kind of thing will force the sheriff to come after us. Who knows how many people might be looking for this guy?"

"Stuff it, Gerald. Why did you even mention my name to him? My son don't need anyone snooping around, and I'll fuck up anyone who tries to mess with him. By the way, this guy must have driven here tonight. Tomorrow, I'll see what cars are left and take his car back to my house. My son Curt does have a knack for making cars disappear."

All the group went back into the bar, leaving the one man standing at the end of the dock. He smoked part of a cigarette and flipped it into the river. "Screw it, the guy's gone." Then he reentered the bar.

Mark had not moved a muscle as he stood in chest-deep water under the dock. It was cold, and he realized he was bleeding heavily from the gash across his shoulder. But it wasn't the cut or blood or even the cold that really scared him. It was the possibility of a water moccasin being somewhere nearby. They were the most aggressive of all the poisonous snakes in North America, and unlike all the rest, they were well-known to go well out of their way to attack a moving body.

As he carefully moved toward the shoreline, he flinched every time he felt anything other than water. He moved away from the occupied patio to the darker side of the building and away from the front entrance. By the time he worked his way from under the dock and through thick patches of palmetto around the building, he was sweating profusely. He remembered that Mark Twain had said something about the worst thing that had ever happened to him was only in his mind. If that were true, he'd already been snake-bit a dozen times over. Even when he could see the front entrance, he had to stay deep enough in the underbrush to remain hidden.

By the time he'd reached the cul-de-sac where his car was parked, he was exhausted. Plus, he was acutely aware of why palmetto was sometimes called "Saw Palmetto." His wet clothes had been shredded. His arms and legs were scratched and bleeding, all of which together caused him to look like he'd been whipped with a cat o' nine tails.

As he'd worked his way through the dense foliage, he'd been thinking about what he was going to do next. When he reached the cul-de-sac at the end of the paved road, he identified the pickup truck that he saw when he first arrived. The bar's sentry was alone and smoking a cigar. Mark could hear Stonewall Jackson singing something about not being angry on the truck's radio. The driver's side window was rolled down to let fresh air in while the cigar smoke kept the mosquitoes away.

Mark quietly moved up next to the truck on the driver's side and literally crawled up to the door on his hands and knees to avoid the man seeing him in the side view mirror. He took a deep breath and reached into the window, pulling up on the door handle and opening it in one fluid motion. The poor man was surprised as Mark assumed he would be. He was frozen in place just long enough for Mark to grab him by the front of his shirt with his left and pull him toward the open door. As the man's face was pulled toward the open door, Mark used his right fist, releasing some of his anger and frustration on the hapless man's face. Although it was probably unnecessary, he used both hands to bang the man's head once against the doorframe.

The poor guy was going to have one hell of a headache tomorrow, but he was definitely out for now. Before he set him back up in his seat, he took the man's belt and used it to wrap around his own shoulder the best he could. The sentry remained unconscious and would be for a while.

The sentry's cell phone was sitting on the center console. Mark used it to dial 911. "I'm at a bar on the river, and there's been a shooting between some drug dealers. You need to come quick." He followed up with detailed directions. "You might want to come in quietly because they've got a lot of guns."

For the first time, breathing a prayer as he did so, Mark reached deep into his tattered jeans, not knowing whether his keys would still be there. They were. Within minutes, he was driving out toward US 19. As he neared the intersection with US 19, he met a half dozen patrol cars running without sirens or flashing lights, closely followed by two emergency vehicles. Mark drove north toward Palatka, laughing all the way and thinking about the surprise awaiting the occupants of the bar.

What Mark didn't know was the moment they became aware there was a raid coming, both Wilson and Lawson ran out onto the patio dock and went down a ladder constructed specifically for a situation like this. A small fishing boat equipped with fishing gear was waiting. They pushed off from the dock and were almost immediately lost in the dark. If by some chance the authorities had approached by boat from the river side, it would be hard to prove they were not legally fishing for channel catfish.

Mark remembered seeing an emergency clinic somewhere on one of the main roads when he'd been looking for auto repair shops earlier. His luck held up, and he found the clinic with only two cars in in the parking lot but an *OPEN* neon sign over the entrance. Knowing that he should be going to a hospital emergency room where the cut on his shoulder might include muscle and would need to be treated by a general surgeon, he hoped he could get treated without leaving a record.

The small waiting room was empty, and there was no one behind the reception desk. The door chimes alerted a young woman, who came out of a door behind the desk. Mark's appearance caught her by surprise, as he also realized how he must look.

"Don't be afraid. I'm not here to rob you. I just need some help."

"What happened to you?"

"It's a long story. I'll tell you, but for now, is there someone who can sew up this cut on my shoulder?"

As he spoke, a young, dark, brown-skinned lady appeared out of the back and looked at Mark with a curious expression. "I can sew you up, but you've got to tell me what happened."

"Okay, but it's embarrassing. I fell out of my boat tonight. I was down on the river fishing by myself when I stood up to cut a ray off the line, I lost my balance and fell overboard. I was holding a knife that cost more than the boat, and I held on to it as I fell. My hand hit the side of the boat, and the knife caught me as I fell. The current took the boat away, and I had to swim to shore. It took me two hours of walking through the thickest palmettos I've ever seen to get back to my car. And here I am."

"Okay, Emma, go ahead and get his information while I get things ready."

By the time he'd completed the paperwork, the second lady came back wearing a paper gown and simply said, "Follow me, Mr. Hoover. By the way, I'm Dr. Maldonado. Mark followed her into a small treatment room after paying Emma cash to cover the visit from his fortunately dry wallet. He was seated on a motorized chair that the doctor reclined by pushing buttons. Using scissors and talking at the same time, she removed the belt and cut away the shoulder and arm of his shirt.

"Sorry, Herbert, I couldn't save the shirt."

"I couldn't care less about the shirt as long as you know how to sew."

Maldonado smiled. "If I can't remember how to do it, I've always got my medical books close by."

"That's encouraging."

She continued to work in silence, but making several grim-looking expressions during the procedure. If she didn't know what she was doing, she was doing a great job of faking it, Mark thought. When she'd finished and the top of his shoulder and arm were wrapped in a tight sling, she finally spoke. "I had to put in several internal sutures where the muscle was slightly cut, but I don't think you'll have any lasting effects from this. After being in the river, you'll need to take these antibiotics and come back in two days to have the bandage changed. I'm curious, Herbert, did your parents name you after the president or the dam?"

"That obvious?"

"No shit, it's obvious. That cut was intentional. You must be walking on the wild side, Mr. Hoover. You need to be more careful."

"That's good advice. I really do appreciate your help."

She followed Mark out past the reception desk where Emma had just given paperwork to a young, frightened couple holding a very young baby. The mom was tearfully telling Emma in broken English that they didn't have money or insurance. "Her temperature just shot up, and we didn't know what to do."

Mark stopped, reached into the pocket of his torn jeans, and took out his wallet. Walking over to where Emma sat, he counted out five hundred-dollar bills onto her desk. "This should cover these people's visit. Give them the change."

He quickly walked out, leaving surprised looks on their faces.

Chapter 29

Al found Carmen Baker's office located in a development on the western edge of Gainesville called Hammock Place. It originally consisted of homes built around a golf course. Now a sizable part of the development included a thriving business district with restaurants and professional offices mixed with apartments and condos. Baker's office was on the first floor with an investment firm on one side and a psychiatrist office on the other. All of the two upper floors were apartments. There was a simple brass plaque embedded in the door stating *CARMEN BAKER, BROKER*, and under that in smaller print, *Farms and Lands.*

Al entered a small room with a sofa, two upholstered chairs, and a marble-topped coffee table. A large magazine display case featuring multiple real estate magazines and journals leaned against one wall. As he walked into the room, Al heard a faint sound of a chime sounding somewhere beyond the single closed door, which led toward the rear of the office. Within moments, that door opened, and Carmen Baker walked into the room to greet him.

Carmen Baker was a slim five foot four in heels. She wore a very conservative pants suit with an open white silk blouse. Her only jewelry was a gold Rolex watch and a simple gold chain necklace. Her long jet-black hair was fashioned into a simple ponytail.

"You must be Al," she said, smiling while looking up at him and offering her hand. Al found himself momentarily speechless before he was finally able to respond.

"Yes, and if I look surprised, I'll admit I was expecting someone much older, maybe dressed in blue jeans and a plaid shirt."

"I came late in my parent's life. To say they were surprised would be an understatement. But they did decide to keep me, for which I'm grateful. Did you just arrive in Gainesville, or did you come down yesterday?"

"I drove down late yesterday and got a room at the courtyard off 75."

"Listen, have you had breakfast?"

"I have, but I can drink coffee all day."

"I haven't eaten anything this morning and I'm starved. There's a good bistro around the corner. How about we walk around there, and you can tell me something about what you're looking for while I eat?"

The restaurant was literally just around the corner. Baker must have been a regular because she was greeted warmly by the hostess, who led them to a table in a quiet nook. Carmen ordered a huge country breakfast with sausage, bacon, eggs, cheese grits, toast and black coffee. Al only ordered the black coffee.

After they'd ordered, Carmen said, "Okay, Al, tell me what you're looking for."

Even though he'd rehearsed what he planned to say the night before, Al was suddenly at a loss on how to proceed. He realized that it was Carmen Baker who was confusing him. Even sitting across the small table from her, he got a whiff of her perfume. He took a deep breath and tried to concentrate as he started his spiel.

"My dad and I are looking together. We like to hunt and fish, but we want privacy. Hunting on almost all public lands has become dangerous. There are just too many yahoos who brag about brush shots and will shoot at the sound of footsteps in the woods. We've looked at maps, and there appear to be huge tracts of private land around the Waccasassa Flats and over toward the coast."

Carmen was nodding as Al spoke, but she was still enjoying her meal. She finished the last of her food, and took a long drag of her coffee before she answered. "I'll have to add that most of the land that appears to be private is owned by the large paper companies. There's very little access for hunting on the company's lands. Ideally, what you're looking for is land that borders the larger paper companies. You get the game that lives on the large areas, and you get your property protected on one side by the company's private land."

"Why don't the paper companies just buy up the adjacent land as it becomes available?"

"They do. In fact, it's one of the things that keeps me in business."

"I guess I'm confused. If there is a tract of land as you describe that comes on the market, what would determine whether you sell it to me or to the company?"

"Money. You see most of the large companies are driven by a fixed bottom line. They don't have much room for negotiation. What they offer is usually lowball. If someone is willing to pay more than the company for a piece of land, who do you think the owner will sell it to? Many times, land is just too isolated or too wet, and even someone like yourself just won't be willing to pay a premium price for it. Paper companies are only interested in dirt that will grow a tree. One question that I need to know before we start looking at tracts is what is your budget and how many acres are we looking at?"

"Maybe at least three hundred acres in size and under two mil."

"Let's go back to my office and we'll look at some maps."

When they stood up to leave, Al took out his wallet to pay.

She waved him off. "I keep a tab here."

When they returned to her office, they entered through the waiting area. Her business area was well furnished, but its purpose was obviously utilitarian. In addition to her desk, a table designed to hold large maps was arranged along one wall. She reached under the table and pulled out a large map that she unrolled across the surface.

"My business is focused on these three counties: Dixie, Levy, and north Citrus. My office and an apartment are here in Gainesville. I like being close to all of the perks that come with living near a large university. From here, I can still maintain easy access to these three counties. The further you go west from here, the more isolated it gets. I'm assuming that's what you'd want. If you want fine dining close by, that's not where you want to be."

"I guess I've heard so much about the Waccasassa Flats that I was sure there would be something there."

"There are two possibilities in Levy County. The one I think would be closest to what you're looking for is west of the Flats. It's bordered by the Waccasassa River and paper company land. There's another tract that's closer to Bronson that might work as well. I'm also going to show you a tract bordering the Flats that's already an existing hunting club. It's just another possible option for you and your dad. Now, here's the deal. I've got to be in court in Bronson all afternoon today as an expert witness for a paper company. I'm free all day tomorrow. Will that work with you?"

"I've come this far. I'll plan on it."

"Great, meet me here at nine tomorrow. You'll need boots or hiking shoes."

Al left Carmen and went back to his motel filled with conflicting emotions. He had to ask himself what the hell was he doing here anyway. Where was this leading? He was already feeling guilty spending time with Baker. He was only using her and obviously wasting her time. So far, he didn't have the courage to use the term "Iron Road" or Moreno and Sons. Would she question where he'd heard the term and question his motives? Or was it a common phrase that anyone from the area would use? At least she'd mentioned a hunting club located on the Flats. According to the maps he'd studied, there was only one main road passing near the area. "I'll give it one more day and see what happens," he finally decided.

Since he had the rest of the afternoon free, he decided to drive out toward Chiefland and drive by the location of Moreno and Sons Salvage. As soon as Al left the city limits of Gainesville, he entered another world. It was easy to see that the university town was an oasis in a rural desert. Apartments, shopping centers, and golf courses gave way for pastures with grazing cattle and ploughed-up watermelon and corn fields, eventually turning into endless rows of planted pine trees.

Realizing he needed gas, Al stopped at a station in the hamlet of Bronson. After filling his tank, he went inside and took a bottle of water from the cooler. As he paid for the water, he asked the clerk if she'd ever heard of the Iron Road.

She laughed and said, "You're on part of it now. If you haven't been run off the road yet, just keep on driving toward Trenton and you'll know why it's called the Iron Road. It's a familiar name for people who live around here."

He left Bronson and turned onto a two-lane state road that led to the small town of Trenton. Al couldn't help but notice how well the road was maintained, especially in such a rural setting. The lanes were wider than usual with flat, well maintained shoulders. There was nothing but pine forest and an occasional pasture but minimal signs of civilization. He was beginning to wonder if Kelly had given him the wrong directions when he was suddenly aware of a huge truck coming up behind him at a high rate of speed.

He watched in amazement in his rearview mirror at how fast the tractor trailer was approaching. It simply moved into the left lane, never slowing, passing him as if he were sitting still. He could see that it was a flatbed with wrecked cars stacked high, one on the other. He stepped on the gas and tried to keep the truck in sight. He reached ninety miles per hour and was still barely able to keep it in sight. Eventually, he saw the truck's brake lights come on. As he slowed down, another truck was accelerating toward him. This truck was a large panel truck. When it accelerated past him in the opposite direction, Al glimpsed the writing on the side as *Moreno and Sons Salvage*.

Approaching the spot where the flatbed had turned off the main highway, he saw a small sign on a corner fence post with *M&S Salvage* and an arrow pointing down a gravel road where the large truck had turned. He could see a cloud of dust the truck had raised on the dry gravel road.

Not sure how obvious he might be, he decided not to follow the truck down the road. He was thinking instead of how he could entice information out of Carmen Baker without ringing the bell on his true intentions. Just confirming the existence of the Moreno and Sons Salvage was an accomplishment and enough for today. Making a U-turn, he headed back to Gainesville.

Instead of going back to his hotel, Al returned to the same bistro where Carmen had taken him earlier in the day. It was well before the dinner hour rush and there were only two tables occupied. He took a seat at the empty bar and ordered a draft beer. The same waitress who'd served them earlier was tending the bar, and Al tried to start a conversation with her.

"I was here earlier today, and the food looked so good I had to come back."

"But you only had coffee."

"Good memory. I had already eaten, but I will be trying the food this time."

"So, you must not live here?"

"No, I live in Atlanta. I'm here to look at some land."

"Well, you've got the right person helping you. You won't believe the people who come in here with her. I mean some wealthy and very famous people. I do know just from what people have told me that she and her family own a lot of land between here and the coast. Even if she is rich, she's always nice and polite to everybody here in the restaurant."

"That's good to know. Now if you'll bring me a menu, I'll see just how good the food is."

Chapter 30

Both Gary and Shela attended their high school classes the day after stealing the Maybach. They were each surprised to see the other. Their reasons for attending school were hard to explain. Somehow, they must have had a seed of obligatory behavior planted in their brains when they were young. They barely acknowledged each other as they passed in the hall, with Gary only saying as they passed, "I'll meet you after school at your car."

Gary was standing next to the Honda when Shela walked up to him and attempted to give him a hug. Gary pushed her back. "For God's sake, Shela. Not here. We don't need any attention."

With a disappointed look on her face, Shela walked around to the driver's side and got in. Gary walked to the other side. "I need you to take me to the Walmart down the road."

Shela waited in the car while Gary went into the store for a short time. When he returned, he had a burner phone and a card to upload call time. As soon as he'd activated the phone, he had Shela give him Curt's number, which he dialed. "This is Gary. Are we good?" Satisfied that Curt had been able to calm down after the previous evening, he told Shela, "Let's go to Curt's house."

Shela obviously had other plans. "Let's go back to the river again."

"Later. I want to talk to Curt before I do anything."

When they reached Curt's house and entered the garage, they found Curt just as he'd been the previous time, buried under the hood of the Mustang, cursing and banging against something. "I've just about had it with this goddam car."

"I'd still recommend taking it back to Taro. It would help with your blood pressure."

"What I'm going to do is take it to the dump," Curt said as he slammed the hood down. "What's the new idea you've got?"

"I'm going to have to go to the library and do some research on one of the computers. I'll give you the details then. We're going to have to go further away this time, probably Orlando."

"Why, aren't there other gated places around Ocala?"

"Curt, that's like returning to the scene of the crime. If you want to go back to Ocala, you're on your own."

"All right, smart-ass, go do your research and then explain why we need to go to Orlando."

"I need Shela to drive me."

"Whatever, I'll be here waiting for your hotshot plan."

Shela drove Gary to the public library, where Gary accessed one of the many computers the library provided its patrons. When he'd found exactly what he was looking for, he wrote some details down on a notepad. When Gary walked out of the library with his notes, Shela was waiting outside, pacing back and forth.

"You took long enough."

"Shela, take me by my mom's trailer on the way back to Curt's house. I need to pick up an address list I made earlier."

When they reached the trailer, Gary said, "Wait just a minute. I'll be right back." It took less than two minutes for him to enter his room and take the revolver that he'd taken from Curt from under the mattress. Holding it carefully with a paper towel, he wiped his own fingerprints off the barrel where he'd held it the night before. He wrapped it in the paper and put it in his back pocket.

Driving on to Curt's home, they found Curt actually smiling when they saw him waiting in the garage with a beer in hand. "I think I've got the son of a bitch fixed."

Shaking his head, Gary answered, "I'd still leave it locked in the garage for a while."

"This time, I'll agree with you, numbnuts. Now tell us about this plan of yours."

A bench seat left from some vehicle that had once occupied the garage leaned against one cinder block wall. Curt and Shela sat on the bench while Gary pulled over a mechanics chair on rollers and sat directly in front of them. It could have been a professor giving a lecture to a class if it hadn't looked so comical. But the plan that Gary rolled out captured their attention. Curt was actually nodding his head in approval as Gary continued to talk.

When he'd finished, Curt actually smiled. "I can't believe I've never thought about doing that. When do we do it?"

"This Friday. So many people are going out to eat on a Friday, we should have a good selection of cars to pick from. We'll go down a day earlier and look at the place."

Gary had already observed that the trunk of the Mustang was partially open. As he walked by, he opened it slightly and tossed the revolver deep inside into a loose pile of clothing. He smoothly and firmly closed it. "Your trunk was open. It's closed now."

It was late afternoon and approaching dark when Shela drove Gary back to his mom's trailer park home. Gary told her there was no need to go back to the lover's lane on the river. His mom worked until ten and usually didn't get home before eleven, so they had plenty of time. And so, Gary was able to make the many wet dreams he'd had in his bed in the trailer finally come true.

He had to force Shela to get dressed as ten approached. He knew his mom would be coming home any minute. Shela was finally walking down the steps of the mobile home when Gary's mom pulled up in her wheezing compact car. She quickly walked up to where Gary was standing on the steps with Shela.

"Isn't it past you kid's bedtimes?"

To Gary's consternation, Shela answered as she walked to her car, "We've already been to bed, thank you."

As Shela drove away, Gary's mom entered the trailer, leaving Gary standing outside with a red face. "Gary, I don't understand what's happening to you. You're becoming more and more like your big brother."

Even with his embarrassment, Gary was infused with a sense of pride when his mom compared him to his older brother, who had always been his idol. He went to bed for a second time, and slept a deep sleep without any dreams.

Chapter 31

After Mark left the emergency clinic, he knew he needed to return home and regroup before he continued to search for the Mustang. He tried to keep his shoulder dry while he showered, but it was difficult. After his shower, the many small cuts and scratches over his body seemed to be less severe than he'd imagined. If he also considered he hadn't suffered any snake bites, it was a positive thing.

His shoulder was beginning to throb, so he medicated himself with a couple of generous Tanquerays with a heavy dose of lime juice. He propped himself up in an old soft upholstered chair and watched an old rerun of *Mama's Family*. Eventually, the combined effect of the night's events—plus the gin—sent him into a well-deserved sleep, still sitting propped up in the chair.

He woke at dawn as the first rays of light began to creep across the river. He ached all over, and his shoulder hurt like hell. But he was okay, and he remembered that at one time, he'd been in far worse condition after barely surviving his last covert Army mission. This time, black coffee and the tincture of time would easily heal his injury.

While he sat on his patio drinking coffee and watching the dawn rise, he reassessed what had happened so far. He probably should have been calling Sheriff Norton, but he still wanted to be sure he wasn't on a wild-goose chase before he called him. So far, there was no concrete evidence linking Lawson's Mustang to the rest stop crime. If he could find the car and compare it to the picture recorded on Ralph Lound's car cam, he'd know for certain.

After leaving Jacksonville wearing black jeans and a long sleeve black pullover, Mark drove south on I-95 and stopped at the hospital to check on Keri. She'd been moved from intensive care to a private room where he found Vera asleep in a chair next to Keri's bed.

"Mark, I guess this is considered to be progress. She's continuing to look better, but so far, she's not responding to any external stimulus. The doctor told me that she has normal brain activity, but it's like she's sleeping and just refuses to wake up."

"Vera, I wish I could be the handsome prince. I'd kiss her and she'd wake up. Like I said before, if Brutus could lick her face, it might get her attention quicker than a prince."

"Well, I am following up on your suggestion. My brother is bringing Brutus up this afternoon. Dr. Goldblatt agreed that it was a good idea."

"That's great, Vera. It can't hurt."

After spending time with Vera, Mark continued on to Palatka. He found the water plant and then Myrtle Street. He started from the beginning of the street and slowly moved down the street thinking he would recognize the house from the description he'd been given. He was beginning to think that maybe he'd been given the wrong description. There were only two blocks to go before the street ended in a cul-de-sac.

The area was filled with old-growth live oak trees stretching out over both the street and houses. It looked like the homes had been dropped down in the middle of a dense forest with the surrounding vegetation making many houses almost invisible from the street. The condition was actually the result of the houses being some of the oldest homes in the city combined with a lack of serious maintenance over the years.

He hit pay dirt in the middle of the last block before the cul-de-sac. Without the blacked-out sign in the front, he might have missed it, because the drooping limbs of the live oaks and the overgrowth of wild myrtle and ancient shrubbery blocked the view of the RV barn behind the house. He turned around in the cul-de-sac and drove slowly back up the street. Most of the houses had multiple older worn-out cars and pickup trucks parked across the front drives and what would have been lawns in their prime. There were no vehicles visible around Lawson's house. A screen porch that was tilted to one side reached out from the house almost to the overgrown sidewalk. A driveway led toward the back of the house, and Mark caught a glimpse of a tall cinder block building with two wooden double doors that were closed. No signs of life were discernible from the street.

Mark's first impulse was to park and walk around the house toward the garage. He realized that directly across the street two men were working on a car with its front end jacked up. A young boy who was eight or ten years old was near the car where they were working. He had what looked to be a homemade bow and was shooting at a cardboard box.

Mark had a sudden flashback to a time when he was about the same age, and he was shooting an arrow from a bow he'd made himself. He'd accidently hit the neighbor's dog with an arrow that fortunately bounced off the dog's ribs without causing serious harm. It had been an early lesson on the responsibility that came with holding a weapon of any type.

Even though the men across the street were absorbed in their repair work, Mark didn't want to risk being noticed, so he drove to the next street parallel to the one he was on. Driving down that street, he passed a deserted metal barn that might have been a repair shop sometime in the past. It, too, was surrounded by overgrown bushes and enclosed by a tall chain-link fence with strings of barbed wire strung along the top. Holes had been opened in the fence, so getting in would not be a problem. Anything of value must have been long since removed from the property. By his estimation, it should have been directly behind Lawson's house. Even so, he decided to wait until dark before he approached the house on foot.

With more time to kill, he returned to the restaurant where he'd had the liver and onions. Today the special was all-you-could-eat fried catfish, hush puppies, and grits. Thinking to himself that it couldn't get any better than that, he enjoyed a great meal washed down with the sweet iced tea.

While waiting for his food, Mark called Al, who answered immediately. "Hello."

"Al, where are you?"

"I'm on my way back to my hotel in Gainesville."

"You didn't waste any time before continuing your investigation. I hope you haven't incinerated anyone yet."

"Not yet. I have met with a very promising realtor who's taking me out to look at some properties in the area of Moreno and Sons tomorrow. Today I drove out to the location of the salvage yard, but I couldn't get close enough to the actual location because I didn't want to be seen snooping around. There was heavy traffic coming and going from the place though. There were some really big heavy trucks of all types on the road. I'll admit I'm feeling a little guilty in using the realtor just to get close to the place. I found out that she knows the area well and also owns a lot of property herself."

"Al, just look and listen, nothing else. It might be a moot point anyway. I may have found where one of the three carjackers lives. I'll know more later. If I'm correct, I'm going to take what I've found to the sheriff and let him take it from there. Don't do anything but look until you've talked to me again. Promise me that.

"I'll try not to do anything stupid."

"You don't sound so sincere."

"Carmen Baker, the realtor is an interesting person, and I'll admit that I'm feeling guilty for using her. I actually enjoyed meeting her. I'll let you know what I learn from her tomorrow."

"Just stay safe. I'll talk to you tomorrow."

It was dark by the time Mark returned to Lawson's neighborhood. He parked next to the abandoned building on the street adjacent to Lawson's house. The last thing he did before he left his car was to double-check to be sure he had a round chambered in his Model 39, a small penlight, and a leather sap that he pushed into his back pocket. This part of the street was quiet with no apparent human activity. The streetlights on this block were either nonexistent or not operating at all, so he was cloaked in darkness the moment he left his car.

Moving up to the side of the abandoned metal building, he worked his way along the side toward the rear. Twice he encountered a pile of debris and had to move away from the side of the building and into the surrounding brush. Once again, he had to stifle his inherent fear of snakes. Here it wasn't water moccasins he feared. This time, his mind was filled with images of rattlesnakes. At least he'd know what was biting him from the rattling noise the snake would make before it struck. When he reached the rear of the building, light from a three-quarter moon provided enough light for him to see the stacks of years accumulation of junk, including the rusted-out hulks of two ancient pickup trucks.

From where he stood, he was able to see the old television antenna to his right reaching above the trees along the back fence. He'd made a mental note of it earlier, thinking it might help in finding the house from the next block. He carefully picked his way through the debris field until he reached the surrounding chain-link fence. It was overgrown with vines that combined with the thick bushes made it difficult to see anything on the other side of the fence.

As he moved to his right along the fence, he recognized a path leading parallel to the fence. Using his penlight, he could see the point where the fence had been cut at the bottom, making room for a person to easily slip through. Risking using the light again, he could see the corner of the RV barn from there.

At the same moment, he recoiled as he pointed his light to his left and two massive pit bulls lunged toward him. By the time Mark had his gun in his hand, he realized the dogs were separated from him by the chain-link fence. The hole in the fence was on his right and not connected to the lot where the dogs were coming from. He was surprised that the two dogs were not barking. There was just a low rumble coming from both of them. They were trained to bite—not to bark—and that was good for Mark as long as the chain-link fence held them back.

Ignoring the dogs, he slipped through the fence and eased along the side of the garage, looking for some sort of opening. There were only two openings. One was the double doors on the house side and the other was a single door on one side of the barn. The upper half of the single door had a window divided into panels. The glass had probably not been cleaned since the garage had been built. Even after wiping some of the grime off a pane of glass, there was still total darkness inside.

Glancing back toward the house, Mark could see lights and hear loud music playing, but no movement. The single door was locked. Using his gun to break a glass pane, he reached in and unlocked the door. The minute he stepped inside and turned on his penlight, he knew he'd hit pay dirt. He didn't need his picture of the car to know that it was the same one that had left the rest stop, leaving pain and death in its wake.

He needed light to take a picture of the car. Knowing he was taking a chance, he found a light switch and quickly took several pictures. When he'd taken the last picture, he suddenly realized that the music had stopped. Quickly, he switched the light off, went back out of the single door, and lay down flat in the dense overgrown shrubbery next to the door. He watched as a porch light came on and a figure walked down the steps, moving cautiously toward the garage. He was holding a shotgun and flashlight. As he approached the open door, Mark could hear him muttering to himself, "I got you this time, you dumb son of a bitch."

Mark realized the man, whom he could now recognize as Frank Lawson, assumed that whoever had entered the garage was still inside. That was fortunate for Mark, because he lay only a few feet from the door. If

Lawson moved his flashlight around at all, he could easily see Mark lying there.

As Lawson stood in the doorway with his shotgun pointing toward the interior of the garage, Mark carefully took the sap from his pocket. In a single fluid motion, he rose from the ground and hit Lawson across the side of his head before he could turn around. As Lawson crumpled to the ground, Mark had a fleeting moment of concern, thinking maybe he'd hit Lawson too hard. Blood was pouring from his head from where the blow had split his scalp open. But he also felt a sense of satisfaction as he remembered what Lawson had done to him. He checked Lawson's pulse and was relieved that it was strong and steady. He took Lawson's watch, then the money from his wallet, leaving it opened next to him where he lay. He was sure that Lawson never saw him, and he wanted Lawson to think he'd been assaulted and robbed by the burglar. There was no way Lawson would report this to the police. The last thing he did was to find the registration inside the Mustang. He took a picture of it and replaced it in the car. Picking up the shotgun as he left, he passed the two snarling pit bulls who were patiently waiting for him by the corner of the fence. They had still not barked a single time.

After taking the shells out of the shotgun and dropping them in a water-filled drum behind the abandoned building, he shoved the empty gun under one of the rusting trucks. He smiled as he headed back to his home in Jacksonville, thinking of ways to anonymously send the location of the Mustang to the sheriff in St. Augustine.

Chapter 32

The next morning, Al met Carmen Baker at her office as planned. Following Carmen's suggestion, the night before, he'd gone to a big box store and bought a pair of hiking boots, thick brown pants, and a shirt. When Carmen came out to meet him, he couldn't help but think that Carmen—dressed in a utilitarian pants suit, boots, and an orange cap with the letter *F* on the front—looked as if she were going on a safari.

"Did you have a good night?" she asked, as Al was focused on how good she looked.

He was not surprised when she led him to a heavy-duty four-by-four pickup truck.

As they drove west toward Chiefland, she stayed just over the speed limit on the two-lane highway. "I've gotten so many tickets between here and the coast, the locals and the highway patrol salivate when they see my truck coming. I've got to be careful, so I won't lose my license."

"You are a fast driver?"

"It's not that I think about driving fast. I just seem to always be running late, and anyone in front of me is an obstacle that has to be passed."

Carmen was easy to talk to, and in seemingly no time, they were passing through Bronson. Sitting so close to her in the cab of the truck, Al would occasionally get a faint whiff of her perfume. He couldn't believe the way she was making him feel. He tried to shake it off, but he still felt like he was having a childhood crush as he talked to her. "Are you originally from this area?"

"Yes. I grew up here, went to school in the county, and then the University of Florida. I did a stupid thing and got married while I was a sophomore and by the time I graduated I was single again. I've been single since."

"Guess we all have to do something stupid to shock us into adulthood."

"I suppose. It certainly moved me along."

"Where I'm taking you now is probably not a good business move for someone who wants to sell you real estate, but you've come a long way to look at property, and I want you to see all of your options. A lot depends on just how often and for how long you're planning to hunt. If you want to come at the drop of a hat and possibly have other people hunt on your land, what I'm going to show you wouldn't work. But in any case, it will give you some options."

Al's curiosity was aroused as they drove down the same road as he had the previous afternoon. Twice they were overtaken by large flatbeds, one loaded with wrecked cars and the other with engine blocks. As each one approached them from the rear, Carmen slowed and moved as far as possible to the right to give the speeding trucks more room to pass. Al wanted to make some comment about the trucks but decided to wait until they reached the place where the trucks had turned off at the *M&S* sign.

As they approached the turnoff point with the *M&S* sign, Carmen slowed and turned off onto the road behind the trucks. At this point, Al was almost speechless, but he managed to ask, "What is the sign *M&S*?"

"Moreno and Sons Salvage. It's been in my family since the 1930s. My brother runs it. I handle the outside investments."

Hearing that statement almost caused Al to pass out. How in hell had he gotten himself into this? Almost inaudibly, and in a choking voice, he said, "You must have kept your married name after your divorce."

"Yes, there are some business advantages in having a different name. Those who know me are aware that I'm a Moreno, but there are others whom I'd just as soon not know up-front."

Al still was overcome with confusion. If he'd been uncomfortable with what he was doing before, he was even more conflicted now. Realizing that he really had no choice, he pulled himself together and asked, "So, this is literally where you grew up?"

"Yes, just down this road. My grandparents started the salvage business in 1930. They were really smart, and they defied all the odds by building a salvage business in such an isolated spot. It has grown steadily since day one. Additionally, my family has gradually bought land. They started with the area surrounding the original purchase, and they've added to it ever since. When they first arrived, most of this area around the Flats were small farms, but the depression wiped them out. My grandparents did just the opposite during the depression. Their business prospered and enabled them to buy land for pennies on the dollar. We own most of the land around the Flats."

Carmen slowed down as they passed where the road split, with one leading to the right and the other continuing straight. She pointed to the right, where Al could see where the road ended at a massive gate with the name *Moreno and Sons* high above. "That's the entrance to the salvage business."

As they continued on, Al could glimpse the tops of large buildings through the trees in the direction of the salvage yard. There was also a military grade fence bordering the road they were on. Eventually, the trees receded, and an open body of water appeared. It was so unexpected to see such a large lake. There was even an island visible far out in the middle.

"A lot of that is natural, and a lot was developed years before anyone heard of rules, regulations, or permitting. If you're wondering about the fence, it's not to keep anyone out. It's to keep the buffalo inside. A loose Herford bull may not be much of a problem, but a bull buffalo running wild could turn over a truck."

As they continued on the same road, Carmen continued, "You can see that the fence changes at this point. From this point on, it's for the privacy of the houses you can barely see on your right. These are the homes my family has built over the years."

All Al could see was a large grove of ancient live oak trees, and the "fence" Carmen was referring to was a limestone wall that extended for a half mile along the road. The structures that had been built over the years had been so carefully designed that they were almost invisible, nestled in among the huge branches that extended out from the century's old oaks. They were constructed of native limestone and weathered cypress, making them appear as if they had grown out of the earth and trees. Carmen slowed again as they passed an automatic metal gate set between two limestone pillars.

"My brother, Leon, built the last house using the same materials my grandparents used. They were sticklers for controlling the building materials. My house is the one next to his. After both our parents died, I kept their house and just gutted the interior and refurnished it."

They followed the narrow-graded road until the limestone fence came to an end and was replaced with tall chain-link fencing. Soon they were surrounded by oak hammocks alternating with groves of planted pines on either side of the road. The road stopped abruptly at a heavy gate that had been built using heavy iron pipes wielded together.

Carmen slipped out of the driver's seat, telling Al to get out as well. She entered a code on a lock attached to a heavy chain that secured the gate. As soon as the chain was removed, the gate swung open and Carmen said, "After I drive through, just pull the gate closed. Don't worry about locking it. We'll come back out this way and lock it then."

The gravel road ended at the gate, and the trail from this point on was only two ruts overgrown with grass.

"You're now inside one of the larger protected natural forests in the state of Florida. There are deer, turkey, black bear, and occasionally a Florida panther. We keep a biologist on our staff who oversees the area and doubles as a game warden. We use best management practices that are approved and monitored by the state as well. As much as my family is about making money, we've always been grateful for the opportunity to own this land. Habitat for native animals in Florida is disappearing fast. Preserving this habitat is our way of giving back. This preserve includes and protects most of the headwaters of the Waccasassa River."

"I'm impressed. But how does hunting encourage preserving wildlife?"

"We only hunt white-tailed deer and wild hogs as a means of controlling the population. Even though we occasionally have native panthers and black bear here, it's difficult to maintain a natural balance. Roadkill effectively keeps the panther and bear populations from overpopulating. So, there's no need to hunt them to control their population. I worry about the future of these animals just based on loss of habitat across the entire state. We also have several lakes that provide what might be the best bass fishing in the state."

After the trail passed through a dense hammock, they suddenly emerged out onto an open vista that included a large lake stretching out in front of them. As Carmen followed the tree line towards the left, a two-story log cabin rose up in front of them. It looked as if it had been transplanted from the mountains of Colorado and set down in Florida.

Parking in a small, designated spot for vehicles, Carmen continued to explain to Al, "This lodge will accommodate ten adults in luxury. You have the option of letting us provide help for cleaning and preparing game, cooking, cleaning, and even bartending if requested. There is also the option of us just keeping the lodge stocked with food and beverage of your choice for as long as you're here and leaving you with total privacy."

She continued to talk as they climbed the steps onto the wide porch and through the unlocked front door. It was a spectacular room with two-story ceilings held up by bare wooden beams. One wall was built of native limestone, enclosing a fireplace large enough to sit in.

"We keep four-wheelers out in a barn behind the lodge. There are maps that show all the trails and hunting blinds, although some guests have no intention of hunting or fishing. They only crave the solitude."

"I had no idea something like this existed in Florida."

"I'm not sure there are any other places like this. The downside is the cost. It's not cheap. As I said earlier, if you want to spend a lot of time in a place, you're better off buying land. If you only want to use a place once or twice a year, this might be more cost-effective. Now let's go look at what you can buy."

They returned the same way they'd come. The rest of the day was spent in looking at two parcels of land that might be suitable for Al's needs. Al's confusion only continued to grow. He tried to maintain interest in the property they were looking at, but it was becoming more and more difficult. He finally had to admit to himself that he was thinking more about her than his purpose for being here. It was dark by the time they were driving back toward Gainesville. They stopped at a hole-in-the-wall Mexican restaurant in Archer to eat and drink cold beer.

Instead of a quick meal, after eating, they lingered on with both of them enjoying the company of the other. The table had been cleared, but they continued to talk. The conversations had been all over the map before Al asked, "I've had two different people who gave me directions mention the Iron Road. Why is that?"

"Simple, because the heavy traffic on that road between Bronson and Trenton consists of metal from vehicles of every type being transported in and out of Moreno and Sons. It started in 1930 and has only grown over the years. My brother Leon and I are constantly turning down offers to go public with the business. We could sell the business tomorrow if we wanted to. Who knows, we might do it someday."

"I can understand why it would be difficult to lose control of something that had been in your family for so long."

"Yes, it would be hard. But back to real estate. How do you feel about what I've shown you so far?"

"Carmen, I like all the options you've shown me. I need to talk to my dad before I make a decision. We have to be on the same page with whatever we do."

"Of course. I understand. I'm not trying to hard-sell you, but if you were to seriously consider buying one of the tracts I showed you, they won't be available for long. Parcels like those are absorbed pretty quickly."

They engaged in small talk on the rest of the drive back to Carmen's office. Al asked her how she and her brother had come to divide their responsibilities with the family business.

"My brother was obsessed with fast cars from the time he could walk. Over our parent's objections, he raced stock cars while he was enrolled at FSU. But Leon isn't stupid. He was involved in a huge pileup in a stock car race somewhere in Alabama. Two other drivers were killed, and Leon's car was demolished beyond recognition. He miraculously walked away without a scratch and watched emergency people dig what was left of the other two drivers out of the wreckage. People who deal with Leon wouldn't believe me when I say that Leon is actually one of the most tenderhearted people I know. Although his appearance can be a little bit intimidating.

"Leon confided in me that after the wreck, while he watched the medics remove the driver's bodies, he had an epiphany. He said that all of the thrill of speed was suddenly gone. He decided to focus on school and ended up with a master's degree in business. But he did know his cars and everything about them, so running the family business just came naturally. He runs the salvage business with an iron fist, but he won't allow anyone to kill a duck, dove, or quail anywhere on the property around the place."

"And how did you end up in real estate?"

"I loved the outdoors. I camped out. I hunted. I fished. My degree was in forestry. Then I got a law degree from Stetson for good measure. Adding to our real estate portfolio has become a mission for me. Fortunately, Leon and I work well together. All big decisions we make together. I give legal input with the help of a small local law firm."

"That's all impressive."

"It's worked well for us so far."

After they parked at Carmen's office, there was an awkward moment before she asked, "I've enjoyed spending time with you Al. When will I hear from you?"

A very conflicted Al replied, "Soon, Carmen. Soon."

Chapter 33

As soon as Carmen entered her apartment, she realized she had a text from her brother, Leon, wanting to meet ASAP.

Carmen replied immediately that she would be there the next morning. They knew each other well enough to recognize the importance of a request to meet.

They met at Carmen's house, where they knew they'd have total privacy. Carmen made a large pot of strong coffee, which she carried out onto a limestone patio looking out from underneath two ancient and giant live oak trees. A green pasture bordered the shore of a lake that extended out in front of them.

Carmen waited patiently for Leon to speak.

"Carmen, our family has been blessed. It all started with our grandparents, Rita and Larry. I wish I'd spent more time with them when I was a kid. They taught our parents well. I hope I'm doing the same with my two kids."

"I don't think you need to worry about that, Leon. You and Betsy are good parents. You're lucky in that at least you have good memories of Rita and Larry. I came along too late to have known them. Tell me, what's really on your mind?"

"Carmen, you know how our business has always adapted to changing times. Mainly to anything automotive- or metal-related. We've flown under the radar for a long time with some aspects of the business. We've maintained our good reputation for being good neighbors and good citizens. I'm not going to give you any details, but recent events have made me realize that it's time to make some changes."

"Leon, I understand that you don't want me to know some things, but remember, I've grown up here and I'm not blind. I'm well aware that the family has always taken risks with certain parts of the salvage business. I've questioned it, but I've kept quiet and left it up to you to manage. And you've given me full control of the real estate business, which as you know has grown significantly. Now tell me what you want to do or not do, whichever it is."

"Carmen, we have connections to some unsavory people. I'm concerned about them making mistakes that might lead back to us. I want to disengage from any connection with those people. That part of the business is so insignificant compared to our national auto parts business and our exports to South America. You add my legitimate auto parts business to your real estate enterprise, and we've got more money than we can ever spend. I simply can't justify continuing to take risks for such minimal returns."

"When will you begin implementing the change?"

"Immediately. The word will spread quickly. We will require full documentation on any vehicle, running or wrecked, that's brought in. We'll refuse anything that's not one hundred percent legit. I may need to use a heavy hand in a few cases, but you don't need to know anything about it."

"That's good to know, Leon. Fortunately, from a legal point of view, the two parts of our holdings are independent of each other. But public perception is a different matter."

"Carmen, there's one other thing I want to bring up. Recently, I've met a young man I'm impressed with. I've been looking for the right person that I think might be a fit for our business. If I bring him in, I'll want you to meet him, and of course there will be a trial period to see if he'll work out."

"Leon, that's okay with me. If he does work out, I may want some help myself. Just know, I'm behind you one hundred percent. I've been hoping that you would make this change without any pressure from me. It's a wise decision. Our family has maintained a delicate balancing act for a long time. Our parents and grandparents may not have been formally educated, but their wisdom has enabled us to survive and prosper through all these years. I hope we can maintain the same level they had in spite of you and I having been educated."

"Okay, it's as good as done," Leon said as they each raised their coffee cups in a toast.

Chapter 34

Their graduation was only a couple weeks away. Shela and Gary were finished with schoolwork and were just waiting for graduation. Shela was scheduled to graduate with honors, and Gary thought he was just graduating, for which he was grateful. They had no problem in skipping school on Friday so they could drive to Orlando with Curt and follow up on Gary's next plan.

They rode in Curt's—or more correctly, the recently deceased Otis Morphet's—Honda. It was early, so they checked in to a small mom-and-pop motel near Winter Park. Gary, who was now thinking well ahead as if he were playing a game of chess, handed cash to Curt and suggested since he was older, there would be less scrutiny if he registered for the room.

Happy to not be using his own money, Curt played his part just as Gary knew he would and registered for a room with two double beds.

The restaurant that Gary had targeted didn't open for happy hour until four. It appeared to be such a low-key establishment from the outside that Gary began to question his own research. It was only a square plain front at the end of a small strip shopping plaza on Fairbanks Avenue. It was set so closely to the sidewalk, there was no visible place for parking. It was identified only by a very small sign—*Le Place*—over the door. No one would ever be driving by and say to themselves, "Hey, that looks like a good place to eat."

Curt was skeptical as well. "You're shitting me! This place is high-end. What, high-end tacos?"

"Curt, that's part of your problem. You're so goddammed shortsighted, you can't see the forest for the trees. Trust me and just watch."

There was a small barbeque across the street from Le Place that had outside seating around a bar. It was early enough for the three of them to get seats with a direct view of the restaurant from across the street. Curt started with beer but was soon into vodka. Shela's ID wouldn't pass muster, so she had to reinforce her Shirley Temples with some pills she produced from her handbag. Gary stuck with a soft drink.

Sometime after 3:00 PM, two men appeared from around the corner of the building that housed Le Place. They were pushing a wooden structure that looked like a combination reception desk and blackboard. Soon after, two men and one young woman came out of the front door of the restaurant wearing identical uniforms.

The first cars arrived before four. The first car was a Porsche Carrera, soon followed by a Bentley convertible.

Curt let out a gasp. "Holy shit."

That was only an indication of the cars that followed for the rest of the night. The three of them watched how the uniformed employees helped the occupants out of their cars, gave them a ticket before getting into the cars, and driving them away to a parking area behind the strip shopping center. They would return with the keys and hang them on a board behind the desk.

Curt was incredulous. "What kind of fucking food do they serve in this place?"

Gary smiled. "Expensive food. That's what makes it so attractive for these people. People with the kind of money they have want to think that what they have is the best. For some people, the more something costs somehow makes it even more exclusive for them. Let's drive around to the lot where they're taking the cars."

Gary realized that Curt was in no condition to drive, so he drove. He went across the street and followed the driveway that led to the parking lot behind the building. The lot was larger than he'd expected, and the lighting was minimal. It was perfect for what they wanted to do. He parked in an open spot and turned off the engine. They watched as the attendants drove the cars into the dark lot, parked, locked the car, and ran back toward the front.

There was a steady stream of cars being brought back to the lot, and he only saw one apparent owner who parked his own car. The owner who was probably in his thirties was driving a new Porsche Macan. Gary couldn't help but smile at the young man, thinking that if he was so worried about his car being abused by an attendant, then he really couldn't afford to be driving it.

Shela was in the back seat and tripping out to the music from the headset that both Curt and Gary had insisted she wear to save their own ears. Curt was so drunk he couldn't understand why they didn't just go ahead and steal a car. Actually, Gary would have liked to do just that, but Curt and Shela were both in no condition to drive. The only option was to return to the motel, let them sleep it off, and keep them sober tomorrow. Over Curt's objections, Gary drove them back to their motel.

The moment they walked into the room, Curt crawled into the first double bed and was immediately snoring like a freight train.

Shela headed for the small bathroom. "Shower time."

Gary undressed and climbed under the covers of the second bed wearing only his shorts and was soon competing with Curt to snore the loudest.

Gary woke up from a deep sleep in the middle of a most realistic and pleasant dream. The dream became reality as he realized that Shela was under the covers and the source of the pleasure was apparent. Pulling her up beside him, it was obvious she was wearing nothing.

"What the hell are you doing? What do you think will happen if Curt wakes up?"

"Don't worry. He's too far gone. You couldn't wake him if you tried. Relax and enjoy."

And so, Gary did just that. Eventually, he drifted off to sleep again.

It was Curt who woke him with a loud "My fucking head is about to explode" as he walked into the bathroom.

At the same moment, Gary realized Shela was still curled up close to him, hidden by the bed covers. The sudden noise had awakened her as well.

"Shit," was all she said.

As soon as Curt had closed the door to the bathroom, she left Gary's bed and climbed into Curt's. Curt's hangover was so bad—he never realized that Shela was not in his bed. Gary just breathed a sigh of relief. He was even more determined to free himself from these two as soon as possible. He sensed, correctly so, that only a thin line separated Curt and Shela from an impending disaster.

Chapter 35

After his encounter with Frank Lawson, Mark was returning to his home in Jacksonville. Now he was confident he'd found the vehicle used in the rest stop murder. He was thinking of the best way to notify Sheriff Norton when he received a call from Keri's mom.

"Yes, Vera."

"Mark, she woke up! Keri's awake. The minute Brutus started licking her face, she smiled. Oh, Mark, she's not brain-dead. Someone from the sheriff's office is on the way here to see if she remembers anything from the rest stop."

Mark had to pull over to the side of the road. He felt like his heart was in his throat, and tears were running down his cheeks. As soon as he was able to regain some degree of composure, he was able to reply to Vera. "Vera, sometimes our prayers are answered. I'll be there in about an hour."

Mark broke every speeding law on the books and reached the hospital in forty-five minutes. Two deputies from the sheriff's office had already arrived and were talking to Keri. Vera, her brother, and Brutus were in a waiting room.

When they stood up to meet Mark, Vera gave him a tearful hug. "She made it."

"When can I see her?" Mark asked as Brutus came up to him and patiently waited for Mark to acknowledge him. It had taken Mark a long time to gain the trust of the big Dobermann.

"Mark, the two detectives are talking to her right now. Even though she was still in a lot of pain, she insisted she wanted to tell them what she remembered. When she woke up, she told me that it seemed like it had just happened and she wanted to give them every detail while everything seemed so fresh in her mind."

Vera's brother Gabriel, an ex-cop, spoke up. "Mark, they promised us that they wouldn't push her too hard. Dr. Goldblatt talked to them as well to be sure they wouldn't stress her unnecessarily."

Gabriel was around five foot ten and well over two hundred pounds. He had a receding hairline, thick neck, and a grizzly, unshaved, reddish face. Mark could clearly see the outline of a large frame revolver under the loose-fitting shirt that he wore. His voice was deep and gruff. Mark couldn't help but think to himself that Gabriel projected a textbook image of what an old, retired cop should look like.

"Mark, you know I handled a lot of assaults like this, but after thirty years on the force, this is the first time it's personal. If I could get my hands on the people who hurt Keri like this, I'm afraid I'd go rogue."

"Gabriel, I can't begin to tell you how much I understand how you feel. Let's see if the detectives will tell us what they've learned."

As soon as Mark uttered those words, he suddenly realized that he'd been so focused on Keri's recovery, he'd neglected to tell the sheriff's office what he'd learned about the Mustang. He knew he couldn't tell the detectives because he would lose his anonymity and he didn't want to link himself or Al so close to the investigation. He'd wait and see if the detectives would share any information with them.

They didn't have to wait long before the same two detectives who'd first interviewed Mark appeared. Vera and Brutus immediately headed back to Keri's room. Mark and Gabriel waited to see if the detectives would offer any information.

Detectives Luhrs and Adams looked much better than they had on the night they interviewed Mark at the hospital.

Their attitude was more relaxed and friendly as well.

Luhrs spoke first. "I can't tell you how happy we are to see the progress Ms. Smith has made. I'll have to say that we didn't expect her to make it. It's the only good thing about this case so far. Ms. Smith clearly remembers what happened up to the second she blacked out. She saw two people—a young man and woman. It was the woman who assaulted her. She says she can clearly see her face in her mind. We have a forensic artist coming as we speak. We'd like to get a composite drawing while it is so fresh in her mind. We are also going to see if Ms. Smith recognizes the female who was recorded on the dashcam."

Mark couldn't help but ask, "Any leads on the car they might have been driving?"

Adams answered, angrily, "No, dammit. The dashcam from the car of the older man who was assaulted was a cheap piece of shit. The car was a modified Mustang, but do you have any idea how many similar cars are out there? We got a partial image of a woman's face. The man and his wife only remember two shadows, but they couldn't identify anyone. The man only remembers that one of the cars already parked was a souped-up hot rod, but he couldn't even identify the make of the car."

Luhrs added, "Again, like I said, if Ms. Smith recognizes the woman on the dashcam, we'll be able to post a pretty accurate picture that someone might recognize. I understand that you were the first person to think of the dashcam. I have to congratulate you on that. Having seen it is there anything you saw that we haven't mentioned?"

Mark answered, "Have you identified the county it was registered in? Ben Lounds told me it started with a *P*."

Adams replied, "We guess that it was *P* for Putnam, but we still haven't found it."

Mark couldn't help but think that there might be something to the theories about police being underbudgeted and understaffed. He only answered, "Let's hope the composite will help identify Keri's assailant."

When he reached Keri's room, she was sleeping with Vera and Brutus sitting close by her side.

"Sorry, Mark. The interview with the detectives took all her strength."

"That's okay, Vera. She needs to rest and be ready for the artist."

"Mark, why don't you and Brutus stay here with her? I need to get Gabriel some coffee and let him go back to Orlando."

"Take your time, Vera. I'll probably go to sleep in the chair." He eventually did close his eyes for a time.

When something woke him up, Keri was staring at him. Mark reached out and held her hand. He started to speak, but she held up a finger.

"Don't say it, Mark. This wasn't your fault. Don't even try to go there. My choices are mine and mine alone. You look worse than I do. Why don't you go home and sleep? I've got to work with the artist anyway. I'm going to be okay. Tomorrow, you can tell me about everything I've missed."

"Keri, I can tell that your common sense hasn't been affected."

Mark waited until Vera returned, and he reluctantly left the hospital and returned to his home in Jacksonville for a deserved night's sleep. Even though he felt a great sense of relief and gratitude, his mind was still in turmoil with the events of the day. Especially troubling was the question of what he should do with the information he'd found. Although he was convinced that the car he'd found in the garage was the car involved, would the sheriff's people take his information seriously?

He finally decided to wait until the morning. With a fresh mind, he could think more objectively.

Chapter 36

Curt was still hungover the morning after they'd cased the Le Place Restaurant. After they'd all showered and dressed, Gary gave Curt some cash and had him go the motel's office and pay for another night. They needed a place to hang out until the restaurant opened in the evening. Gary knew that Curt couldn't afford to get as drunk as he'd done on the previous evening. They found a breakfast place nearby and spent the rest of the morning drinking coffee and helping Curt sober up.

As soon as they'd returned to the motel, Gary made some excuse about needing something for a sore throat. He left Curt and Shela in the motel room watching a rerun of some mindless sitcom while he walked across the street to a big chain pharmacy. Using the burner cell phone, he'd bought earlier, he carefully typed in a message just as Leon had instructed him to do. He bought a box of cough drops for authenticity and returned to the motel room.

When he used his card and opened the door, he had a brief flash of naked bodies pulling up sheets. At least Curt was trying to cover himself.

A full naked Shela stood up and said, "Curt, why don't you invite Gary to join us?"

This only angered Curt, who replied, "The hell he is. Get out, Gary, and give us a little privacy."

Suppressing a smile, Gary backed out of the room and closed the door. "Take your time, guys. I'll just get a little more fresh air."

Gary waited at a picnic table next to the motel's parking lot. When Curt finally emerged from the room, he had a sheepish look on his face. "We just got bored. I hope Shela didn't embarrass you too badly."

Gary couldn't help but laugh. "That's okay. I'll survive. I need to explain how we're going to steal a car. If Shela is dressed, let's go back inside and we'll go over the details. We both have to be on the same page to make this work."

They waited until after 6:00 PM to return to the restaurant.

They had to wait a few minutes before they found the right seats at the bar. Gary wanted to be seated so they would have a good view of the Le Place restaurant directly across the street.

Gary had already insisted that Curt was to stay clear of any alcohol. What Shela did didn't concern him as long as she didn't bring any attention their way. She was already taking something as indicated by her glassy stare.

After about thirty minutes, Gary saw what he wanted. A jet-black Porsche Cayenne Turbo GT stopped in front of the restaurant's door. An older bald-headed man got out of the driver's seat and a twenty-something dark-haired girl climbed out of the passenger's side. The man left the Porsche running and handed the keys to a young man who immediately drove the car away.

Gary looked at Curt and nodded. "Showtime, Curt. Get in position and watch for my signal."

Curt went a short distance down the street before he crossed and slowly walked toward Le Place. He stopped on the sidewalk at the outer edge of the building that housed the restaurant. Casually lighting a cigarette, he looked as if he were waiting for an opening in traffic so he could recross the street. But at the same time, he was closely watching as the young man who had parked the Porsche returned with the key and placed it on a hook on the board leaning up against the wall of the restaurant.

Gary waited patiently until three cars almost simultaneously stopped in front of Le Place. There were only three attendants working to park the cars. Suddenly, there was a moment when all three of the valets were either going or coming from the parking lot. Gary gave a thumbs-up to Curt, who was now watching Gary sitting across the street.

At the signal, Curt, who had slowly moved closer to the front door of Le Place, quickly walked past the door of the restaurant and took a couple steps to his left. He took the set of keys belonging to the Porsche from the board of keys leaning against the wall. He continued walking nonchalantly down the sidewalk away from Le Place.

When he reached the driveway leading to the rear of the buildings, he followed it back to the dark parking area, passing one of the returning valets. He clicked the key, and the Porsche blinked back at him as if to say, "Here I am."

Exiting on the dark street behind the strip mall, he headed west. He was soon followed by Gary and a high-flying Shela.

Chapter 37

Mark's phone woke him up just as the morning light was reflecting off the river.

"Good morning, Mark—or I should call you Dad?"

"Morning, Al. Because you recognize me as your dad, you can call me anything you want. I'm calling you Al, but what I'm also saying is 'son.'"

"I wanted to update you on what I've learned. I didn't call you last night because it was a strange day and I wanted to sleep on everything before I talked to you. Give me an update on Keri first."

"Al, I planned to call you this morning. Keri's awake, and it looks like she's going to be okay. She has been moved out of intensive care and into a private room. Her mom tells me they'll be moving her again into a rehab center that's next to the hospital. She'll still be getting hands on nursing care, but she can be evaluated for whatever rehab she may need."

"That's the best news of all. I'm so happy for you all."

"Thanks, Al. Now update me on what you've learned."

"Let me tell you what I learned and what I saw. After you've heard it all, I'll tell you what I'm thinking." Al continued to relate all the details of his meeting with Carmen. Mark could only shake his head as Al continued to talk.

When he was finished, Mark asked, "Okay, you've told me what you've found. Now tell me what you think."

"Mark, I simply can't reconcile Carmen as being a part of a chop shop. Granted, I didn't meet her brother, who runs the salvage business. It's just hard to believe that a business that's been operating nationally for so many years can continue to hide illegal activity. The business is a pillar of the community. My secretary checked, and Moreno and Sons Salvage has maintained a Better Business Bureau rating of A+ from the start. Also, the term 'Iron Road' is a well-known local term because of the heavy traffic of wrecked cars being brought to the business. I'm beginning to think there may be another place off this road that's hiding a chop shop."

"Al, I'm sensing that you were impressed by this Carmen lady. Is that affecting your judgment?"

If Mark could have seen Al's face turn red, his question would have been answered.

"If I'm honest with myself, yes. I'll admit that's got to be a factor. Not only was she drop-dead beautiful, she was smart, self-assured, and apparently very successful at what she does."

"Al, let's look at our priorities. Granted, I'd like to hold a chop shop, or whoever profited from Keri's car being stolen, accountable. But my first priority is to find the pair who killed the guard and assaulted Keri. I've been busy myself. I'm pretty sure the sheriff's office has identified the pair that are responsible. Keri was able to give a good description, which, added to the image on the elderly man's dashcam, gives us a good semblance of the woman. This picture is going to be made public. I've also located what I believe to be the car they were driving. I think it's only a matter of time before they're caught."

"That is good news. Before I dig any deeper into Moreno and Sons, I'll wait for the couple who hurt Keri to be caught. They may tell the authorities where they took Keri's car. For the moment, I probably need to go back to Atlanta and practice being a lawyer in case my career as a private eye doesn't work out. For the time being, I'll let Carmen know that we'd be more interested in reserving their hunting lodge than buying land."

"Al, that sounds good. I'll keep you updated."

Chapter 38

Gary had mapped out the route they would follow with the stolen Porsche. Getting out of Orlando from John Young Parkway to State Road 50 West seemed to take forever. He was relieved that Shela had apparently maxed out on whatever chemical concoction she was using. She was sleeping and snoring loudly.

By the time they had reached State Road 41, it was nearing midnight. It would be another hour before they reached Williston. As Gary had instructed him to do, Curt was waiting outside an all-night convenience store. He'd already purchased a six-pack of beer and was close to finishing it off. Gary wasn't surprised; it just reinforced his desire to separate himself from the pair.

Shela woke up as soon as Gary parked next to Curt, who was sitting in the Porsche with the radio cranked up on loud, obnoxious, punk rock. The idiot wasn't even trying to hide the beer can he was drinking from. Before Gary could say a word, Shela woke up and climbed into the Porsche with Curt, berating him as she did.

"What the hell, Curt? You got to ride in a nice car, and I've had to ride in an old economy one. Give me one of those," she said as she opened one of the remaining cans.

Gary had to smile as he said, "Okay, Shela. I guess I'll have to drive the rest of the way without your scintillating conversation."

Shela was already bouncing to the loud music coming from the high-end speakers in the Porsche, and Gary's remark went unanswered. He was thinking to himself that this was working out just as he'd planned.

"All right, Curt, Leon is expecting us. I'll follow you. Watch your speed."

Curt drove responsibly and stayed within the speed limits the rest of the way. Even so, Gary stayed a respectable distance behind the Porsche just in case an alert trooper had gotten a BOLO on the Porsche. The Iron Highway was largely deserted this time of night as they passed through Bronson and were driving toward Trenton.

Gary began to worry and hope that his trust in Leon was justified. He couldn't help but remember what Curt had said the first time they'd arrived at Moreno and Sons Salvage. "Gary, people have come here and never been heard from again." There was no reason to doubt that Leon was a hard man, but something he couldn't explain gave him confidence that Leon was not a threat to him.

Driving ahead in the Porsche, emboldened by the alcohol, Curt was telling Shela it was time for them to take back control. This time, he and Shela would drive the stolen car into Moreno and Sons. Gary could cool his heels waiting for them outside the compound. Gary had already told Curt he'd called Leon and alerted him they were coming.

It was after 1:00 AM when they turned off the main highway and approached the gates of Moreno and Sons. As they'd neared the turnoff, Gary closed the distance between the two cars so when they stopped in front of the towering gates, he was directly behind the Porsche. Curt quickly climbed out of the SUV and walked over to the phone mounted on the wall. The minute he took it out of its box, floodlights lit up the night.

After a moment's disorientation, Curt stammered into the phone, "This is Curt. I've got a another good one."

After waiting a moment for an answer, he returned to the Porsche and waited some more. They didn't have to wait long before the gates opened, and Ethan emerged on a golf cart as usual.

Driving the cart up to the passenger door of the Porsche, Ethan motioned for Curt to follow him. But before he led them inside the gates, he drove over to where Gary was sitting. Gary had lowered the driver's side window. Ethan stepped off the golf cart and walked up to Gary, who was still not sure what was going to happen.

Surprised, it was the first time Gary had seen Ethan smile, and the smile immediately put him at ease. "Gary, Leon wants you to wait out here. Don't worry. You're good. There's no reason for you to go in with those two. Some things you don't need to see or hear. This is just part of the separation process. They'll be a while though. You might want to relax and take a nap until I get back."

Somewhat relieved and knowing he had no choice, Gary made himself comfortable and waited.

Feeling important once he realized Gary was indeed going to wait outside the gates, Curt followed Ethan up to the warehouse as before. "You see, Shela? You just have to take charge."

But Shela, who was far smarter than Curt, was starting to get some bad vibes. As they'd approached Moreno and Sons, she'd quickly sobered up and remembered all the things Curt had told her about the place. Curt had paid no attention to the way Ethan had walked up to Gary's window and spoke with him.

She had seen the smile on Ethan's face as he'd talked to Gary. There had been no such smile when he'd rudely told Curt to follow him in. So now she was regretting having left Gary in the Honda. In fact, she wished she was sitting outside the gates with Gary. Now she had no choice but to exit the Porsche and follow Ethan and Curt into the building.

Ethan pointed toward the open door leading into Leon's office. As soon as they were inside, the door closed behind them. Leon was sitting at his desk. He was looking at a sheet of paper he was holding in his hand. He was not smiling.

By now, even Curt was starting to feel some of the same apprehension that Shela was feeling. He started to speak, but Leon curt him off. "Did you kill or assault anyone tonight?"

"No, no, of course not. We just brought you a good car."

"What do you mean by 'brought me a good car'? If you think I somehow deal in stolen cars, you've got the wrong place. I run a legitimate salvage yard."

"But I thought—" Curt started to say before Leon cut him off again.

"Then what's this all about?" Leon said in a quiet voice as he slid the paper he was holding across the desk.

Curt picked up the sheet of paper and stared at it for a full minute before he handed it to Shela with a trembling hand.

As she looked at a full facial picture of herself, her eyes grew wide. She was barely able to read the words underneath the picture: *Anyone recognizing this person, please contact the St. Johns County's Sheriff's Office.* In a weak voice, she managed to ask, "Where did this come from?"

Calmly, Leon explained, "The woman you nearly killed got a good look at your face. There was also a dashcam shot of you as well. You are both fucked, and you've got to go."

Curt managed to speak in a horse voice, "Go where?"

As Curt spoke, the office door opened and Ethan and three other men entered the office. They came up behind Curt and Shela, and bags filled with a sicky, sweet-smelling gas was pulled over their heads before either one could stand up or resist. They both lost consciousness immediately.

Chapter 39

After his conversation with Al, Mark realized he had to get the information he'd found about the location of the Mustang to either Sheriff Norton or the two detectives, Luhrs and Adams. In order to remain anonymous, Mark drove to a Walmart some distance from his home. He bought a burner phone, returned home, and activated it.

Just as he started to make the call to the sheriff's office, he suddenly realized that he didn't have Lawson's house number. He remembered the street name, but he realized he'd never seen a house number. Even so, Mark thought he could give enough details to enable authorities to find the right house. Earlier, Mark had looked up the website for the sheriff's office and found the number designated for crime stopper tips.

Holding a thick napkin over his mouth, Mark called the crime stopper number. As soon as he was certain he was speaking to a live individual and not a recording, he quickly said, "Please record this call. This is to be directed to Detectives Luhrs and Adams as well as Sheriff Norton. It is in reference to the recent murder at the I-95 rest stop. The modified car driven by the suspects can be found in Palatka on Myrtle Street near the water plant. There is an old RV barn behind the house of Frank Lawson. The car is inside the barn. These people are all armed and dangerous. Did you get all that I said?"

"Yes, I have what you said. What else can you—" was all the operator could say before Mark closed the call.

He walked down to his dock, reaching out into the river, and started to throw the phone out into the water. He hesitated and decided to wait before he got rid of it. It might have been useful again before all of this was over.

Feeling like a burden had been lifted from his shoulders, he was confident that the sheriff now had more than enough information to find the killers. Maybe it was true that wisdom came with age. He knew there had been a time when he would never have shared any information with authorities and would have exacted his own form of justice. He also realized that Keri's recovery was a big factor. If she hadn't survived, he might not have been so wise.

Driving to the hospital to see Keri, he thought about Al. Something Al had said—or maybe it was his tone of voice, worried Mark. On one hand, he was proud of Al's strength and decisiveness, but Al reminded him too much of himself when he was younger.

Wisdom for himself had been very slow in coming. He hoped that maybe for Al, it would come much quicker.

Chapter 40

Curt and Shela began to regain consciousness at the same time. It was like the momentary confusion a person sometimes experiences when waking up from a deep sleep. It didn't take long for each to realize they couldn't move, but were held firmly in place by something.

Curt was the first to recognize Leon's voice. "Okay, time to wake up and watch the show."

As soon as they each were able to focus on their surroundings, it was apparent they were bound together tightly with duct tape and were sitting in a golf cart. Their surroundings made no sense. Leon and Ethan were standing on either side of the golf cart, looking at what could have been a stage for musical performances. The floor of the stage was a thick, single piece of solid metal. The roof of the stage was made of a similar piece of solid metal.

The stage seemed to be set inside what looked to be a giant's toy erector set. Any thoughts that the stage was for performing was easily discounted by the towering stacks of broken-down vehicles in all stages of age and disrepair. The surrounding ground was littered with broken glass and smaller pieces of metal.

As soon as Leon was convinced they were both awake and conscious of their surroundings, he gave a signal with his arm. The sound of a heavy diesel starting up was followed by a large forklift appearing from behind them. The forklift approached a wrecked hulk of a car and lifted it up as if it were made of cardboard. It carried the car over to the stage and set it down carefully in the middle.

As the forklift began to back away, they heard the sound of another machine close by rumble to life. This sound was more of a loud hum. At first, it was hard to tell where the sound was coming from until it suddenly became clear. The roof of the stage containing the junk car, slowly, inch by slow inch, was moving downward. The stage was acting as a hydraulic press powered by electric motors. Just moments after the descending roof of the press contacted the top of the car, the windows all exploded outward.

Curt and Shela both watched wide-eyed as the car was slowly crushed to a four-foot piece of solid metal. The forklift quickly removed the crumpled-up vehicle. Curt finally blurted out, "Why are we watching this?"

Leon smiled as he spoke. "Because you're both going to be in the next car."

Curt almost passed out, and Shela lost control of her bladder. Urine ran down her legs and into her shoes. The forklift had already deposited the crushed car and had picked up another wreck. It stopped in front of the golf cart where Curt and Shela were sitting and lowered the car to ground level. It only took a moment for two men to throw them both in the back seat of the car and the forklift continued carrying it toward the compactor.

By this time, both Curt and Shela were going crazy. They were so bound up with duct tape, they had no use of their hands, and even their legs were bound together. Both were screaming and sobbing at the same time. When the motors of the hydraulic press began to hum, the sounds only intensified as the press descended inexorably toward the roof of the car. When the press touched the roof of the car and the windows exploded, showering Curt and Shela with glass, their screams had reached an earsplitting crescendo.

Then the motors of the press suddenly stopped. What followed was a profound silence.

Leon let the silence continue uninterrupted for a couple of minutes before two men pried open the rear door of the car. Curt and Shela were huddled on the floorboard, shaking like leaves in the wind. They were both in a state of shock and unable to speak. When they had to be lifted out of the car, one by one, they had wide-open eyes that were totally blank. The duct tape that bound them was removed, giving them both freedom of movement again. They still had to be lifted into the golf cart. After being driven back up to the warehouse, they were led into Leon's office and seated in the same chairs as before.

Speaking to Ethan, Leon said, "Bring them a cold bottle of water."

It only took a few seconds for Ethan to return with two bottles of water. He had to open it for them because their hands were still shaking so badly, they were unable to do it themselves. "Stay here, Ethan. I want you to hear what I'm telling them."

By now, both Shela and Curt were overwhelmed with gratitude, realizing how close they had been to a horrible death. Shela was crying as Curt managed to speak.

"Why?"

"I want you both to remember how good it feels to be alive. I also don't want you to forget how it feels to be so close to death. Both of you look at me and listen carefully to what I say. You have never been to this place. You have never heard of this place, and you will never come again. You do not know Gary Anders and you'll never speak to him again. If you are ever identified by this picture and charged for the murder at the rest stop"—he held up the composite picture as he spoke— "you will have no knowledge of Moreno and Sons or Gary Anders. If you try to connect us or Gary to your actions, your legal status will be the very least of your problems. My reach extends into any prison in this state you might be privileged to visit."

Leon stood up, indicating he was through with them. "Ethan, get them out of here before I change my mind."

Ethan helped them to stand on shaky feet and led them out where the Porsche was still sitting next to the loading dock. Curt's eyes expressed surprise to see the car still there. It was beginning to dawn on him now that Leon was deadly serious about everything he'd said.

Ethan motioned for Curt to get back into the driver's seat. He had to walk Shela around to the passenger side and help her up into the seat. Curt was still a little confused that he was back in the Porsche. When Ethan said, "Follow me," Curt summoned enough courage ask about Gary and the Honda.

Ethan tersely replied, "Forget Gary and the Honda."

As Ethan continued to lead them back toward the main gate, it became clear to Curt that he was leaving in the car he'd expected to exchange for a ton of money. The main gate was open, and Ethan motioned for Curt to keep going as he passed through. He saw the surprised look on Gary's face as the Porsche passed by the Honda waiting outside the Gate. Although he was leaving in a stolen car and had little money, Curt was suddenly exhilarated to be alive as he stepped hard on the gas.

After leaving Moreno and Sons, they drove in stunned silence. The silence only lasted for three or four miles until they were sure they were safe. Shela was the first to make a sound, and it was in the form of a primeval scream so loud that Curt slowed the Porsche and stopped by the side of the road.

The scream lasted for almost a minute before she ran out of air and stopped. "It's all that little asshole's fault. Gary set us up. He probably thought that Leon would finish the job, and he'd steal cars by himself. Oh, Curt, let me tell you what else that prick did. He *raped* me! I've been ashamed to tell you."

"He *what*?" Curt's face turned red. "I'll kill the son of a bitch! I took him under my wing and helped him out. Now look how he's paid me back. He even has my fucking car."

Shela pounded the dashboard with her fist. "What can we do?"

"He's going to have to come down this road. We'll find a place next to the road where we can't be seen. When he comes by, we'll pull out behind him. This car is so much faster than Otis's old car, and I'll run him off the road when he tries to outrun us. Even if I have to ram him from the rear and fuck up this car, I don't care. I just want to hurt him bad."

"Curt, he's not the only one we have to get rid of. That bitch saw me and can remember my face. That's the only way they can get us for the rest stop deal. We need to find out where she is and make sure she never gets a chance to identify me."

"Okay, one thing at a time. Let's get this little shit first. We'll look for her next."

They drove a short distance before turning into a two-rutted lane leading into the pines. Curt turned the Porsche around and parked just inside the tree line. The pines and the dark color of the Porsche provided camouflage from the view of vehicles coming from either direction. Curt turned off the engine, and they waited in the dark for the little shit to appear.

Chapter 41

As the Porsche with Curt and Shela disappeared into the night, Ethan motioned for Gary to follow him through the gate and on to the warehouse. He was still confused and didn't understand what was happening. He didn't feel threatened or that he was in any danger, even though he could clearly see Curt's face as he'd passed by in the Porsche. Although he only had a brief glance, he was sure Curt's face was a ghostly white.

Leon was waiting behind his desk when Ethan led Gary into his office.

Leon was smiling as he said, "Sit down, Gary. Let's talk. First, I want to tell you that I don't think you'll need to worry about either Curt or Shela again. Now that you've become an experienced car thief, what's your opinion of the business?"

Gary didn't hesitate to answer. "I like the money, and I need the work, but it's a dead end. I think it would only be a matter of time before I'd get caught, or worse, end up like Otis Morphet. I'd rather stay broke."

"Gary, you're wise beyond your years. It's taken me a lot longer to reach the same conclusion. I'm not going to go into details, but Moreno and Sons is no longer accepting cars of dubious origin. Our operation will require full and legal documentation for any vehicle brought to us. Since its beginning, this business has limited its employees to a very few. You can't imagine the full extent of our operations. I'm only looking for smart people I can trust implicitly. I've had someone look at your background. I think you've been underestimated all your life. Did you know that you are about to graduate at the top of your class?"

"No, sir. I thought I was lucky to graduate at all."

"After you graduate, would you be interested in working for Moreno and Sons on a trial basis? I can promise you the compensation will be better than you'd make stealing cars. Not to mention, it will be a lot safer and legal as well. If you want, I could facilitate helping your mom get a good job and a place to live nearby."

Gary was overwhelmed with what he was hearing. "Mr. Moreno, I'm not sure what I have to offer. I really don't know anything about your business."

"That's not a problem. You'll learn. I've watched you adapt and survive under very challenging conditions. I'll have you start as a personal assistant doing odd jobs for both me and my sister you haven't yet met. I want you to go back to Palatka, graduate, and think about what you want to do. I know this is a lot to take in at once. I don't expect an answer this minute. In the meantime, you can do some research on Moreno and Sons. I think you'll be surprised at what you find."

The door to the office opened, and Ethan came in and handed an envelope and a set of keys to Leon. Leon handed the envelope to Gary. "Take this as payment for services rendered tonight. It should help you through your graduation. I also want to trade out the car you're driving for something safe. Were you aware that Otis Morphant's Honda has an expired tag? I can't believe it hasn't been stopped. If the car had been stopped, it would still be registered to Otis. It would have been a shitshow for whoever was caught driving it. It's going to disappear. I'm going to loan you a car that's safe to drive. If you ever do get stopped, it's a company car, and you just say you work for me. Bring it back here with your decision after your graduation."

Ethan led Gary back outside the warehouse. There was a generic Chevrolet sedan sitting in the spot where he'd left the Honda. Ethan handed Gary the keys, smiling as he did.

"Gary, I'm not sure what Leon sees in you. But I trust him with my life. If he thinks you can be an asset to this business, I will go along. I can tell you in all the years I've known him, he doesn't trust many people. I hope you can justify that trust. If you do, you will never find a better boss and friend. One last suggestion: Instead of going back through Bronson, go the other way on the main highway. Trenton is only a short distance, and from there, you can go east to Gainesville and on to Palatka. I really don't think Curt would be so stupid as to ambush you on the way back to Bronson, but that Shela is batshit crazy."

I agree, Gary thought as he took Ethan's advice and took the alternate route back through Gainesville and on to Palatka. He was still overwhelmed by Leon's offer. Somehow, he knew he was at a crossroad, and he hadn't even graduated from high school. This was going to be a lifelong decision.

If Gary could have seen the Porsche sitting in a dark abandoned driveway next to the Iron Highway near Bronson, he would have been more thankful for Ethan's advice on taking a different route home.

Chapter 42

Al checked out of the Gainesville hotel and drove back up I-75 toward Atlanta. Dreading the call, and with mixed emotions, he called Carmen's office.

Carmen answered, "Hello, Al, did you talk with your dad?"

"Yes, I did. We considered the options, and after I described your lodge, he is sold on the idea of leasing your place instead of buying land and having to deal with setting up and taking care of a place."

"I hate to miss out on a sale, but that's probably the smartest thing for you to do. Do you have any specific times you're considering?"

"We're both going to look at our calendars as soon as I get back to the office." Al could sense the disappointment in her voice when she replied, "Again, you need to let me know as soon as possible. We stay booked a year ahead unless we get a cancellation, which rarely happens. Al, I really enjoyed spending time with you. When you do come back, I'd like to take you over to the coast for some real Florida seafood."

"That sounds great, Carmen. I will talk to you soon."

Al experienced feelings of guilt all the way back to his Atlanta office. By the time he reached Atlanta, he knew what he was going to do. It was probably not the smartest thing, but once he worked it out in his mind, his course was set. As he expected, Kelly was waiting for him in his office.

"So, are y'all going to sign your paycheck over to me since I've been doing all the work?"

Al could only laugh, "Kelly, you know you'll be well compensated. How about you bring me up-to-date on all this work you've done?"

The rest of the day was spent playing lawyer. The only thing of significance was the grand jury's refusal to indict the man who'd killed the teenage carjacker. But the poor guy was still facing a civil lawsuit filed by the kid's family. Al and others in the firm had anticipated it and already had plans to counter it. They had firm evidence that the DA, who was seeking the grand jury indictment, was not only giving the family instructions on how to file the civil suit, but it was also with his former law firm. Al took some pleasure knowing that this might very well cost the DA his job and maybe even his license.

He stayed at his desk until the office had emptied out. Taking out the file Kelly had previously compiled on Dennis Swilley, he read through it carefully to refresh his memory of the addresses she'd listed for Swilley. He'd wanted to have Kelly see if there was any new information on Swilley since he was left tied up on a sidewalk. But Kelly was too intuitive, and he knew her radar would go off if he mentioned Swilley. Deciding to take the bull by the horns, he went back to the place where he'd started before.

So it was that later in the evening, Al was walking into the Purple Rose Tavern on Peters Street for the third time. The place was frozen in time. Mac was behind the bar and looked exactly as he had before. As all good bartenders were programed to do, he recognized Mark immediately.

"Mark, what brings you back to the dark side of Atlanta? You obviously have very discriminating taste."

"Hello, Mac. I'm not sure there's a distinction between the sides of the city," Al said as he took a seat at the empty bar. Mac was pushing a tall glass of beer across to him almost before he was seated.

"Let me guess, Al, you're still looking for Dennis Swilley."

"That's very perceptive of you, Mac. Yes, I am looking for him."

"Well, I will tell you that you're not the only one looking for Dennis."

"Any idea who else wants to find him?"

"Al, you must have heard about the trouble he had a few days ago."

"Only what was on the news. Someone left him tied up in front of a fire of some sort."

"Al, what do you know about the fire?"

"Mac, I guess someone must have saved Dennis from a burning building."

Mac smiled and nodded. "There were two cars inside the garage that burned down. The owners of the two cars had not been paid as expected. They want to find Dennis and extract some money from him. Dennis hasn't been seen since he left the sidewalk. The guys looking for him are bad news. If you think the gangbangers who tried to rob you were bad, they are choir boys compared to these guys. The leader is a huge bald headed black man they call Big T. He's got a reputation for using violence and cruelty just for the fun of it. I'm not sure it would be wise to be anywhere near Dennis right now. I sure as hell don't want to see him anywhere near my place anytime soon."

"Mac, like I said before, I'm not looking to hurt Dennis. In fact, I may be able to help him with his current problem. I just need to find him and talk to him. I doubt that he'd return to the house where the fire occurred. I do have an address for a girlfriend, but the bad guys may have it as well."

"I really couldn't say but then again, the bad guys are not that smart. They may not know anything about Swilley's girlfriend. I'd just be damn careful."

Al finished his beer and left the Purple Rose thinking about what Mac had told him. He'd looked at an Atlanta map and knew how to find the girlfriend's house. It was located on a side street off Piedmont. It was not a bad neighborhood, but its old glamor was offset by the motel like apartment buildings that had grown up along side what had once been grand homes.

The girlfriend's home was an apartment over a two-car garage located behind a stately old home. The garage doors were the original wooden doors, with an intricate design, that were designed to be opened manually. There was a faint light showing through a curtain in the living quarters on the second floor. Al decided to park a short distance down the street and just watch for a while. It turned out to be a wise decision. Soon after he'd stopped, a black Lincoln Town Car slowly eased down the street and stopped next to the curb near the garage.

Al stayed low in his seat and remained still. There was something ominous about the black car and when no one got out of the car Al immediately sensed trouble. At this point all he could do was wait and watch. He sat waiting for over an hour before everything suddenly went south.

A small compact car pulled up in front of one of the two garage doors. A young dark-skinned woman wearing a green scrub suit got out of the compact and unlocked one of the garage doors. Using handles on the door, she lifted it and it retracted into the ceiling. While she was lifting the garage door, three men suddenly emerged from the Town Car and lifted the woman off her feet and rushed her into the garage. She didn't have a chance to resist or even scream as they covered her mouth to silence her. From where he was sitting, Al couldn't see the interior of the garage, but he assumed there must be stairs inside the garage that led to the apartment above. The garage door was left open, but the interior of the garage still remained dark.

For Al, it was decision time again. He knew he had no obligation to do anything. He should just drive away. But he couldn't. In an obtuse line of reasoning, he felt he was partially responsible for putting Swilley in this situation. This was not going to end well for him or his girlfriend. He double-checked his Colt to be sure it was cocked with a shell in the chamber before tucking it into his waist and quickly getting out of his car. He walked down the sidewalk toward where the Town Car was parked. When he reached the car, he walked up to the driver's side window which was tinted so darkly that he couldn't see inside. He tapped on the window and as he had suspected the driver had remained in the car. The window silently lowered revealing a bald-headed man with a heavy mustache. In an irritated voice he said, "What do you want?"

Before he'd finished his sentence Al had pushed the barrel of his Commander up under the man's chin with such force the man had to lift himself up in his seat to avoid the pain.

Quietly, but firmly, Al said, "You've never been closer to dying than you are right now. Understand?" Wide-eyed the man could only nod in affirmation. "Put your left arm outside the window and use your right hand to give me the cell phone. Good boy, now the car keys next." As soon as Al had pocketed the cell phone and car keys, he had him use his right hand to remove his belt. "Now put both hands on the top of the steering wheel." While keeping his Colt pressed firmly under the man's chin, he used his left hand to wrap the belt around the man's arms just above his elbows. Once the belt was secured, Al pulled it tight with so much force the guy let out a moan.

Leading the man to the rear of the car, he popped the trunk open. Anticipating the man's reluctance to get into the trunk, he hit him across the side of his head with his gun. While he was stunned, Al searched his jacket to be sure he didn't have a gun. Then he shoved him into the trunk and closed it firmly. Wiping the cell phone to be sure he hadn't left his fingerprints on it, he threw it across the street into a flower bed. The car keys remained in his pocket.

Approaching the open garage door with gun in his hand, he took a deep breath and went inside.

Chapter 43

Once Curt had the Porsche parked in a hidden spot off the highway, he turned the car's engine off, and they waited for Gary to pass by. They were enveloped in darkness while they both were still traumatized by the events that had just occurred. As they sat without speaking, a medley made up of lack of sleep, alcohol, extreme stress, and seething anger overwhelmed them both. Within five minutes, they were both fast asleep.

The first tints of dawn were visible on the horizon when the roar of a flatbed trailer loaded with wrecked cars jolted Curt awake. His head was pounding, and all he could utter was "Shit! Wake up, Shela. I can't believe this."

Shela was a lot slower waking up, but she finally recognized where she was before she spoke. "Okay, we missed the little turd. Let's get the hell out of here and go find the girl. Gary will have to wait."

Before they reached Williston on the drive back across the state, they discussed how they could find the woman Shela had assaulted at the rest stop. Shela said, "I remember Gary said something about her being in the hospital in St. Augustine. I think there's only one big hospital there. I'd say that's where we should start."

Curt shook his head. "We don't even have a gun remember? Gary took it."

Shela smiled. "If you'll take me by my aunt's house, I'll get us one."

"Your aunt has a gun?"

"She has a bunch of guns. My uncle was a big hunter. I once looked in their bedroom closet. I was actually looking for money, but I saw the guns stacked in a corner behind some clothes."

"But so what, Shela, if the woman is still in the hospital? We can't walk in with guns blazing."

"You're right, Curt. I'm also going to get a big knife from my aunt's house. That's what we'll use in the hospital."

"Your aunt will let you walk in and take guns and a knife and walk out?"

"She won't even be there. She works at a doctor's office."

Shela's aunt lived on a quiet street lined with modest but well-kept smaller homes. Curt parked in a carport next to the house. Shela got out and said, "Follow me."

She took a key from under a doormat, unlocked the door, and went in with Curt following right behind. There was one large closet in the master bedroom, and it only took a moment to locate several long guns leaning in a corner.

"This will do fine," Curt said as he brought out a .223 caliber Ruger Mini-14 with a twenty-round clip. He totally ignored the other high-caliber hunting rifles. "Now where are the shells?" he asked as he looked at the shelves lining the closet. He found them stacked behind a large hatbox. There was a full box of twenty rounds plus another half box.

"Holy shit, Shela, look at this," he said with a wide grin as he opened the hatbox and took out a Colt Python revolver. "Otis had one of these, and he told me that it's one of the best revolvers ever made."

Rummaging further around the closet shelves, he finally found a box of .357 Magnum shells. "We're in business now. Let's go check out the hospital."

Before they left the home, Shela went into the kitchen, and after rummaging around in drawers, she picked up a long-curved filet knife she wrapped in a towel.

When they reached the hospital, Curt parked toward the rear of the main parking lot. He backed into the parking space so the tag would be less visible. "Shela, you'll need to stay in the car since they have a picture of your face." For once, Shela agreed with Curt.

When he went through the main entrance, the first thing Curt did was to find a small gift shop where he bought a local newspaper. The first page of the local section had the same picture of Shela that Leon had shown them, featured prominently on the page. Reading the accompanying article, he immediately found the victims' names, which included Keri Smith's name.

Now that he had a name, Curt approached the information desk and told the clerk that he wanted to visit Keri Smith.

The lady looked closely at Curt before looking at her computer. Curt quickly realized that he probably did look like he'd been chewed up and spit out.

Still frowning, the lady told Curt, "Ms. Smith has been moved to the rehab center. You'll have to go there and see if she's allowed to have visitors."

"Thank you," Curt said as he made a hasty retreat, not wanting to draw any more attention to himself. He remembered seeing signs pointing in different directions when they approached the hospital. One sign had listed

Rehab Center, so he knew it must be close by. Before he left the hospital lobby, he found a restroom and looked at himself in a mirror. He had to admit, he looked like shit. What could he expect after the last forty-eight hours? Splashing water on his face and straightening his wrinkled shirt and trousers, he went from looking like a bum to simply looking disheveled.

As he approached the Porsche where Shela was waiting, the first thing he saw was Shela playing with the Colt Python. She pointed it playfully at him as he got back onto the car.

"Shela, you idiot. What the hell are you doing?"

"I'm just practicing. You know, like Bonnie and Clyde."

"Give me the damn gun," he said as he took the revolver from her hands. Opening the cylinder, he saw that she had loaded all six chambers. These two guns are only a last resort."

"That's what I said, just like Bonnie and Clyde."

"Well, I'm not ready to end up like Bonnie and Clyde. If we can eliminate the woman and Gary, we'll be home free. No one can prove we had anything to do with the rest stop. Even the picture they have of you is only an approximation. It's not a real photograph. So just for a little while, let's stay focused."

It only took them a moment to see that the rehab center was just across from the main hospital. As they drove around the rehab center, they could see that it backed up on a tidal marsh that led to the Matanzas River. The two-story building looked like a high-end hotel. A walkway circled the entire building. Two sides of the building were bordered by the tidal marsh. Parking areas bordered the two other sides. A set of stairs led to the second floor on two sides of the building.

Parking at one end of the building, Curt walked to the section of the building where the service entrances were located. He was surprised to see one double door on a small loading dock was left partially open. It was obvious that this facility was not considered to be a high security zone. Returning to the front of the building, he found the main entrance. The lobby was small, with windows separating it from a business office. There was a small shop providing drinks, coffee, and sundry items on one side.

Approaching one of the windows, he could see two women behind desks and another looking into a filing cabinet. The lady at the cabinet saw him and approached the window.

"Can I help you?"

"Yes, my aunt was just moved here from the main hospital. Keri Smith?"

"Yes, the miracle lady. What a strong person. All the doctors were saying she shouldn't be alive. She's on the second floor in 227. You'll have to go upstairs and see if she can have visitors. She still has a long way to go. There is an elevator down the hall, or you can use the stairs outside to get to the second floor."

"Thanks," Curt replied. Returning to the end of the building where the loading docks were located, he entered the open door on the dock. Seeing no one, he went down a service hallway. The smell of cooking and the sounds of pots and pans meant he was near a kitchen. Before he reached the kitchen, he came to a set of stairs leading up to the second floor. Hearing footsteps approaching, he quickly went up the stairs. Opening the door onto the second floor, he found himself in a hallway with rooms leading off either side. The doors to most of the rooms were closed. Room numbers were 248 and descending as he walked down the hallway. He passed several people as he walked nonchalantly down the hallway. No one paid any attention to him. He approached Room 227, just past the exits to the outside stairs. The door to the room was closed, so he turned around and returned to the stairs leading back down to street level.

As he neared the loading dock, he passed another door just as an orderly was taking out a bag of trash, which he threw into the dumpster adjacent to the dock. The orderly was in no hurry to get back to the door because it was designed to close very slowly unless pressure was applied. Curt waited until the orderly went back inside. He caught the door before it closed completely. He stood there thinking for a moment before he put a shoe in the door to be sure it would not close.

Walking to the other side of the sidewalk, he broke off a thin branch from the shrubbery lining the sidewalk. Using a little force, he jammed a small piece of the branch into the dead bolt locking mechanism of the door. The door would now close, but the bolt that locked it was jammed by the piece of shrub preventing it from locking.

Knowing they had time to kill before night, Curt drove them to the beach, which was only a short distance away from the hospital. He made a quick stop at a drug store and bought a couple items for Shela. He backed the Porsche into a parking space on the side of a motel, and they entered through an unlocked side door. A small grab-and-go food court on one end of the lobby was open. It also served as a bar, and Curt quickly told the young woman behind the counter he was staying in the hotel and wanted to start a tab.

Shela, who was now wearing dark sunglasses and a scarf covering her psychedelic hair, was waiting on the unoccupied pool deck. They stayed there until well after dark, eating finger food and drinking. Shela was out of any pharmaceuticals and had to rely on martinis while Curt remained somewhat functional by only drinking beer.

Another couple had seated themselves at a nearby table. Just before Curt and Shela stood up to leave, the woman left to use the restroom, and the man got up to make a trip to the bar. As she passed the table where the couple were sitting, Shela casually picked up the woman's beach bag that was hanging on her chair. They walked out of the side door they'd come through earlier, got into the Porsche, and headed back towards the hospital.

Soon after leaving the motel, Curt and Shela were standing next to the same door that Curt had jury-rigged earlier. Shela was carrying a towel under her arm. The towel concealed the long-curved filet knife. Holding his breath, Curt pulled on the door, and it opened silently. They both went inside and found the staircase leading to the second floor.

Chapter 44

With gun in hand, Al entered the garage of Swilley's girlfriend's apartment. The open door allowed enough light in to see the staircase at the rear. Slowly easing up the stairs, being careful to put his weight close to the wall to lessen the chance of squeaky boards, he reached the top. They had obviously been in a hurry because the door at the top of the stairs leading into the apartment had been left partially open. Al stood there and listened.

The moan he heard made the hairs on his neck stand up. For a fleeting instant, he started to turn and run like hell. Instead, he took a deep breath and slowly entered. He was in a very small hallway that was open on either end. The sounds were coming from his right, so he went to his left. It was a good choice, because he was standing behind two black men and one white.

They were looking down at two pitiful figures who were bound up with clear packaging tape. More tape had secured them to wooden chairs. The woman was sobbing, and the man Al recognized as Swilley was moaning. Al could clearly see blood dripping from his right hand. One of the two black men was leaning down toward the woman. He was holding a bloody pair of kitchen shears as he was reaching for the hand of the sobbing woman. As soon as he had her defenseless hand in a firm grip, he started to move the kitchen shears toward her fingers.

Knowing he had to act, Al stepped into the room behind the men, gun raised. "Drop the shears, now!"

Turning, the three men looked at Al with surprise. The largest of the three was the man with the shears. "Who the hell are you?"

"No matter who I am. All three of you get down on your knees."

The big black bald man whom Al had already figured to be the alpha of the three spoke again, "You really think you can make us get down? There are three of us and we have guns, too." As he spoke, his hand was reaching into his coat.

Al's question of what he would do if he were ever put in a life-or-death situation was answered when he aimed carefully and fired a 245-grain soft-nosed .45 caliber slug into the big man's kneecap, blowing it into slivers of bone. He was only eight feet away and couldn't miss at such a close range.

The man went down but was still trying to pull his gun out of his coat. Al fired the second time—this slug blew out the shoulder socket of his gun arm. Not wanting to lose his advantage, Al took a step toward the other two men, who stood frozen in fear.

"Both of you use your left hands and take out your guns, very slowly."

They complied.

"Good. Now throw them on the sofa behind you, and get down on the floor."

This time, the two men wasted no time dropping to their knees. Meanwhile, the big man was finally aware of the degree of his injuries and was beginning to moan along with Swilley.

Taking no chances, Al took the man's gun out of his shoulder holster and threw it onto the sofa with the guns while keeping his Colt trained on the other two men on the floor.

Using the shears the big man had dropped, Al cut the tape binding Swilley and his girlfriend.

Swilley was holding his hand where he was missing a finger. "Who are you? Why are you helping us?"

"We'll have time to talk about that later. Where did they get this tape they used on you?"

The woman understood immediately what Al meant. "The kitchen, I'll get it."

In a short time, they had all three men secured. They even wrapped a piece of tape around their heads covering their mouths. Al silently motioned for Swilley and the woman to follow him into the separate room, which served as the bedroom.

Al spoke in a quiet voice, "I don't want them to hear what I'm going to say. I know why these guys are after you—"

He was interrupted by Swilley, who blurted out, "I recognize your voice! I'll never forget it. You're the one who was going to set me on fire!"

"Yes, and I'm also the one who carried you safely out of the garage. It would have been a lot easier to have left you in the trunk of that car. I'm here to offer you another lifeline. These men are not going to let you go. Your finger—or rather your lack of a finger—should be all the proof you need. You both know who they are and can identify them. You will never be safe remaining here in Atlanta. I'm going to offer a deal. I know you have family in West Florida. I'll help you get there safely in return for a small favor on your part. If you aren't interested, I'll leave right now, and you both can work out your future options of living in Atlanta.

The woman spoke. "How do we know we can trust you?"

Al smiled and looked at her. "What's your name?"

"Donis."

"Donis, you don't know that you can trust me. But at the moment, I don't think you've got many viable options. You might take into account the small fact that I've saved Dennis twice now, and I'm offering to do it again with you included."

Dennis had picked up a dirty T-shirt from the bed and was squeezing it down tightly on his hand. "What's the 'small favor' that you want from us?"

"I'll give you details later when we're in a safer place, but basically, what I want you to do is simple." Al continued to reveal a short outline of what he planned to do.

After he'd finished explaining his plan, Swilley and Donis looked at each other for a moment before Donis shrugged and said, "He's right. We really don't have a choice."

They went back into the room where the three men were squirming on the floor. After ensuring that the three men were sufficiently bound, Al took the wallets of the three men and removed the cash. He didn't even try to count it, but the big man had a large wad of bills. The only other thing he took was the driver's license of the white man. While he was doing that, Donis and Swilley were both filling a suitcase with a few clothes and personal items.

When they started to go back down the stairs into the garage, Donis stopped and returned to the three men on the floor. Picking up the shears, she approached the big man, who was moaning and bleeding from his shoulder and knee. She grabbed one of his fingers and tried to cut it off with the shears. She didn't have enough strength to sever the finger, only cutting the skin and causing blood to flow from his hand. The man was hyperventilating as she dropped the shears on the floor.

Standing back up, Donis muttered, "Too bad, I really wanted a finger."

Al returned to the Lincoln, started it up, and backed it up next to garage. When he opened the trunk, the man inside kicked out violently with his legs. Al was anticipating the man trying something. Before he opened the trunk, he'd found a hammer hanging on a wall. Using the hammer, he stayed far enough back so the attempted kick was far short of its mark but left his leg in a defenseless position.

Al swung the hammer down onto the man's kneecap. The sickening crunch of bone was followed by a howl of pain. Al violently pulled the man—whose arms were still locked behand his back by the belt—out of the trunk and onto the concrete floor of the garage. Donis handed Al the roll of tape, and he managed to securely tape him up. The last piece went over his mouth, and the stream of threats were finally cut off.

After closing the garage door, Al handed the keys for the Lincoln to Swilley. "You drive that car and follow me. Donis, where are the keys to your car?"

"In the ignition. I was going to drive it into the garage."

"Okay. I want you to get in and follow me. I'll go slow. Stay close behind me."

Swilley started to object, but Al cut him off. "You do what I say or you're on your own. Just try to stay with me. If we get separated in traffic, just go south on I-75. Take 41 just north of the airport. There's a motel on the northwest corner. If we get separated, we'll meet up there. If you think you can just drive away, think again. I'll go back, untie those men, and personally help them hunt you down."

Donis reluctantly got into her car and followed Al up the street to his car. Donise's "car" was actually a car that Dennis had stolen from a car lot in Macon. He'd simply put a stolen tag on it and given it to Donis, so she'd have a ride to her job. She worked as an X-ray technician at an orthopedics clinic. She reluctantly felt that she was somehow obliged to him for the gift. He didn't tell her it was stolen until she'd been driving it for several months. From that point forward, she started looking for an excuse to give the car back and cut him loose. What was happening now was a nightmare.

They left the neighborhood followed closely by Swilley in the Lincoln. While Al was driving, he was questioning his own actions. He was truly afraid that the cartel violence he'd left in Tampico was a part of him that he'd never be able to escape.

Swilley and Donis did a good job of keeping Al in sight. When they reached the parking lot of the motel, Al took the keys to the Lincoln and told Swilley and Donis to wait outside. He used the driver's license he'd taken from the man at the apartment as identification. It was late, and the clerk was not paying any attention to the photo on the license.

Stripping money from the cash he'd taken from the big man, he paid for two days in advance. He took two room keys back out to where Donis and Swilley were waiting. He had Swilley park the Lincoln on the darkest part of the lot and led them to a room located toward the rear of the motel.

Opening the room door, he led them in, giving Swilley one of the keys and keeping one for himself. He'd already counted the cash he'd taken from the men. It was just under ten thousand dollars. He held up the large stack of bills.

"This can all be yours in addition to the favor you'll be doing for me. Here's a couple hundred for food. Don't leave this place except to eat at the restaurant next door. Do not attempt to hot-wire the Lincoln and drive it. I'm sure the owners are not going to be going to the police anytime soon. It should be safe where it is for now. You won't hear from me until day after tomorrow. I know you can walk away if you choose. Just remember you won't get a better chance to get out of your predicament."

As Al left them at the motel and drove back to his condo, he was well aware they might choose to bolt, but that would be their problem, not his. His plan was mapped out. If they wouldn't help him, he was confident he'd find someone who would.

Chapter 45

It was nearing 11:00 PM when Curt and Shela entered the dark hallway at the back of the rehab center. The strong smell of cafeteria food still hung heavy in the air. But it was quiet, and they saw no one as they quietly ascended the stairs to the second floor. The rehab center, unlike the hospital, had open visitor hours. Family members were allowed to stay overnight in the patient's rooms. Each room allowed for a reclining chair to be used for a family member.

They cracked open the door at the top of the stairs and looked down the empty hallway. They could hear faint sounds of television sets coming from rooms with partially open doors. The lights in the hallway were subdued compared to the lights earlier in the day. They opened the door and entered the hallway just as a door halfway down the corridor opened and two figures left a room and walked toward the elevator in the other direction.

Curt and Shela froze and leaned flat against the wall. The couple leaving the room reached the elevator and disappeared without ever looking back toward them. When they reached Room 227, the door was closed, and there was no sound from inside the door.

Curt whispered to Shela, "This is your chance to finish what you started. I'm going to open the door, and you go straight toward the bed. I'll watch the hallway while you use the knife. Remember, we don't want her to wake up this time."

"Don't worry. She's as good as gone."

Curt opened the door to Room 227 and Shela slid inside, moving slowly in order to get her bearings. The lights in the room had been dimmed, but she could easily see the bed on the right side of the room and a large recliner next to it. Dropping the towel that concealed the knife, she took another step toward the bed while raising the knife high over her shoulder to generate power.

Suddenly, from out of the foot of the bed, a figure that looked like a demon from hell lunged toward Shela. As she felt a searing pain in her left arm, she caught a glimpse of red eyes and white teeth. The weight of the animal pulled her to the floor. She tied to free herself, but the animal was shaking its head back and forth as large teeth dug deeper and deeper into her flesh. In fear and desperation, she flailed out with the knife she was still gripping in her right hand. She was able to drive the blade into the skin of the animal until she finally plunged it deep between its ribs.

It took Curt a few seconds to comprehend what was happening before he entered the room and attempted to kick the animal. At the same time, Keri woke up and pulled out the heart monitors she was attached to. That immediately set off an alarm at the main nurse's station as well as automatically turning on all the lights in the room.

Curt's efforts finally caused Brutus to relinquish his hold on Shela as Curt helped her to her feet, blood pouring down her arm. For a moment, Keri stared directly into Shela's eyes and felt the palpable hate flowing from her. If there had ever been a question of Keri identifying Shela, it was answered at that moment.

Curt reached down and picked up the towel and wrapped it around Shela's arm. "We need to get the fuck out of here, *now*."

Shela didn't object as Curt led her back down the hallway just as the elevator opened and three orderlies came running down the hallway toward Keri's room. Curt and Shela left the same way they'd entered. Because of where they'd parked at the end of the lot, they had to pass directly in front of the main entrance. Two security guards turned and watched as the Porsche roared by. Leaving the area, they could see multiple vehicles with flashing lights converging on the rehab center.

Shela was silent as she clutched her arm tightly.

Curt only muttered, "They got a good look at this damn car. We're running out of options."

Chapter 46

After he'd left the information about the Mustang with the sheriff's office, Mark spent the afternoon with Keri and her mom. Keri was still heavily medicated, and most attempts at conversation ended with her slipping off to sleep.

As dark descended, Mark told Vera that he was going to take a break, but he'd come back later and take her to her motel. He promised her that he'd sleep in the reclining chair and stay with Keri all night. This would give Vera her first chance for a good night's sleep in a real bed instead of a chair.

Mark returned to the center later and found Vera nodding in the recliner and Keri sleeping soundly. Vera's hotel was within walking distance, but Mark offered to drive her instead.

They both left Keri's room just as Curt and Shela entered the other end of the hallway. Mark dropped Vera off at her motel's entrance and returned to the rehab center, stopping on the way back to get a large cup of coffee from an all-night diner.

As he approached the rehab center, he saw flashing lights converging in the same direction. At first, he assumed they were emergency vehicles heading for the hospital before realizing they were descending onto the rehab center. Stepping hard on the gas, he made it into the parking area before police had it cordoned off. He sprinted toward the entrance, but as soon as he realized it was blocked by officers, he used the outside stairs to reach the second floor.

The entrance door was locked. He could see several officers standing in the hallway. Now he was getting desperate. If something had happened to Keri after what she'd already experienced, how could he live with it and how could he ever face Keri's mom?

In frustration, Mark pounded his fist against the door. One of the deputies heard and saw him. Luckily for Mark, the deputy didn't shoot him but instead calmly walked over and opened the door.

Mark could only ask, "What's happening?"

By now, another deputy had approached and asked, "Are you a relative of someone on the floor?"

"Yes, I am. Has anyone been hurt?"

"If you count a dog as being anyone, yes."

At that moment, Mark saw Detective Luhrs walking toward the group of officers.

Luhrs saw Mark at the same time and walked over and spoke to the officers before turning his attention toward Mark. "It's okay, guys. I know him. Mr. Price, you're turning up everywhere I go."

"It may be because we have mutual interest. Tell me what's going on."

"Well, we're just trying to reconstruct what happened. We do believe Ms. Smith is living a charmed life. Two individuals entered her room—a man and a woman Ms. Smith swore was the one who attacked her at the rest stop. She was asleep but woke up just in time to see the woman coming toward her bed with a knife in her hand. She was a quick thinker, because she had enough presence of mind to pull her heart monitor loose, and it immediately set off all kinds of alarms.

It was the dog that saved her. The woman had no idea that the Dobermann was sleeping next to her bed. It attacked her before she could reach Ms. Smith. She stabbed the dog pretty bad, but he still held on tight. The man kicked the dog in the head pretty hard. When he let the woman go, they ran. There were people running to the room because of the alarm set off by the monitor, and the couple must have realized they had no choice but to leave while they still could. We got a view of the car they were driving. We think it matches a car that was recently stolen in Orlando."

"Ms. Smith is okay?"

"Yes, she's okay, but the dog is hurt pretty bad. Two of the deputies are already taking him to an emergency veterinary clinic that's only a block away."

"Is it okay for me to go in now?"

"I don't see why not. Ms. Smith has already told us all she can."

When Mark reached Keri's room, the door was open, and an orderly was mopping up the blood from the tile floor. There were traces of tears on her cheeks when Mark entered the room. "Mark, they hurt Brutus really bad."

"Keri, if Brutus can survive water moccasin bites, he'll make it through this." As Mark said it, he was thinking how Keri was far more concerned about her dog than she was her own well-being. "Brutus saved your life. I'm just sorry I couldn't have been here. But at least your mom didn't have to witness any of this."

"Mark, I think if my mom had been here, she would have attacked them before Brutus did."

"Keri, I have no doubt about that. She was looking forward to a good night's sleep. There's no need to bother her tonight. Tell me what you saw."

"Mark, there is absolutely no doubt. That was the woman who attacked me at the rest stop. I'll never forget her face. Why did she come after me?"

"Because you could identify her. Now she'll really be desperate. You are the only person who can put her at the rest stop. I'm going to make sure the sheriff keeps someone here until the pair are caught."

What Keri couldn't see was the rage that was growing in Mark when he answered, "I'm going to see if I can offer any help to the detectives."

Detective Luhrs was still standing in the hallway talking to two sheriff deputies. When he saw Mark, he asked, "You think she's okay?"

"She's a strong woman. She's more concerned about her dog than anything else. Will you be keeping someone here to guard her? Now that there's no doubt about her being able to identify the killers. They may be desperate enough to try again."

"Yes, we'll keep someone here until the couple are caught. But I don't think they'll be back anytime soon."

"You're probably right, but thanks for the guard anyway."

Mark did a good job of concealing his emotions while he talked to Luhrs. As he headed for his car, he knew he'd waited too long to act. The rage he'd kept bottled up began to surface.

Chapter 47

Curt went south on US 1. He stopped at an all-night pharmacy where he bought a bottle of peroxide and a big roll of gauze. He poured the peroxide over the bites in Shela's arm and wrapped it with the gauze. She was stoic and showed no emotion or reaction to the pain. They continued on toward Palatka. Curt was imagining every car they passed to be a state trooper, but they made it to Palatka and Frank Lawson's house on Myrtle Street without any incident.

Curt went into the garage, and after shoving things around, made enough room to drive the Porsche inside and park it next to the Mustang. His dad, Frank Lawson, had heard them drive up and was standing on the small rear porch watching them. After he'd closed the garage doors, Curt led Shela inside. She was carrying the beach bag she'd stolen from the woman at the motel across her shoulder.

Frank had obviously been drinking heavily. "What the hell is going on?" Pointing at Shela, he continued, "You're the girl in the posters they showed on the news." Turning to Curt, he almost yelled, "You've got yourself in a real pile of shit! I hope this bitch is worth it. I want you to get her out of here. I've got enough problems of my own. I don't need yours."

Curt pleaded with his dad. "We need help. We don't have any place to go."

As some faint vestige of parental responsibility rose up in Lawson, he was silent for a minute before he replied, "You could go down to the old bar on the river. It got shut down after some asshole turned us into the sheriff. You know where it is. Take your Mustang and I'll find a way to get rid of that Porsche. I might just get a new tag, paint it, and drive it myself." He motioned to Curt. "Come with me, I want to talk to you in private."

Looking directly at Shela, Frank said, "I need to talk to my son in private. Wait here."

Curt followed him into an adjacent room containing a large TV set facing a well-used reclining leather sofa with multiple cup holders. When he'd made sure that Shela hadn't followed them, he turned to Curt.

"There is another option. We could turn this bitch in and claim she acted on her own. Or even better, we could help her overdose and leave her sitting in the Porsche a long way from here. Maybe they haven't even connected the two of you."

Curt shook his head. "No, Dad. I couldn't do that to her."

"Son, you're a fool. Are you so pussy-whipped that you can't see how much trouble she's got you in?"

At that moment, Shela appeared in the doorway. "You think I can't hear what you said through these thin walls?" She was holding the beach bag with her injured arm. Her right hand was stuck deep in the bag, and it emerged holding the Colt Python. Without any hesitation, she pointed it at Frank and pulled the trigger twice in succession. The recoil from the .357 Magnum load forced the barrel upward, sending the second round into the ceiling.

The noise in the small room was deafening. For a moment, no one moved. Frank was the first to move as he clutched his stomach and fell forward. Curt was next to move as he grabbed for the gun in Shela's hand. "Shela, why did you have to do that? He was going to help us."

"The *hell* he was. I heard what he was saying. If you hadn't objected to what he was suggesting, I'd have shot you first."

Curt walked over to his dad, who was now lying motionless on the floor. Curt had never felt as alone as he did at that moment. Even when his parents had separated, he had not felt so abandoned. Realizing there was nothing he could do for his dad, he simply said, "Let's go."

Chapter 48

Driving far faster than the law allowed as he left the rehab center, Mark reached Palatka in record time. He was convinced that the couple would return to Frank Lawson's house in Palatka. He was perplexed at why the authorities had not found the Mustang or the driver. If his tip had been followed up on, they should be behind bars by now. What Mark didn't and couldn't know was the local sheriff just received a warrant to search the home. A team consisting of deputies from both counties were prepared to execute the warrant early the next morning.

When he reached Myrtle Street, he drove slowly by the house. This time, the neighborhood was dark and quiet. A pickup truck was sitting in the driveway of Lawson's house. Mark could see light coming from the interior of the house.

This time, Mark decided to park a couple of houses down the street. It put him in the cul-de-sac where there were no streetlights. He was relieved that he didn't need to park over on the adjacent street and navigate the treacherous path along the abandoned garage like he'd done before. Knowing he needed to approach cautiously, as soon as he reached the house, he eased along the side of the house opposite the side with the driveway.

He was halfway down the length of the house when two loud shots rang out. Mark froze, waited, and listened.

Although the shot was loud, the sound was contained inside the house enough that it probably couldn't be heard by anyone in the neighborhood. Or it just might be a common occurrence in this part of town. The sound of the shot was followed by someone yelling, followed by silence.

As much as he hated doing it, Mark carefully pushed himself through a clump of overgrown azaleas planted many years ago. The thick bushy shrubs stretched along the full length of the house. A faint light was visible through two windows. What had once been roll-down window shades had deteriorated, and even though they had been pulled down, they had enough holes and cracks permitting some limited view of the interior. He could make out a sofa backed up to the window facing a big-screen TV. At first, he thought the room was empty until he saw a stream of blood leading away from the sofa, followed by a hand reaching out as if hoping someone would take it.

Mark moved out of the azaleas, brushing off the spider web that had become ensnared in his hair. Hoping that the spider was no longer in the web or his hair, he moved quickly to the rear of the house.

Just as he neared the end of the house, the Mustang roared out of the garage, wheels spinning and custom mufflers emitting a growl like a caged animal discovering an open door.

By the time Mark rounded the rear of the house, the Mustang was a block away and still accelerating. He knew there would be no way to return to his car and have any chance of catching or even following the fast car. Making a quick decision, he entered the back door of the house and could immediately hear a loud moan coming from the adjoining room.

Frank Lawson was curled up on the floor, clutching his stomach with both hands. Mark approached the man who was obviously in agony. Being careful not to step in the expanding pool of blood, he carefully lifted him so that he was sitting up with his back leaning against the sofa.

When Lawson looked up to see who was helping him, he immediately recognized Mark.

"You're dead."

"Close, no thanks to you. Who shot you?"

"My son's girlfriend, Shela. She poisoned his mind. I can't believe he left me here. He didn't try to help me."

"Let me look at where you're hit," Mark said as he tried to move Frank's hands enough to see where the bullet had entered.

Lawson's shirt was soaked with blood, but Mark could see where the bullet had entered. The entry point was just under his rib cage on his left side. Because of the amount of blood loss and the sight of blood continuing to pour through Lawson's fingers where he was holding them, Mark knew that his spleen had been hit. Mark also realized he would bleed out long before any help could reach him."

"Help me. Call 911, please!"

"Tell me where your son is going, and I'll help you. I saw him leave a minute ago."

"I don't know where he's going. I've got no more control of him. That bitch does."

Mark stood up, and as he started for the door, he simply said, "Okay, Frank, good luck with that stomach."

Lawson was becoming noticeably weaker, and when he spoke again, his attitude had changed. "Okay, I told them to go to the old bar on the river. It's the place where you got out alive. It got raided, and we closed it down for now. There's still some food and stuff there."

His voice was now reduced to a whisper. "Now hurry, Call someone to help me. I'm getting cold." Those were Frank's last words as his eyes seemed to roll up in his head and freeze in a sightless stare.

Mark left Frank Lawson lying there leaning against the sofa, ran to his car, and headed for the St. Johns River bar.

Chapter 49

Making sure they had moved the rifle and ammunition to the Mustang, Curt and Shela left his dad's house with tires spinning and headed south on US 19. The uneasy silence between the two was palpable. Curt couldn't dismiss the overwhelming sense of desperation he'd felt since leaving his father dying on the floor. Maybe he and Shela really were no different from Bonnie and Clyde. His mom had always stretched out her arms to him, but he'd blamed her for leaving his dad. For the first time since he was a child, he wished he could talk to her and somehow turn the clock back.

Shela sensed that this was not the time to engage Curt in conversation. He was usually a motor mouth, but his sullen demeanor was confusing. Maybe she shouldn't have shot his dad, but Curt had always told her what a shit his dad was. So, why would he care if she shot him? Anyway, it was done, and they needed to figure a way out of this mess.

They turned off 19 and were soon approaching the end of the paved road. At that point, the dirt lane that led to the river was blocked with plastic drums like the ones road repair crews use. In addition to a long string of crime tape across the road, there was also a sign painted on one drum that read *CRIME SCENE.*

"Get out and move a drum so I can drive in. After I'm in, put it back in place." The tone of Curt's voice told

Shela that this would not be the time to argue with him. When they reached the bar, Curt parked in a spot under the cover of the front porch entrance. They took the guns out of the Mustang, plus an unopened bottle of vodka that Shela had grabbed from Frank's kitchen counter as they'd left his house.

There was crime tape everywhere. It looked as if the sheriff's office was decorating the building for Christmas. Fortunately, in spite of the excess with the crime tape, the deputies didn't feel a need to put a lock on the front door. So, Curt and Shela simply tore their way through the tape and entered the bar.

Everything of any real value had been confiscated and moved out. Curt led Shela into a hallway leading from the main room. There were several rooms off the hallway. At the end were two rooms with beds in each. It didn't take much imagination to realize what the rooms had been used for. It was probably the questionable use of the rooms that accounted for why the beds were not perceived to be of any resale value by the authorities.

"Curt, you expect me to sleep on this bed. I'm not sure these sheets have ever been washed."

"Then you can have the floor."

Shela had finally had it with Curt's sour mood. "Screw you. I'm going to find something to mix this vodka with." She walked back into the main room. She went behind the bar and started searching. It didn't take her long to find a large bottle of tonic. It had been opened but was almost full. After opening the vodka, she poured a large amount into a bar glass, followed by a touch of the flat tonic water. Continuing her search under the bar, she came up with a tub of stale popcorn and a jar of pickled pig's feet.

Curt had followed her into the room and saw what she'd found. "Okay, I'll take some of that vodka."

Hoping that Curt's mood was improving, Shela helped him take the drinks and food to one of the remaining tables where they began to work on the bottle of vodka. The alcohol soon helped Curt forget how dire their situation was. Again, they were talking about how they were going to get their revenge on the "Little Asshole," Gary Anders, as soon as the current shitstorm blew over. Their optimism was shattered when they heard the faint but growing volume of sirens approaching the river.

Chapter 50

As soon as Mark approached the turnoff leading to the river, he stopped by the side of the road and used the burner phone he'd kept. Calling the 911 number, he began with, "A man has just been murdered. His name is Frank Lawson. He lives on Myrtle Street."

Mark went on to give the precise location. "He was shot by his son's girlfriend. They are also the pair who killed a guard in St. Johns County and earlier tonight attempted to attack a woman in a rehab facility in St. Augustine. They are hiding in the riverside bar that was recently raided by the sheriff. They are armed. This is not a crank call."

As soon as he'd finished the call, Mark drove to the end of the paved road, stopped, got out of his car, and looked carefully at the broken crime tape. When he walked closer to the drums, the light from his car's headlights provided enough light to clearly see that one of the drums had been dragged off to one side and then moved back in place. Now he was sure this was where the couple had come. He returned to the same spot near the end of the paved road where he'd hidden off the side of the road once before.

He leaned his seat back and made himself comfortable and settled in to wait. He hoped this time his call would be immediately followed up on. He didn't know how he could paint a better scenario for the authorities to follow. He was truly worried about what his next step would be if his information was not taken seriously this time. If the law didn't show up soon, before dawn, he'd end this himself, regardless of the consequences.

Closing his eyes, his mind went back in time as a kaleidoscope of faces of those he'd killed both in anger and in duty flooded his mind. Mark truly wanted the violence that had followed him most of his life to come to an end.

When he heard the distant sound of rapidly approaching sirens, he felt a great sense of relief as if somehow he'd been given a momentary reprieve from the violence that had been such a large part of his life.

Chapter 51

The first thing Shela did when they heard the sounds of the approaching sirens was to grab the closest weapon, which happened to be the rifle they'd brought inside.

Curt made no attempt to stop her. The revolver was lying on the table. Without thinking, Curt picked it up.

Meanwhile, there was little hesitation on the part of the deputies. Within seconds, the entire building was illuminated by bright searchlights followed by a voice amplified by a bullhorn device.

"We know you're in there. You need to come on out now. We don't want anybody to get hurt."

Shela had hidden herself behind the bar. She aimed the rifle toward the front entrance and fired off three shots in rapid succession. Curt was stunned by the shots.

"Shela, no! What are you doing? We can't fight them."

The amplified voice boomed again. "You're making a big mistake. You've got nowhere to go. Throw your guns out the front door. We don't want to hurt you."

Ignoring Shela, Curt lunged toward the front door, pushing it open while screaming as loud as possible, "I'm coming out! Don't shoot!"

He threw the revolver out onto the floor of the deck outside the entrance door as he went through. Shela screamed as she ran from behind the bar and fired at Curt at the same time while shouting, "Come back and fight, you pussy!"

Two rounds from the rifle hit Curt in the back, with one of them severing his descending aorta. As Curt fell, he uttered, "Mama." He was dead when he hit the floor.

Her mind working in a different universe, Shela followed Curt through the door onto the deck where she was illuminated by the searchlights. She was firing the rifle as rapidly and maniacally as possible at whatever demons were trapped in her head.

Leaving the deputies with no choice, multiple shots were fired with precision and Shela fell across Curt on the floor. She was smiling as she fell across Curt.

Minutes before, from his hidden vantage point, Mark had watched the deputies approach the river and rush in toward the bar. He could clearly hear the gunfire that soon followed. He waited a while longer, and as soon as a truck with *CRIME SCENE* on its side passed, he smiled and drove away.

Chapter 52

Dawn was nearing as Mark drove back toward St. Augustine. When he reached I-95, he had to make a decision—and he did. He was dead tired and emotionally exhausted, so instead of going back to the rehab center, he headed north toward his home. Now that the assailants were no longer a threat to Keri, he didn't feel the need hover at her side.

Mark took a long daytime nap before he was retracing his steps down I-95 to the rehab center. Before he left his home, he'd looked up the emergency veterinary clinic. Luhrs had said it was within a block of the hospital, so it was easy to find.

Going into the clinic, he could hear a cacophony of sounds, consisting mostly of barking dogs. A young lady dressed in green scrubs was manning the reception desk. She looked like she hadn't slept in days.

"Can I help you?"

"I'm checking on the status of a Dobermann name Brutus who was brought in last night."

"Oh, is that his name? He's a beautiful dog, and from what the deputies said last night, he's a hero as well. Let me see if the doctor has a moment. Your name?"

"Mark Price."

"Have a seat, Mr. Price. It's been a long night here."

The only other occupants in the waiting room were a young boy, maybe ten or eleven, sitting between his mom and dad. He was clutching his mom's hand, and his cheeks were covered in tears. When Mark looked toward them, the dad who was obviously angry said, "We think our neighbor poisoned our son's young cocker spaniel. The dog chased his cat that was in our yard. He only wanted to play with it. We think we stopped the dog from eating much of the piece of meat."

Mark shook his head and replied, "I'd save the meat, have it tested, and report it to the police." But true to his nature, Mark thought to himself, *It's not what I'd do though.*

At that moment, the doctor entered the waiting room and went straight to the anxious family. He was an older man also wearing green scrubs. His demeanor was kind and gentle as he spoke to the family. Mark's first thought was that he looked more like a priest than a doctor.

"Good news, folks. Cougar is going to be okay. We got his stomach pumped out before any real damage was done."

The smile on the young boy's face could have lit a hundred rooms. And as soon as the parents finished thanking the doctor, he turned to Mark. "Now that I know his name, I'll be able to talk to Brutus a little better. All his wounds are superficial with the exception of the single stab wound. I had to open him up to get to the main source of the bleeding. I can't guarantee anything yet, but I feel good about his chances. He'll need to remain as still as possible for a few days. I understand that he may have saved his owner's life."

"He most definitely saved her life."

"And thus, 'man's best friend'—or in this case, 'woman's.'"

When Mark reached Keri's room at the rehab center, both she and her mom were watching the evening news.

As soon as Mark entered the room, Vera excitedly blurted out, "Mark, did you see the news? They found the people who tried to kill Keri. It sounds like they were both killed in a shootout. They even think they have the gun that was used to kill the guard."

"That's good news, but I have even better news. I stopped at the veterinary clinic on my way. The doctor thinks Brutus is going to make it."

With a big smile, Keri said, "Yes, that's the best news of all."

The three of them stayed glued to the television newscast for the rest of the evening. It was still too early in the investigation to get many of the details. It was reported that an anonymous phone call had led the authorities to the suspects. When that was being reported, Keri looked toward Mark with a curious glance. Mark refused to make eye contact.

Mark even got a call from Roe, who had seen the news as well. She, too, was skeptical when she asked Mark if he had any idea how the killers had been found.

"Roe, that will be a conversation we'll have on the dock when it's only the two of us."

During the course of the evening, the two women let Mark know that the hospital was ready to discharge Keri send her to a rehab center near her home in Orlando. Keri was excited with the prospect of going home.

Vera added, "I'm sure my brother will drive back up and ferry Brutus home as soon as the vet thinks it's safe for him to move."

When Mark said it was time for him to leave, Vera discreetly left the room to give them privacy.

Keri spoke first. "Mark, whatever you do, just realize that none of this has been your fault. If you can't accept that, I'll never visit you again. Remember what I said to you that night in Orlando when we were looking for my sister's killer? 'We are only the very best of friends.' You will always be my friend."

"Thanks, Keri. You get well and we'll plan a getaway."

Mark kissed Keri on her forehead and left the room, not forgetting to give Vera a big hug. "Vera, you're a world-class mother. Just let me know if I can help with anything."

Mark left the rehab center and returned to his riverfront home in Jacksonville. There was some sadness in leaving Keri, but he knew there were limits on their relationship.

What really was bothering him now was Al. He'd tried a couple of times within the last couple of days to call him, but he'd not gotten a response. Now that he was aware of Al's capacity to take risks, his concerns were only amplified.

Chapter 53

Driving the sedan Leon had loaned him, he reached his home in Palatka in the early morning. His mom was asleep, and even as much as he wanted to talk to her, he just didn't have the heart to wake her up. She was always dead tired after she finished her shift at the restaurant, so he let her sleep and went to bed himself.

The smell of bacon frying greeted him when he woke up and joined his mom in the trailer's tiny kitchen.

"Gary, you must have come in late last night."

"I did, Mom. I had a long two days. I need to have a serious talk with you. I just got a real job offer and I have a big decision to make."

"For real, Gary? I'm really proud of you. Did the food mart offer you a job?"

Gary had to smile when he answered, "No, Mom, it's a lot bigger than the food mart. I'd have a starting salary of eighty thousand during a trial period. If I can handle the job, then I'll get double that."

Dot had to grab the counter when Gary mentioned the salary. It made her head spin. "Gary, someone's playing a joke on you."

"No, Mom. It is for real. The thing is, I'd have to move across the state. They even offered to get you a good job somewhere close by. Wait a minute. Let me show you something." He went back to his bedroom and got the stack of cash Leon had given him. Walking back into the kitchen, he spread it out on the small table.

Dot was stunned. "Gary, is this legal?"

Gary told a little white lie. "The job is all legal. They want me to come back after I graduate next week and give them a final answer. You can come with me and see for yourself."

Dot was having a hard time comprehending all this information at once. The change she was seeing in Gary was perplexing. It was as if he'd morphed into an entirely different person. He was self-assured, confident, and the little lost meek boy that had been her son was gone.

Gary graduated with honors that he learned about when he agreed to attend his graduation. He only agreed to attend the ceremony to please his mom. To his surprise and delight, his big brother made a special trip home to attend.

Days before graduation, the community was rocked by the news of Shela and Curt's deaths. The stories that were circulating told a wild tale that was hard to believe. Through the entire time, Gary held his breath wondering if he would somehow be connected to the two. A few classmates were aware that he was acquainted with them both, but he was able to dismiss it as anything but a passing and casual relationship. He expressed total surprise at the crimes they were accused of committing. Inside though, he was conflicted. On one hand, he felt a sense of relief to be free of their influence. But he also felt a deep sadness at the unnecessary loss of their lives.

Gary returned to Moreno and Sons Salvage the day after graduation. Leon took Gary over to Carmen's house and left him.

Carmen spent over three hours talking to Gary before she drove him back around to Leon's office. Leon had already given Carmen limited information of how he'd come to know Gary.

When Carmen came back to the office with Gary, she nodded at Leon and simply said, "He's good to go. I think you found a winner." It was a final stamp of approval.

Over time, Gary Anders became Leon's right hand in the business, which was now one hundred percent legitimate. Gary was only one of a very few people, outside of family, who were ever accepted into the inner circle of Moreno and Sons Salvage. His future as a businessman and later as a prominent figure in the state of Florida is a story for another day.

Chapter 54

A mobile home park was located on the west side of the Iron Road. It was just a short distance up the main highway from the secondary road that led directly to Moreno and Sons Salvage. The park had been built years ago and housed a few of the day employees of the Moreno business as well as isolationists who couldn't afford to buy their own secluded piece of paradise but still wanted to be as far away from other people as possible. The size of the park combined with the traffic from Moreno and Sons across the highway generated enough business to support the small convenience store.

It was late afternoon, and Al was sitting in the gravel parking lot of the store. Dennis Swilley and Donis both sat in the back seat of Al's SUV. Swilley appeared to be tense and nervous as he spoke. "As soon as we're done here, you'll give us the money and forget about us, right?"

"Absolutely. I don't think you've got any reason to be concerned. They'll either give you cash for the Town Car, or they'll tell you to get lost."

"I told you before, I've never brought a car to this location. I've brought a couple to Tampa. I've just heard rumors about this place and the Iron Road."

"Well, it's time to find out whether the rumors are fact or fiction. Be optimistic. If they do pay you for the Town Car, it's extra money in your pocket."

Donis remained silent while thinking to herself, *How the hell did I get myself in this place?*

Dennis drove the Town Car, followed by Donis reluctantly driving the compact. They followed the directions until they found themselves sitting in front of the huge, gated entrance to Moreno and Sons. The gates were closed, and Dennis sat for a few moments before he saw the phone next to the gates. Getting out of his car, he picked up the phone and pushed the red button underneath. He could hear the phone buzzing. He was about to give up and replace the phone when he heard a voice answer, "Yes."

In a shaky voice, Dennis replied, "I have a car to sell."

The voice answered, "Why are you bringing it here?"

"I heard that this is the best place to sell a car quick."

"Just wait in your car."

Dennis went back to the Town Car and waited for several minutes before the massive gates opened and a huge black man driving a golf cart emerged. Coming up to the window of the Town Car where Dennis had the window rolled down, he stopped and looked carefully at him before he spoke. "Have you been here before?"

"No, but I've taken cars to Tampa."

"You follow me inside." Pointing toward Donis where she was sitting in her car, he said, "She can wait here."

Following the golf cart just inside the gate, Dennis passed a building that looked like an office building. There were still some cars parked next to it. Winding around the first building, he could see several buildings. Past them, even as it was getting dark, endless rows of vehicles were stacked high, one upon another as far as he could see. Eventually, they stopped at a loading platform of a huge warehouse. The parking area was as large as a football field, and parked on one end were several tractor trailers as well as specialized trucks for hauling autos.

The man who led him in motioned for him to get out of the Town Car and follow him inside. He led Swilley up onto the loading dock and into the cavernous building. Inside, he opened a door into a small office and pointed inside.

Swilley entered the office and found himself looking at a man sitting behind a desk with a questioning look on his face. "Sit down. I'm Leon Moreno. What's your name?"

"I'm Dennis Swilley," he replied. As he sat down, he noticed two things at once. The large black man stayed in the room and remained standing just behind his chair. Secondly, there was a .45 caliber M1911 Colt handgun laying on the desk in front of him.

As soon as he was seated, the man behind the desk asked, "You said you have a car to sell?"

Swilley answered in an uncertain voice, "Yes, it's a new model Lincoln Town Car."

"Okay, let me have a look at the title and registration."

Sweat suddenly began to bead up on Swilley's forehead. "I—I don't have a title."

Leon seemed to take offense with Swilley's answer.

"You don't fuckin' have a title? So, what the hell are you coming here for? Are you telling me you want to sell me a stolen car? What in God's name made you think you could bring a car with no records to Moreno and Sons? This business is and always will be a legitimate one. Also, I'm not sure who you did business with in Tampa, but it sure as hell wasn't us."

By this point, Swilley was wishing he and Donis had run when they'd had a chance. He didn't feel good about where this conversation was going. It was not at all what he'd expected.

Leon looked at the man standing behind Swilley. "Ethan, make a copy of his driver's license and any other ID he's got."

Leaving no room for argument, Ethan said, "Give me your wallet. Don't worry. I'm not going to take your money. We just want to know who you are so that if we ever need to talk to you, we'll know who to look for."

Ethan left the room with Swilley's wallet, leaving him alone with Leon Moreno, who said, "You know I don't like the idea that anyone else might have some misplaced notion that we deal in illegal vehicles. It might be a poor career choice to make assumptions like that especially if you repeated the rumor."

Leon opened a drawer behind the desk, took out a flash drive, and inserted it into the computer on his desk. He turned the monitor around so that Swilley could see the screen.

The video that started playing was grainy and poorly focused. But there was no doubt about what he was watching. Two burly men were forcing a man into an old beat-up sedan and handcuffing him to something inside the car. The car was sitting on what appeared to be a stage, but its purpose became clear as the upper part began to slowly descend.

Swilley watched in morbid fascination as the roof of the car began to cave in. When he saw an arm stretch out of the car's window in a last-ditch effort to plead for mercy, Dennis didn't want to watch, but he was transfixed on the gruesome scene. As the car was crushed, the arm extending from the window was cut cleanly off. It toppled to the floor next to the car, which was now reduced to a compacted mass of metal.

Only then did a shaken Swilley look away from the screen. He had to fight the urge to throw up, but somehow he managed to hold it back. At that same moment, Ethan returned to the office with Swilley's wallet and handed it to him. The fact that he was getting his wallet back gave Swilley some hope that he was going to be okay.

Leon had been watching Swilley the entire time. "You know that video scares the shit out of me every time I watch it. That's a rough way to die."

All Swilley could do was nod his head like a bobblehead in agreement.

What Swilley didn't know was that the video was staged. True, he saw a man placed in the car, but he didn't know that he had been removed and replaced with a mannequin. The arm that was cut off was the mannequin's plastic arm. The entire video was poor enough quality that an observer didn't have enough time to realize that the arm didn't move, nor was there any sign of the blood that would have been apparent if it had been real. The fear instilled by the possibility of being crushed was so strong, it always had the desired effect. Only Ethan and a couple more trusted employees were aware that Leon Moreno had never killed anyone. It was simply advantageous for Leon to project an image of intimidation and fear to the few questionable characters he had to deal with.

Leon looked at Ethan. "Take him back out, Ethan. If he wants to ever do business with us in the future, he'll know to bring proper documentation."

With that statement, Swilley was dismissed from Moreno and Sons for what would be the first and the last time he would visit the site. He followed Ethan back out through the front gates where Donis was waiting. His thoughts jumped from being happy to be alive to regretting that he didn't get any money for the Town Car.

Al was waiting across the highway at the convenience store. When he saw Dennis returning in the Town Car, he smiled and waited for them to park and get back into his car.

"So, I see they didn't take the Lincoln."

Dennis was still in a partial state of shock, but he still replied, "No shit, that Moreno guy scared the crap out of me. I don't care what you may have heard, that's not the place to take a stolen car. Now, I've done what you wanted."

"Yes, you have, Dennis, and I thank you," Al said as he handed a wad of money across the seat to Dennis. "What are you going to do with the Lincoln? I'm sure you won't be driving it back to Atlanta anytime soon."

"I'm going to leave it right where it sits, unlocked with the keys in the ignition. Donis and I are going to Tampa where I have family to try to start over there."

After the pair drove away in her compact car, Al took a deep breath and called Mark, who answered on the first ring. "Al, I've been trying to reach you."

"Sorry, I've been on a mission. I have seen the news about Keri's assailants being killed. I guess that brings some degree of closure for you both."

"Yes, it does, but the best part is how well she's recovering. It looks as if Brutus is going to make it as well."

"That's great. Now let me tell you what I've learned." Al continued to explain to Mark all that had transpired over the last few days. Mark listened in silence as Al told Mark how he'd enlisted Swilley to help in his plan to investigate Moreno and Sons. Al conveniently left out the details of the dangerous encounter at the garage apartment.

"Mark, I didn't take any chances. I just saw this as an easy and safe way to see if Carmen's family business was legitimate. From all that Swilley told me about his experience after trying to sell a stolen car to Moreno himself, they are definitely not a chop shop. The Iron Road is a long stretch of highway. The chop shop could be anywhere off this road.

"Okay, Al, you've satisfied your concerns about Carmen's family business. What's next?"

"Well, for now, I'm going back to my office in Atlanta to get some work done. I'll talk to you later about maybe scheduling a week or two at the hunting reserve here."

"That sounds good, Al. Just stop playing detective, okay?"

Chapter 55

Al would never know how much he'd underestimated Swilley. Swilley had driven a short distance down the road to the small village of Trenton after he'd left Al at the convenience store. He and Donis waited to give Al time to leave before they returned to the convenience store. Instead of leaving the Lincoln, Swilley got back into the big car and headed back to I-75 and north to Atlanta. Donis followed in the stolen compact. Swilley, egged on by Donis, who had no intention of leaving Atlanta, was convinced they could find a way to stay safely in Atlanta. It seemed as though he had no memory of what had happened at Donise's apartment.

Swilley knew that the only real threat to his long-term safety was the man in the apartment who had removed his finger. The big man had been born as Terrance Nace Thomas, but his street name was TNT, or as his close associates dubbed him, Big T. Behind his back and well out of earshot, sometimes he was referred to as Little T. While nature had bestowed him with a massive body, it had left him compromised by leaving him with a small penis. The small member was emphasized by his otherwise huge body. This fact alone probably contributed to his perpetual state of anger. God help any woman who might be inclined to comment on the subject of size.

As soon as his associates had freed themselves in the apartment where Al had left them, they had taken Big T to an emergency room for treatment. Because his wounds were clearly a result of gunshots, the police had to investigate. But since the victims would not give any information, there was no crime to charge them with. The police wrote it up as simply gang-related. Both Big T's wounds required surgical intervention, but he was immediately released to outpatient care.

He was beside himself with anger. Not only had he been bested in front of his men, he had also lost his new Town Car. He was consumed with only one thing. He would somehow get his hands on that little son of a bitch Dennis Swilley. Big T smiled to himself as he imagined the things he'd do to him. After he'd done Swilley in, he'd track down the guy who shot him. He'd already been told by the doctors that he'd have a pronounced limp. The consequence of that encounter would be visible to everyone for the rest of his life. But in spite of his efforts and contacts, he still couldn't find a trace of Swilley or the guy who shot him.

If Big T had only known how close he was to Swilley. Collier Heights was a small residential neighborhood in West Atlanta. It was an old neighborhood built among trees and rolling hills. The house on Jones Road was built on a lot that sloped downward from the street. A driveway led down to the back of the house and a double garage on the lowest floor.

The Town Car was sitting in one of the spaces with three people leaning into the trunk. The trunk wall behind the rear seats had been removed, and pieces of the trunk were scattered across the floor. Donis, Swilley, and a tall, thin man—with a dark beard that was hardly noticeable against his dark skin and heavy sideburns—were intently focused on their work.

The tall man, Angus Green, was Donis's big brother. Donis and Angus had been orphaned at a young age. Angus, who was eight years older, had raised Donis. They had survived some tough times together. He would do anything to protect his little sister and only living blood relative. That was why he was breaking a lot of rules to do what he was doing now. Angus worked for a demolition business that demolished everything from a simple house to condemned skyscrapers. And with that job came the training in use of explosives. He was good at what he did and well paid as well.

Earlier, when Angus learned what happened at Donise's apartment, he was ready to confront Big T single-handedly, but Donis was able to dissuade him and look for another way to handle Big T. Angus was the one who suggested a way to do it. Swilley was all in on the plan, believing it would solve all his problems.

Angus was tuned into his sister's moods, and it was apparent to him that she was trying to hide something. At the same time Dennis was complaining about the lack of beer in the house. Angus told Dennis, "There is a store a couple blocks away. How about you get whatever you need and pick up some subs for us all while you're there."

Dennis quickly took Angus up on the suggestion and left. Angus looked at Donis. "Now tell me what's bothering you."

"I could take all night, but I'll condense it. Dennis Swilley is getting crazier every day. It starts with him giving me a stolen car to drive. I'm sure if I ever got pulled over, he would swear he didn't know me. I've suggested we go our separate ways, but he says we'll never be parted. He's threatened to beat the shit out of me if I mention anything about separating again. He is planning to continue dealing with stolen cars. He tells me it's the only way he's ever been successful even though it almost got us killed. I want no part of any of that. So, how do I get rid of him?"

Angus listened in silence before he finally spoke. "Donis, how are we planning to get rid of Big T?"

Donis thought for a moment and then smiled. "I understand."

Now the trio were placing plastic containers of gasoline behind the back seat of the Town Car. Angus had rigged a way for the gas to be ignited remotely. A timer had been ruled out due to the uncertainty of the timing, and they also wanted to control the location of any explosion to reduce the possibility of innocent victims. The only downside was the necessity for the detonator being within proximity of the Town Car.

When the work on the Lincoln was almost completed, Donis said she wanted to go upstairs and get away from the fumes for a while. She exchanged glances with Angus before saying, "Dennis, come up with me. You look like you could use a drink."

Dennis didn't need any more encouragement and left the garage with Donis leaving Angus to finish up rigging the car. As soon as they'd left, Angus turned his attention to the stolen compact car that Donis had been driving.

Big T got a call late the next evening. He was sitting in his favorite chair doped up on coke to ease the pain from his recent surgeries. A couple of men, including the original driver of the Lincoln, were in the room with him.

"Is this Big T?

"Yeah, who's this?"

"I thought sure you'd recognize me, Big T. This is Dennis Swilley."

To his credit, Big T kept his cool. "Yeah, man. You done me bad, you know."

"Yeah, I know. But you didn't do me much good either. I gotta forget my dream of being a concert pianist. I just want to make it all good again. You know that guy that shot you and kidnapped me and Donis? He made me take the car. We just got away from him, but I know how to find the guy. I left your car back at the same place. I even got it washed and detailed real good for you. If you'll give me a couple of days, I'll have your money."

Big T was listening, but he didn't give a goddamn if Dennis wanted to kiss and make up. It was too late for that now. If he could get his car back and maybe some cash, he'd still kill the asshole. Plus, he'd find out who the other guy was.

"You say my car is sitting at your girlfriend's apartment?"

"Yeah, same spot."

"Here's what I'm going to do. I'll go get my car, and as soon as you bring me cash money, we'll talk."

"Okay, T. I just want us to be okay. You know we work good together."

Big T tried to stand up but needed help from one of the guys. "We're going for a drive." No one dared question him. They helped him get into a modified car of some unrecognizable make and followed his directions back to the garage apartment where the car was last seen.

Angus had already shown Dennis how to use the simple detonating device. The moment Dennis closed his call to Big T ,he left Angus's home in Donise's compact car. He wanted Donis to ride with him, but Donis had a severe migraine resulting from the gas fumes in the basement. At least that was what she told Dennis.

Just as Swilley had promised, the big Lincoln Town Car sat in the same spot as if it had never been moved. As Big T was helped into the rear seat, he smiled for the first time in several days. The same driver was happy to get into the driver's seat, and even with a brace on his knee where Al had hit him with the hammer, he was able to drive the car with minimal pain. Before he got into the Lincoln, Big T told the driver of the car who had brought them to get some pizza on the way home. "Get some cheese sticks, too. We gonna have a celebration."

The driver started the Town Car and remarked, "He even filled up the gas tank."

"Yeah, he overfilled it. I can smell the fuckin' stuff."

Driving away from the neighborhood, they didn't see the small compact car with no lights following a short distance behind. The route they were driving led through a deserted commercial area when Big T's cell phone rang.

"Swilley, what the hell do you want now?"

"I just wanted to say goodbye, Little T."

A buzzing behind his seat was the last sound Big T heard as the Lincoln burst into a ball of fire. Simultaneously, the compact car Swilley was driving exploded in a blinding flash. The Town Car rolled into a concrete culvert while the compact car stopped in the middle of the road. There were no witnesses, and both vehicles burned until only the smoldering frames were left.

At the same time the cars were burning, Donis and Angus sat on his patio enjoying a fine bottle of Merlot.

Chapter 56

Al sat at his desk in deep thought after finishing his conversation with Mark. Mark had agreed to spend a week at the Moreno's hunting lodge. Although Mark had been an avid hunter growing up in Florida's Panhandle, he no longer had a desire to hunt anything. He had no problem with others hunting, but he fervently hoped he'd never have to kill any living thing for the rest of his life. Just the quiet and solitude of the forest would be an enjoyable diversion.

He had also been enthusiastic about having Roe and Angel come as well. The thought of inviting Keri crossed his mind. He had talked to her after she'd gone back to her home in Orlando. He was pleased to know that both she and Brutus were making a full recovery. Knowing that Keri needed more time for the memory of her assault to fade, he chose to not invite her. There would be other times.

Now all Al had to do was to call Carmen and set it up. He couldn't understand why he was as nervous as a high school kid making a first date.

When Carmen answered his call, she asked, "Where have you been? I was afraid I'd scared you off."

"Sorry, it took longer than I'd expected to coordinate with my dad. We're ready to reserve the lodge."

After Al and Carmen worked out the time and details, Al said, "I'm looking forward to that seafood on the coast."

Carmen was smiling as she replied, "So am I."

Thomas Willis was a college athlete, a Vietnam War veteran, a practicing dentist, a university professor, and an author. He lives in south Florida with his wife Ruth.

In the first book of the Mark Price series, when Mark has those he loves the most in life brutally taken from him how far will he go to extract revenge? How far does a young woman have to fall in a dark world of drugs and sex before she is able regain her pride and dignity? And how does a man sitting on death row for a crime he is innocent of, retain his sanity as his execution date nears? In *Marks Way*, these stories are all connected in a rollercoaster ride of vengeance and vindication.

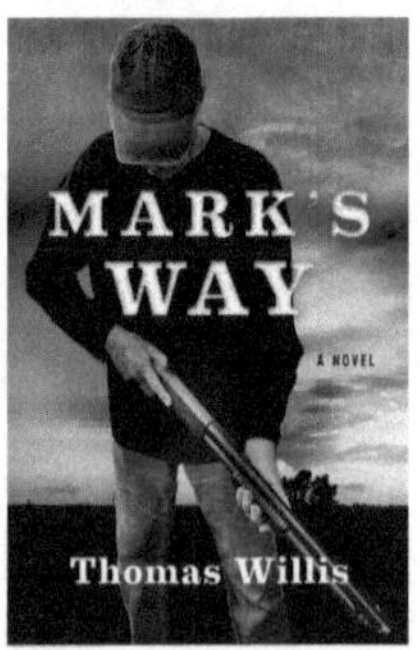

Last Night in Tampico is a story of how Emelia Rojas, a victim of human trafficking, finds the strength and will to survive even at her darkest hour.Her survival is tied to Mark Price, a man with a dark and violent history, Roe Estes, a young woman with a tumultuous past who now works as a DEA agent, and a Haitian/Chilean immigrant, Samuel Oreste, who has been caught up in events beyond his control. The unlikely trio follow a convoluted and dangerous trail that leads them from El Paso, Ciudad Juarez, West Palm Beach, and finally Tampico Mexico. The story alternates between Mark's questionable military actions in the past and the present search for Emelia and the cartel that holds her. The end of the odyssey results in a bittersweet and life changing event for them all.

*Book two in
the Mark
Price series*